Otto Penzler Presents

God Save the Mark by Donald Westlake

The Quiller Memorandum by Adam Hall

Hopscotch by Brian Garfield

A Time for Predators by Joe Gores*

*forthcoming

HOPSCOTCH

BRIAN GARFIELD

A Tom Doherty Associates Book

New York

HOPSCOTCH

Copyright © 1975 by Brian Garfield

Introduction copyright © 2004 by Otto Penzler

First published in the United States by M. Evans and Company, Inc.

This book is printed on acid-free paper.

Book design by Michael Collica

A Forge Book
Published by Tom Doherty Associates, LLC
175 Fifth Avenue
New York, NY 10010

www.tor.com

Forge® is a registered trademark of Tom Doherty Associates, LLC.

Library of Congress Cataloging-in-Publication Data

Garfield, Brian, 1939–
    Hopscotch / Brian Garfield.—1st ed.
      p.   cm.
    "A Tom Doherty Associates book."
    ISBN 0-765-30920-3 (hc)
    EAN 978-0765-30920-4 (hc)
    ISBN 0-765-30921-1 (pbk)
    EAN 978-0765-30921-1 (pbk)
      1. Fugitives from justice—Fiction.   2. Intelligence officers—Fiction.
    3. Official secrets—Fiction.   4. Retirees—Fiction.   I. Title.

    PS3557.A715H67   2004
    813'.54—dc22

                                                        2004047163

First Forge Edition: September 2004

Printed in the United States of America

0   9   8   7   6   5   4   3   2   1

For Henry

| INTRODUCTION |

Sometime during the middle of the Cold War, a strange transformation occurred in the authors who produced espionage fiction. Until the conclusion of World War II, virtually every writer of significance in the long, noble history of the spy story had attempted to portray his own country as honorable and heroic, and its enemy as utterly vile and, its anagram, evil.

No espionage novel written by an English or American author, that I can recall, ever portrayed Nazi Germany in a sympathetic light, as a nation filled with decent, honest people who simply favored a different political system that went amok. No writer suggested that Nazism was a brilliant form of government in a philosophical sense, but that its leaders had failed to implement it properly, much to the detriment of the German people.

The fiction that featured intellectual battles between Nazi spies and their democratic counterparts invariably depicted the contest as a straightforward struggle between the forces of Good and Evil.

Earlier spy stories by English and, less commonly, American, writers treated their foes (France, usually, but also Russia) as ruthless emissaries of Satan who came to their countries to rape, pillage, and use any foul methods available in pursuit of their dastardly desires.

The successful resolution of WWII and the spread of Communism apparently changed all that. While the tyranny of Nazism was justly abhorred, the equally virulent Communist states of the Soviet Union and China were somehow regarded differently by espionage writers (not to mention journalists and academics, but that's another story).

As time has passed and more information has become available, we have learned that the number of people who were killed by Stalin and Mao, directly by execution or indirectly by starvation and other means, far exceeds those charged to the blindingly evil Hitler.

Outrage at the cruel excesses of left-wing totalitarianism, an overt slap in the face of humanity has not, however, often been reflected in the work of contemporary espionage writers. There are exceptions, of course, such as John Gardner, Adam Hall, Ian Fleming, Frederick Forsyth, and the great Charles McCarry, but they are just that: exceptions.

Moral relativism with regard to Germany would not have been accepted by most of the population in the United States or Great Britain, yet it has been applauded by publishers, critics, and readers alike with regard to the Soviet Union. (The same may soon occur with regard to Osama bin Laden and Saddam Hussein, but that's also another story.)

The brilliant John le Carré has invested his Soviet spies with uncommon intelligence and the behavior of gentlemen. Eric Ambler did the same. So did Robert Littell. Ken Follett bent over backwards to do it. And here, in *Hopscotch,* so does Brian Garfield.

Miles Kendig, the protagonist, is miffed about his treatment by the CIA and decides to write a book, telling more secrets than he ought to hint at, much less disclose. He then decides to hold an auction, apparently quite willing to sell it to the Soviets if they outbid the United States. Mikhail Yaskov, the Soviet agent with whom Kendig has been sparring for many years, is presented as a funny, folksy foe. It's a friendly game of chess, no more. No matter that those secrets could cost lives. No matter that the Soviet Union, in the person of Nikita Khrushchev, had threatened to bury the U.S. Kendig appears to have no loyalty to the country that gave him a successful career and a good life. Indeed, Garfield has created a character who almost seems to hate his own country—not what readers would have expected when the enemy was fascism.

To be fair, Garfield doesn't seem to like anybody. When he speaks of humanity, he has Kendig think: "If you compressed all the matter in a human being, closing down the spaces between electrons and nuclei, you would end up with a heavy mass about the size of a one-eighth carat diamond, and far less useful."

Garfield knocks the Swiss (quoting Harry Lime in *The Third Man*), noting "in Switzerland . . . the street workers laughed and they worked. And as Orson Welles and Graham Greene had pointed out, all that energy and spirit had produced, in five hundred years of peaceful civilization, the cuckoo clock."

He slaps the French a little, too. "In France, [Kendig] passed easily for a Frenchman because it never occurred to the French that a foreigner could speak the language properly."

Encompassing an entire continent, Kendig "had no liking for Latin America and he had said as much at least once. . . ."

And Cuba specifically: "Sometimes it surprised him that everything south of the border hadn't gone Communist by now. It was only that the Cubans had set such an inept example and because Che had been such a visible idiot. They had the temperament for it, though. Tyranny suited them."

There are no compliments for the Russians either: "Russians do not smile politely; they smile only when amused. It makes them appear rude to outsiders." Furthermore, "It was amazing how many Russians still thought the United States was a land of sweatshops, scarlet letters, and purple sage."

The political overtones of such novels as *Hopscotch* and *Six Days of the Condor* by James Grady, in which the enemy is the CIA (which slaughters people without conscience) are confusing as they attempt to equate the morality of a free democratic society with that of a repressive dictatorship (Garfield notes the only distinction between the West's leadership and the East's is that the West's is more petty).

Nonetheless, these books have an entertaining excitement to them. While *Condor* is more terrifying, *Hopscotch* has a genial tone that makes the entire series of events, with lives at stake, seem like a giant board game. It's great fun to be with Kendig as he fools the suits at the CIA, as he plans his next moves and his escapes, and as he has a genuine chance to prove he's still really good at what he does. The novel (and the film it inspired) may be unique in the history of espionage thrillers in that not one person does—or receives—so much as a scratch.

The novel won the Edgar Award from the Mystery Writers of America in 1976. The plot was perfect for the movies and the rights were bought immediately. Several writers tried and failed to convert it into a screenplay until Garfield himself took over as a producer and correctly realized that the film would work better as a comedy than as a straightforward thriller.

It took twenty-six drafts to get it right, but the final screenplay by Garfield and Bryan Forbes is first-rate. While the critics were not enthusiastic, audiences made it a box-office success.

Walter Matthau was signed to play Miles Kendig. Of course, he was funny. Walter Matthau walking across a room is funny. Glenda Jackson as his love interest isn't exactly a thrill a minute, but his two CIA colleagues, Myerson, the boorish character played by Ned Beatty, and Cutter, the respectful one played by Sam Waterston, are impeccable—as is Herbert Lom as Yaskov. The less said the better about the rampant nepotism, with Matthau's son boringly playing Ross, another CIA operative, and his daughter-in-law playing a pilot so ineptly that it is excruciating to watch her hunt for charisma. Ronald Neame directed the 1980 film.

Garfield was pretty hot in Hollywood in those days, largely due to the enormous success of *Death Wish* in 1974, which made Charles Bronson a star as big in America as he had been for some time in Europe. The sequels enjoyed some success, though they became more and more cartoonish.

There are a couple of little inside jokes in the novel. Glenn Follett is a CIA operative. Garfield and Follett had made a private agreement to use each other's name in their next respective novels. As good friends, it may not be a surprise that neither portrayed the other in a very favorable light, and he is described as "an idiot." Garfield was also a close friend of Donald E. Westlake, and at one point Kendig goes to a movie theater that happens to be playing *The Outfit,* a film based on a book by Westlake (written under his Richard Stark pseudonym). A character in the film is also named Westlake.

Once a hugely prolific writer, Garfield produced books under eight different pseudonyms (Bennett Garland, Alex Hawk, John Ives, Drew Mallory, Frank O'Brian, Jonas Ward, Brian Wynne, Frank Wynne) in several genres, mainly Westerns and suspense novels.

There was a sequel of sorts to *Hopscotch*. The main characters in his short story collection, *Checkpoint Charlie,* had made their initial appearance in the novel. Garfield is an accomplished short story writer and won his second Edgar for "Scrimshaw" in 1980. He also served as the president of the Mystery Writers of New Mexico.

Born in New York City on January 26, 1939, he lived for many years in Arizona (he earned both his B.A. and M.A. from the University of Arizona) and in Los Angeles, where he spent several years working in the film industry. He now lives mainly in New Mexico.

—Otto Penzler
New York

hop•scotch, n. A children's game in which a player moves a small object into one compartment of a rectangular diagram chalked on the pavement, then hops on one foot from compartment to compartment without touching a chalk line, and picks up the object while standing on one foot in an adjacent compartment.

scotch (2), v.t. To crush or stamp out, as something dangerous; to injure so as to render harmless.

In Paris the gambling was hidden but easy enough to find. This one was in the fifteenth arrondissement near the Citroën factory. The thick door had an iron ring for a handle; a thug absurdly disguised as a doorman admitted Kendig and there was a woman at a desk, attractive enough but she had a cool hard air. Kendig went through the tedium of establishing the credentials of his innocence—he was not a *flic*, he was not Sicilian, he was not Union Corse, he was not this or that. "Just a tourist. I've been here before—with Mme. Labrie. There isn't a message for me by any chance?"

There wasn't. Kendig paid the membership admission and crossed to the elevator. *There will be an interesting message for you tonight at the Club Rouge.* It had been typed, no signature; delivered to his *concierge* by an urchin clutching a five-franc note.

He went up in a lift cage piloted by a little fellow whose face was the texture of old rubber dried grey by a desert sun: the look of an Algerian veteran. The old fellow opened the gate on the third *étage.* *"Bonne chance, M'sieur."* Behind the smile was a leering cynicism.

Kendig's fathomless eyes looked past the tables at a desolate emptiness of his own. The crowd was moderate, the decor discreet, the costumery tiresomely fashionable. Soft laughter here, hard silence there: winners and losers. The bright lighting leeched their faces of color. Kendig drifted among the felted tables. A croupier recognized him from somewhere and smiled; he was in the uniform—the tuxedo that only appeared to have pockets; to discourage temptation. Kendig said, "They've moved the poker?"

"You must speak with the *maître*." The croupier glanced toward a largish man in black who loomed over the neighboring wheel.

Kendig had a word with the *maître* and had to show his bankroll to the cashier behind a cage. He bought five thousand francs in rectangular chips and the *maître* guided him officiously past the tables to an oak door with massive polished brass fittings. Beyond it Kendig found the game, six players around a table that accommodated eight chairs. A houseman stood in the shadows.

There was one woman in the game; he knew who she was but they'd never met. He knew the American, Paul Jaynes; the others were strangers.

Jaynes gave him a debonair greeting and the others glanced at him but Kendig hung back until they had finished the hand. They were playing seven stud—unusual for a room like this. And the house wasn't dealing.

The woman won the hand and gathered the pot; the *maître* bowed his way out and Kendig pulled out one of the empty chairs and sat down with his chips. His place was between Jaynes and the woman, with the woman on his left; he knew Jaynes's manner of play and it didn't trouble him to be downwind of the American.

"Been a while," Jaynes said with his beefy smile and Kendig nodded acknowledgment. Jaynes had a deep suntan and a huckster's compulsion to touch anyone to whom he spoke. He was a film producer of independently financed sex-and-sandal epics.

The others had the same look: businessmen, promoters—two Frenchmen, a German, a Swede. The woman he knew by sight and reputation; he'd seen dossiers on her—she'd spent a few years as patroness of American exiles in Algeria before she'd tired of the game or been frightened out of it by the professionals. She had been married to a banker but there'd been a divorce and she'd reverted to her maiden name.

"Pot limit of course," Jaynes told him, laying out the ground rules. "Check-raise. It's not table stakes—you can go into your pocket if you want to. Or you can tap out. We try to make it easy on ourselves." He smiled; it was a little nervous—it looked as if he might have started with a larger stake than he had now. "Ante twenty-five francs to the player. The house takes one ante for its cut."

"Seven stud or dealer's choice?"

"Seven only."

The woman said, "We decided by majority when we began."

"Suits me." It didn't matter.

The game proceeded. He tried to take an interest in it but most of it came to him like the adult voices you half-heard when you were a small child dozing in the next room. It was one of the things he found soothing about gambling: its detachment from everything. He folded out of three hands on the first round of each; on the fourth he caught a pair of wired jacks in which he had little faith but he strung them along to the sixth card before he dropped out, unimproved; that cost him three hundred francs.

"You're getting cool cards for a newcomer," the woman said apologetically. "You must be disappointed."

He made a soundless reply, a courteous expression. She was wrong, actually; disappointment only follows expectation and he'd had none of that.

After the first half hour he was a thousand francs in the hole and had won only two hands. There had been one extravagant pot;

he had not participated in it; the woman won it. That was what the game amounted to—like surfing; you endured the ordinary waves while you waited for the occasional big one. The players who approached it professionally would have none of that—they played every hand to win—but the big ones came their way too and whatever their denials it came to the same thing. The woman was pushing the big ones hard and he saw she was the player to beat.

The Frenchman Deroget tapped out and left the table in vile spirits. He left nine thousand francs in the game. When the Frenchman was gone Paul Jaynes said, "More than two thousand dollars. Not much for a game like this one—but too much for a shrimp like him. I've heard it around that he's in pretty deep. They'll be keeping a close eye on him." He meant the casino: if a man committed suicide his pockets would be stuffed quietly with money to discourage any idea he might have killed himself over his losses.

A few hands came Kendig's way and he raked them in without particular joy. He was only marking time.

The fifth card of the hand was dealt around; Kendig's was a queen and it gave him three hearts face-up. The woman had two nines in sight but she checked them. Kendig checked as well; Jaynes had a pair of fives showing and was eager to bet them—he was cheerfully transparent about it. There were a thousand francs in the pot by then; Jaynes opened the round's betting with a hundred-franc wager and two of the players beyond him called the bet; the German folded and then it was *Mlle* Stein's turn and she saw the bet and raised five hundred francs. It made a nineteen-hundred-franc pot and when Kendig saw the raise it doubled the size of the pot; and Kendig raised the limit. "The raise is three thousand eight hundred." About a thousand dollars by the day's exchange rate.

Jaynes called the raise without hesitation but he didn't raise back; it meant he had his third five but not his full house. The Swede and the Frenchman folded their hands. The woman smiled a little, thought about it and then called the raise. It ended the round's betting and there was a good sum on the table now: a little over fifteen thousand francs. Two cards remained to be dealt to each player; there would be two more rounds of betting in the hand.

Mlle Stein's card was another four-spot and gave her two pair in sight, nines over fours. The Swede dealt Kendig the king of spades—no visible improvement of his three-hearts-to-the-queen. Jaynes bought the jack of diamonds: his third suit and no evident help for his matched fives. The three-handed betting began with the woman: she counted out five thousand francs into the pot. It could mean anything. Either she had her boat and wanted to build the pot or she didn't have it and wanted to frighten her opponents into not raising.

It was Kendig's turn and he knew every card that had been shown. The hearts were a screen; he had two more queens wired in the hole and he hadn't seen a single king or deuce anywhere in the table's up-cards. Caution dictated a straight call but he made the ten-thousand-franc raise and it folded Jaynes and then the woman was smiling again with her valentine mouth and she bumped him back: "I think I must raise you twenty thousand."

It was as much as some men made in a year. Kendig shrugged and turned to Paul Jaynes. "Can you cover my check?"

"What bank?"

"American Express. Paris branch."

"Will it buy me a peek at your hole cards?"

"No."

Jaynes said, "You've got enough to cover it of course." He said it with a bit of an edge on his voice: not quite a threat.

"Yes." Kendig had a hundred thousand in that bank and a lot

more than that in Switzerland. Most of it had come from gambling of one kind or another. Jaynes knew that much about him. Jaynes said finally, "All right. You can play shy here."

"Thank you." Kendig said it without inflection; he really hadn't cared that much. He pulled the woman's stack of twenty thousand shy and said, "Call."

"What, no reraise *M'sieur?*" She was amused. It meant nothing about her cards; she was too good a player to coffeehouse any revelations.

The final card was dealt face-down and of course the woman had to come out betting; it would have made no sense to sandbag and in any case the bet only encouraged one's opponent to believe it was a bluff: checking the bet couldn't be a bluff.

She bet twenty-five thousand and Jaynes nodded tautly, covering Kendig. Kendig didn't have to perform any calculations to know there were one hundred and ten thousand francs in the pot which the woman could collect if he folded his hand. If he were to call the bet it would make it a 135,000-franc pot—nearly thirty-five-thousand dollars. She had been reading him for the heart flush but if he raised she would have to change her thinking.

He looked at Paul Jaynes. "Blank check?"

"The size of the pot? Christ that's more than I have to pay a top star for two weeks' location work." Jaynes looked at the three men who'd dropped out of the hand. "Anybody want to lay a side bet against Kendig?"

The German had been very impressed by the woman's play tonight; and perhaps he wanted to prove something because she was a Jew. . . . The German said, "Fifty thousand francs?"

"You're faded," Jaynes said. "All right, Kendig."

Kendig looked at the woman. She was watching him, waiting without expression. He said, "Raise the pot."

"I don't have that much in chips." But she was smiling.

"It's not a table-stakes game," Kendig said.

She studied him. He'd doubled the pot and it would cost her 135,000 francs to call his bet. It was a big pot now and if she called the bet it would be a hundred-thousand-dollar pot—that much on a single poker hand. Kendig had never wagered as much in his life; such a hand came only once in a lifetime, win or lose. It didn't matter. His mind began to drift. He accepted the woman's scrutiny, neither evading it nor challenging it. Jaynes looked on, agape, hands trembling with anticipation. The German watched with his face as stiffly controlled as that of an addict who was declining a fix three weeks after taking the cure. The Frenchman and the Swede were hardly breathing.

She had two pair showing; she probably had her full house; she might even have four nines or four fours. Kendig was a stranger betting with another man's money—a man he didn't appear to know too well—and she'd know Jaynes well enough to know he wouldn't shill for anybody. So it was honest play and she had to make her decision on the assumption that Kendig wouldn't bluff with Jaynes's money. She had therefore to conclude Kendig had four queens.

She did not call his raise; she folded her hand. "Well done, M'sieur."

Jaynes buttonholed him at the bar. "Well?"

"She didn't pay to see it."

"But I did, didn't I? At least I offered to. How was I to know whether you had that much in the bank?"

"Why should I have lied about it?"

That stupefied Jaynes. "You had four queens. You must have had."

"I'll tell you this much. I had three queens going in."

"Then you bought the fourth queen on the last down-card?"

"I don't know," Kendig said. "I never looked."

"The hell you didn't. I saw you look at it."

"I shuffled them around. That wasn't the seventh card I looked at."

Jaynes smiled slowly. "Jesus H. Christ. How the hell could you keep from looking?"

Kendig shrugged. The plain fact was he hadn't cared; but it wouldn't be worth the effort to convince Jaynes of that.

"Well we both did all right, didn't we," Jaynes said.

Kendig escaped into the *toilette* and afterward went back into the poker chamber to collect his winnings. The woman was alone at the table adjusting her hair in a handbag mirror. She must have been close to fifty but she hadn't begun to go to seed. "You're leaving?"

"Leaving this game."

"That's hardly sporting." But it was not said unkindly; she was smiling. "You don't take much of an interest in it, do you."

"I suppose not."

"Such a shame," she murmured. Then her smile changed. "I don't know which is worse—a helpless puppy or a lost American. The only thing you really want is to get home, isn't it."

"What makes you think that?"

"I've never met an American who didn't. Why don't you?"

"Perhaps I will."

"You'll feel better then."

"Will I?" He nodded to the houseman, who swept the chips into a sack and went away with them after Kendig finished making the count.

She said, "You *are* the one who hounded my trail in Algiers, aren't you?"

"I was one of them. For a little while. They moved me out after a few months."

"And now?"

"I'm retired," Kendig said.

"I see." She didn't believe it for a minute but she was amused rather than angry. "Our Swedish friend just finished telling me what a success you've been on the Continent. Gambling, motorcars, skiing, flying aeroplanes. You've a rather interesting sort of retirement."

"Yes," he said because that was easier than denying it.

She pushed the cards together and her hands became still: she stared at his face. "Would you care to come home with me tonight?"

"Thank you," he said, "I think not." He executed a slight bow and left the room.

The cashier was waiting for him. "*M'sieur* prefers cash or our cheque?"

"Cash, please."

"It is a dangerous sum to be carrying on one's person, *M'sieur*."

"All the same I'll have it in cash if you don't mind."

"As *M'sieur* wishes."

The *maître* approached, burly and discreet. "*Monsieur* Kendig? *Téléphone, s'il vous plâit. . . . Par ici.*"

He took it in someone's office. He picked up the receiver but didn't speak into it until the *maître* had backed out and shut the door. "Yes?"

"*C'est vous*, Kendig?"

"*Oui.*"

"*Ici Michel.*"

Kendig recognized the voice. It was Mikhail Yaskov. Now Yaskov spoke in English:

"You received my note then."

"Yes."

"I should like to meet with you, old friend."

"For what purpose?"

"To discuss a matter which may prove mutually beneficial."

"I doubt the existence of any such matter, Mikhail."

"Nevertheless perhaps you will humor me?"

Kendig's shoulders stirred. "Why not then?"

"It must be *tout de suite* I am afraid. I am only in Paris another twenty-four hours."

"Tomorrow then?"

"Tomorrow," Yaskov said, his voice very controlled. "I shall be with the *messieurs* Citroën and Mercier. Do you know them?"

"Yes." It wasn't far from here: the intersection of the quai André Citroën and the rue Sebastien Mercier, just below the Mirabeau bridge on the left bank. It was a workers' neighborhood, narrow passages leading back, their drab walls daubed with Communist slogans. Fitting enough.

Yaskov said, "We shall meet at Number Sixteen, yes?"

Sixteen hundred hours: four o'clock in the afternoon. Harmless enough. "All right, Mikhail."

"I assure you the transaction will interest you."

Kendig doubted it but he made no reply. "I'll see you tomorrow."

"Yes. *Bonne chance,* old friend." A soft chuckle and then the line died.

Kendig cradled it and went out and collected his envelope from the cashier. Jaynes waved at him eagerly from across the room but he only waved back and followed the *maître* to the lift; he rode down in the cage with the old Algerian veteran and went out into the night with a pocketful of money.

| 2 |

But she wasn't discouraged that easily. She was waiting by her car at the curb; she held a cigarette imperiously, waiting to have it lighted. The car was white, a Volvo 1800 a few years old—the super-charged grand-touring coupe they had stopped making in '72. It didn't quite suit her; she was more the Jaguar or Ferrari sort—something juggernauty.

When he held his lighter to the cigarette she drew the smoke slowly into her mouth. Her hair was fashionably Medusan; she had a full ripe body and an earthy manner—saloons, cigarettes, cards, beds.

"Well good night again," he said and began to turn away.

She ignored it. "You have a first name, don't you?"

"I suppose so." Everyone always called him Kendig. "It's Miles."

"Miles Kendig. I rather like that—it has a strong sound. Come on then, get in. I'll drop you wherever you like. You won't find a taxi in this quarter, not at this hour."

". . . Thank you." He said it grudgingly and went around to hold the driver's door for her.

She managed the car with poor driving rhythm; it was not an implement to which she'd been born—he suspected she'd grown up amid chauffeurs and taught herself to drive at some point in order to expand the boundaries of her independence but it wasn't anything she'd ever done for pleasure.

He made conversation because evidently she expected it. "You live in Paris all the time now?"

"Live? I imagine one could put it that way. Living is something most of us postpone, isn't it. We sell the present for a chance at a future where we may do our living when we're old and we've lost the talent for it."

"You don't strike me as a woman who's saving up for her retirement."

"Well I was fortunate. I have an ex-husband who settled my pension on me prematurely. Did you ever meet Isaac?"

"No."

"Tycoon, banker, merchant prince. I'm sure you know the type. They're always terrified by their Ozymandian dreams. The future must be guaranteed forever. Ninety-nine-year leases and thousand-year trust funds. It's bloody depressing."

She drove along the quay. There was a good moon but it was very late for lovers; the evening was silent and uninhabited but for the *clochards*, the human flotsam in rags sleeping in the streets underneath the globular streetlamps that hung like rotted melons on their corroded stalks. The woman said, "They disturb your friend Jaynes, the *clochards*. For some reason they frighten him. Would he have us house them in the best hotels, I wonder? Then where would all the Americans live?"

Her laughter was mocking but not unkind. He didn't respond but he couldn't share in her contempt for Jaynes's compassion: he couldn't deceive himself any longer into mocking anyone else's convictions. He could only envy them.

Past the *Tour Eiffel,* Napoleon's tomb, up the Saint Germain, a tourist's route across the island beneath Notre Dame—the architectural gestures of an ambitious past. His eyes opaque, Kendig watched it all flow past; watched the woman's animated face hovering above the wheel. A tiny Renault squirted in front of her and she shouted at it: *"Cochon!"*

Then they were on the right bank threading the maze below the Opera; his hotel was only a few blocks distant. She hadn't asked where he was staying but evidently she knew. She slid the sports car in at the curb a block short of it. "You honestly didn't care, did you."

"About what?"

"Your cards. The size of the wager."

He turned his hand palm up.

"Remarkable," she said.

"Is it."

"You find it an effort merely to grunt a word or two, don't you, Miles Kendig. Yet like the ashes of Alexander you were once Alexander. An exciting reputation precedes you, you know."

He looked at her. "What the hell." It was said of her that in her bedroom in Neuilly there was a statuette of a Punjabi idol clutching his distended giant member. "I'll go to your place."

"You needn't have made it such a bloody concession," she said angrily; but she put the car in gear.

———

In another few years she might become one of those middle-aged divorcées who take up with young Continental gentlemen who teach Italian. But she had not yet degenerated into that sort of female impersonation; she was vital and she stirred what juices had not atrophied in him. "At least you're not a zombie *there*," she told him. He took no particular pleasure from the knowledge.

In the morning he pushed away his plate of breakfast untasted and left her, on foot, strolling in any direction through the *Bois*. She had smiled gently but she'd made no demands when he got up to leave: she was interested but not desperate, she was willing to be casual about it and he thought he might even come back to her some time.

After a while he ambushed a taxi and rode into the snarled center of Paris, made arrangements to have his winnings transferred to Switzerland for deposit, walked to his hotel and met the *concierge* and paid tomorrow's rent as if he believed there would be a tomorrow.

In his room he stripped and bathed and took the trouble to shave; the little daily routines reassured him a bit. In the mirror his face showed the years: every crease. He still had a full head of hair, pepper-grey now; his face was rectilinear, all parallel planes, and his eyebrows were two bushy triangles over his slanted eyes. It was a middle-Caucasion face that had served him well in the chameleon years. In France he passed easily for a Frenchman because it never occurred to the French that a foreigner could speak the language properly. He had posed at one time or another as an Italian, an Arab, a German and a Croat.

From eleven until three he sat in the room waiting, neither reading nor smoking nor otherwise stirring his consciousness. At three he went out.

———

He had a *croque monsieur* in the Deux Magots and took the bus along to the rue de la Convention, dismounted at the quay and had a look around, more through habit than from any particular caution. A woman in dusty black hawked tickets to the *Loterie Nationale*. Lower-class Frenchmen sat at dirty checkerclothed tables before a pair of cafés and a *brasserie*, drinking table wine. A block distant a group of street workers leaned on their tools, never laughing, seldom working, ogling a girl who strolled by—just another girl who worked the bars and the men in them, a brittle black-haired borderline alcoholic who probably couldn't remember the faces of the men she'd bedded in the past week; but she held the workers' full attention until she disappeared. In Switzerland, Kendig recalled, the street workers laughed and they worked. And as Orson Welles and Graham Greene had pointed out, all that energy and spirit had produced, in five hundred years of peaceful civilization, the cuckoo clock.

A coachload of tourists decanted along the quay and Kendig moved around, keeping out of the way of the Americans taking slide photos and Super-8 movies of one another. He was thinking: if you compressed all the matter in a human being, closing down the spaces between cells, the spaces between electrons and nuclei, you would end up with a heavy mass about the size of a one-eighth karat diamond, and far less useful.

Yaskov came along, elegant in a suede jacket with a Malacca cane in his spidery hand; he gave Kendig the benediction of his grave nod. Russians do not smile politely; they smile only when they are amused. It makes them appear rude to outsiders. Kendig fell in step and they walked out to the center of the bridge and down the steps onto the tiny island. The park benches were deserted. "So nice to see you again," Yaskov said. His gleaming skin was stretched over the bones almost to the point of splitting. In the profession he was an *éminence grise*; his name commanded respect in all the agencies. He was not the sort of Russian who would be surprised to learn that America was no longer a land of sweatshops and scarlet letters and riders of the purple sage. (It was truly amazing how many of them were still like that.)

Yaskov's urbane English was almost perfect. "You won a great sum of money last night, yes? It was your good fortune I sent you there."

"Well I'm deeply grateful." Kendig was wry.

Yaskov too was a gambler; his face never betrayed him. "I'm distressed to see you so lackluster, old friend."

"It's only post-coital *tristesse*."

"For so many months?"

He was tired of the roundabout game. "Then you've been keeping tabs on me. Why? I'm out of the game now—you know that."

"By choice, is it?"

"I'm sure you know that too."

"Actually I'm not sure I do, old friend. My sources in Langley haven't always been reliable. It's said you were retired—involuntarily."

"Is it."

"Is that true?"

"I don't see that it matters whether it's true. I'm retired—that's truth enough."

"You have fifty-three years."

"Yes."

"Absurd," Yaskov said. "I myself have sixty-one. Am I retired?"

"Do you want to be?"

"No. Avidly no. I should be bored to distraction."

"Would you now."

They sat down on a bench. A barge drifted past laden with what appeared to be slag. Its aftercabin had a Citroën 2CV parked on the roof and a line of multihued washing strung like an ocean vessel's signal pennants. The barge's family sunned on the afterdeck—a fat wife, three children—while the husband manned the tiller and smoked. Generations of them were born, lived and died aboard the canal barges. It was a peaceful life and a bastion of unchange.

A little motor runabout zipped past the barge, disturbing its tranquillity with the sharp chop of its frenetic wake.

Kendig said, "What's your offer, Mikhail?"

"Life, old friend."

Kendig grinned at him. "And the alternative?"

"I did not invite you to join me here on such a pleasant day in order to impose ultimata upon you," Yaskov said. "I make no threats at all. The alternative would be of your own making, not of mine. I simply offer to revive you. I wish to bring you back to life."

"The resurrection of Miles Kendig." His tongue toyed with it. "A fine title for an autobiography."

"Don't be evasive."

"What is it you want, then? Are you short a defector this month?"

"Oh defection is such a degrading transformation, don't you think? In any case I should imagine you'd be just as bored in a Moscow flat as you are here. My dear Miles, I'm offering to put you back into the game. Back into action. Isn't it what you want?"

"As a double agent I'd be of very little use. I have no access to my former employers."

"Double agents are tedious little people anyhow," Yaskov said. "They're required to be so colorless. I don't think it would suit you at all. No, it's really quite straightforward. I should like to run you in the field. As my own agent. I can assure you the members of my string regard me as a most amiable Control. How does it strike you?"

Kendig tried briefly to put some show of interest on his face. Yaskov did not speak further; he left his invitation dangling like a baited hook.

The barge disappeared round the bend on its leisurely passage to Le Havre. The little powerboat came zigzagging back upstream, splitting the water with its razor bow, planing and slapping gaily.

The sun on Kendig's cheek was soporific. He didn't want to have to think.

Yaskov began to draw circles on the pavement with the rubber tip of his cane. It was a subtle rebuke. It forced Kendig to speak. "It wouldn't be worth it to me, I'm afraid.

"We'd make it worthwhile of course. There's plenty of money."

"Money costs too much when you have to earn it that way."

"Then what is it you want? Power?"

"God no."

"I could let you run a string of your own if you like. You might even rise to the policy level in time. Doesn't that intrigue you? The possibility of making policy for your former enemies?"

"Sounds tedious to me."

"Our kind has been on this planet for perhaps two million years," Yaskov said, "and during all but one percent of that period we lived as hunters. The hunting way of life is the only one natural to man. The one most rewarding. It was your way of life but your government took it away from you. I offer to return it to you."

"It's self-destructive lunacy, that's all it is."

"Well my dear Miles you can't lead our kind of life and expect to live forever. But at least we can be alive for a time."

"It's all computers now. World War Three will be known as the Paperkrieg. There's no need for my kind of toy gladiator any more. We're as obsolete as fur-trapping explorers."

"It's hardly gone that far, old friend. Otherwise why should I be making you this offer?"

"Because you can't face obsolescence—you won't acknowledge it the way I've done. You're as redundant as I am—you just don't know it yet." Kendig smiled meaninglessly. "We've seven'd out. All of us."

"I don't know the expression but you make it clear enough."

"It's to do with a dice game."

"Yes, of course. You're beginning to annoy me. You're not merely disenchanted; you're condescending. I don't need to be patronized. I suspect behind your smokescreen of boredom you're resisting my offer out of some absurd vestige of chauvinistic scruple."

"It could be that. Who knows." When Kendig had learned the game he'd had Truman and the Yaskovs had had Stalin; it had been easy enough to discern which of them wore the white hat and which the black hat. Now there was none of that left. The only distinction was that the West's leadership was more petty than the East's. It wasn't even a game for the intelligence operatives any more; it was only a nihilistic exercise, going through the motions out of habit, answering not to any sense of mission or principle but only to the procedural requirements of bureaucracy. There was no point to it any more. But Yaskov might be right; Kendig might have hated his side too long to be comfortable with the idea of working for them. He didn't know; he didn't really care.

Yaskov brooded toward the enormous monolith of the *Radiodiffusion* which cowed the right bank beneath it. "Well it was an intriguing idea to me. I did hope you would take an interest."

"You'd better forget it. I'd be no good to you—I'd put my foot in it anyway."

"Certainly you would if the work didn't excite you. I won't press you again but you might bear in mind that I won't have closed the offer."

It meant only that the idea of recruiting him had been Yaskov's own. Probably he hadn't cleared it with his superiors. Therefore its failure would not reflect on Yaskov. It meant Kendig was in no danger from them; there'd be no retribution. Somehow the realization angered him.

Yaskov stood up and prodded the cement with his cane. "You were one of the very best. I feel quite sad." Then he walked away.

He sat on the bench without stirring. Pigeons flocked around, then drifted away in disappointment when he had nothing to feed them. Yaskov's high narrow figure dwindled along the quay and was absorbed. Traffic was a muted whirring hum on the *pont*; a thin haze drifted across the sky and Kendig stared among the trees with empty eyes. Recollections drifted through his mind. Lorraine— a dreadful woman with a dreadful name. The caper along the Danube when they'd brought Rozhsenny out in the rain with the Soviet guns spitting blindly in the night. The old man, and the idea of suicide that had hung around him always. Kendig had no scruple against it. A man always ought to have the right to remove himself from the world at his discretion.

But it had no appeal. There was no challenge; it was too passive. He didn't want to be dead: he was already dead. Yaskov had strummed a chord there. To be alive might be the goal. But it was harder to find, all the time. He'd done everything to provoke his jaded sensibilities. High risks: the motor racing, skiing, flying lessons, the gambling which had been satisfying until his own capacities had defeated its purpose: he'd always been professional at whatever he did and his skills were the sort that took the risk out of it after a while. He'd bent the bank at Biarritz a month ago and since then he'd lost all interest in it. And he'd long since given up the athletic challenges. They'd all got to looking the same way— the way bowling had looked when he'd been a college freshman. As soon as he'd discovered that the object of bowling was to learn how to do exactly the same thing every time, he'd lost interest.

He thought part of it was the fact that there was no human antagonist. There was no "other side" with which to compete. He had a quarter century of playing the running-dog game and it had educated his palate to its own flavor; his appetite had been trained to crave human conflict: the chess game of reality with stakes that weren't tokens, rules that weren't artificial.

At one time he had tried to get reinstated.

They'd sent him into the Balkans on a very chancy mission but the objective had some meaning so he'd volunteered for it. He'd accomplished the job but he'd been injured badly—it had been critical for a while—and his cover had been blown. After he'd convalesced he'd done some office work and then they'd put him out to pasture on early retirement. Eighteen months later he'd asked for reactivation but he was too old, they told him, too old and too hot. And in any case Cutter had taken his place and wasn't about to relinquish it. They didn't want any part of him. They'd offered him a sop—a time-filler desk over at NSA with a fair GS rank and salary, punching decodes through computers. A bloody file clerk's job.

When the sun tipped over it got chilly and he left the islet. Snatches of things ran through his mind in a jumbled sort of order and he made a desultory game of tracing the pattern they made. They came without chronology from the retentive cells. The suicide note left by the screen actor George Sanders: "I am leaving because I am bored." Fragmentarily a poem by Stephen Crane which he hadn't read since he was a sophomore; he was sure he didn't have it right: "A man said to the Universe, 'Sir, I exist!' 'Yes,' replied the Universe, 'but that fact does not create in me a sense of obligation.'" At any rate something like that. . . . *I wish to bring you back to life. . . . The resurrection of Miles Kendig. . . . My dear Miles, I'm offering to put you back in the game. Back into action. Isn't it what you want? The hunting way of life is the only one natural to man. I offer to return it to you.*

Well it was something Yaskov didn't have it in his power to restore.

But it was the first time in months he'd felt things churning and he kept toying with them while he slouched up the rue

Lecourbe toward Montparnasse. It was the first time his dialogue with himself hadn't taken the flavor of a talk with a stranger in the adjacent seat of an airliner: an exchange of meaningless monologues, half of them self-serving lies, the other half mechanical responses and none of it designed to be remembered beyond the debarkation ramp.

He ate something in a café and had two Remy Martins and walked all the way back to the hotel. There were no personal things in sight although he had resided in the suite for nearly two months; its occupant had kept himself hidden from it.

The telephone.

"*M'sieur*—a gentleman wishes to see you."

"Who is he?"

"I do not know, *M'sieur.*"

"I'll be down. Ask him to wait." He wasn't about to invite to his room any man who wouldn't give his name.

The rickety cage discharged him into the dusky lobby and he saw Glenn Follett in the reading chair in the alcove. Follett charged beaming to his feet, hearty ebullience filling his dewlapped Basset face. "Hey old buddy—long time no see, hey? How they hanging?"

It made Kendig wince. Follett pumped his hand enthusiastically and reared back: tipped his head to one side and tucked his jowly chin in, contriving to look affectionate and conspiratorial at once. "My goodness you do look well." He said it in the voice of a man telling a polite lie. "Life of luxury in retirement, hey?"

"What do you want, Glenn?" It was a question to which he already knew the answer because he didn't believe in the sort of coincidence that would drop Follett on his doorstep within hours of his meeting with Mikhail Yaskov. But he asked it anyway because it was the best way to shut off Follett's backslapping spout of painful old-buddy pleasantries.

Follett waved his arms around. He was utterly incapable of

talking without the accompaniment of vast gestures. "What do you say we have a drink or two?"

"I've already had a drink. We can talk here."

Follett shot a glance toward the *concierge* behind the desk. That was twenty feet across the lobby. Kendig said, "He's a little deaf and he's only got about forty words of English. Stop looking around—the lamps aren't bugged."

"Well if you say so, sure. Hell. Well then let's have a seat, hey?" Follett led the way back into the alcove and Kendig trailed along reluctantly. Follett sat down with his elbows on his knees so he could flap his hands when he talked. "Damn good to see you again. I mean that."

"Come off it."

"Well Christ Kendig, it *has* been a long time, and here we are both living in the same town. I mean it's good for old friends to get together—we ought to do it more often, you know?"

Kendig said, "You had a tail on Yaskov today, didn't you."

Follett grinned unabashedly. "Sure. Why else would I be here?"

"All right. Get it off your chest. I haven't got all night."

"The hell you haven't. What have you got, Kendig—a vital business meeting? A hard-breathing tryst? Don't give me no bullfeathers. You haven't got a Goddamned thing to do except go upstairs to your little ten-by-twelve room and stare at the walls. I'd think you'd welcome some company from an old officemate."

Kendig just watched him. Follett made a face and dropped his voice several decibels. "All right. What was it about?"

"What was what about?" He didn't want to give Follett the satisfaction.

An exasperated jerk of head, pinch of lips. "The meet with Yaskov, old buddy."

"Ships and shoes and sealing wax."

"Why are you making it so hard for me?"

"Maybe it amuses me."

"Then why aren't you smiling?" Follett flapped his palms. "Come on now. What did he want?"

"The same as you. He thought it would be pleasant if a couple of old friends got together and reminisced about the good old days."

"I see." Follett wasn't buying it; he was just inviting added comment but Kendig didn't make any and finally Follett said, "You'll have to do a little better than that."

"Why?"

"Because it won't wash."

"That's not what I mean."

"Then say what you mean, all right?"

"What I mean," Kendig said, "why will I have to do better than that? Why do I have to tell you anything at all? I don't work for you people any more."

"Come on, Kendig, don't force me to make threats."

"This conversation's getting tedious, wouldn't you say?"

"We can make holy hell for you. Is that what you want?"

"I can't see you bothering to do that. Not with me."

"You're not enjoying this. Just tell me what I want to know and I'll go away."

"You'll go away anyway. Sooner or later."

"You're an exasperating son of a bitch."

"I know."

"Should I offer to buy it then?"

"No."

"I didn't think so. Then tell me this. What is it you want?"

"To be left alone."

"Is that what you told Yaskov?"

"Maybe."

"Everybody wants something. What do you want, Kendig?"

"I just told you."

"Nuts." Follett became still; he examined his hands. "You're just about the most expendable human being on earth right now, I suppose you realize that. You're no good to anybody, not even yourself. I don't think there's anybody in the whole world who'd ever miss you. Except maybe Mikhail Yaskov. What kind of deal did you make with him?"

"I didn't make any deal with him, Glenn."

"Then why not tell me what he wanted?"

"Because it's your job to find that out. Not mine, any more."

"What am I supposed to do? Ask Yaskov?"

"Why don't you? It might be fun."

Follett put his hands on his knees preparatory to rising. "It's not smart to alienate your friends. You might need us some day."

"I doubt that."

"I'll have to report back to Langley. They'll have to decide what to do about you. If they think you've made some tie-up with the other side they'll probably cut orders to have you terminated. Although I wouldn't recommend it, frankly. I don't think you'd be worth the trouble. You don't matter any more, Kendig. You're washed up." With an expansive gesture of dismissal and disgust Follett lurched from the chair and plodded away. Kendig got up and watched him go out to the street. Then he went over to the lift and returned to his room.

He got into bed and lay half-dresed staring at the ceiling. *Everybody wants something. What do you want, Kendig? You're no good to anybody. You don't matter any more. You're washed up.*

Something was taking shape: an elusive thought, an unfamiliar emotion.

After a long while he dozed. When he came awake he found he had his arms around one of the pillows. He put it back where it belonged and switched off the light.

They'd got some mileage out of him and thrown him out like a used car. Yaskov had come along and kicked his tires and made an offer but when Yaskov had tried the ignition the key wouldn't turn. Then Follett had come along and loked at the dilapidated rusty hulk and sneered: All used up. Throw it on the junk heap.

He drowsed but something kept him from falling asleep. He kept shifting position; he had to wipe the sweat off his face with the hem of the sheet.

Everybody wants something. What do you want, Kendig?

My dear Miles, I'm offering to put you back in the game. Back into action. Isn't it what you want?

Isn't it what you want?

Unfamiliar sensations rubbed against him. He began to descend uneasily into sleep but that was when the anger burst its housing and grenaded into him.

He sat up, switched on the light, reached for his watch. It was three in the morning.

Why not rub their noses in it?

The idea was as fully shaped as Minerva from the brow of Jupiter. "Hell," he said aloud. "Why not?"

They'd take it to be a suicidal gesture—they'd look at the record and they'd have to reach that conclusion. It would take them a long time to realize he wasn't inviting suicide. He was challenging them to the ultimate game and he meant to win it.

He padded to the desk and began to write quickly on the hotel stationery—a crabbed scrawl that looked like something unreeling from a seismograph.

They'd set the hounds on him for this. They'd come after him with raging vengeance. They'd set fire to the world if they had to: they'd drop everything else in the frantic rush to nail him.

He felt the race of his pulse and heard a sound he had forgotten: his own laughter.

| 3 |

The security man gave Leonard Ross a vague smile of recognition; all the same Ross had to run his card through the ID machine before it granted him the dubious asylum of the fourth floor.

As always Ross found it discomfiting. Myerson's outer sanctum was as forbidding as a penitentiary: not the clean chill of sterile modernity but the grey austere drabness of nineteen-fiftyish technocracy. The chairs were tubular steel affairs with seats padded in Naugahyde and they looked civilized enough but there was no way to relax in them. Ross sat rigidly upright, buoyed a little by the fact that he was the only visitor waiting to see Myerson—perhaps he wouldn't have to cool his heels too long.

The secretary opened the inner door. "Mr. Myerson will see you now." *The doctor will see you now*—he went in as if to a dentist's chair. The secretary preceded him, swinging smartly with a high-hipped stride; Ross hadn't met her often enough to know her name although if she'd been ten years younger he'd have made a point of it. She rapped out a discreet code on Myerson's door and pushed it open. Ross tried to march right in with some show of confidence but he wasn't sure it was convincing. Myerson was in charge of his department but Myerson was also the Agency's hatchet man. You were never quite sure that a summons to the fourth floor wasn't going to be your last one.

Myerson was rummaging in a four-drawer cabinet built into the wall. "Sit down, Ross."

The chairs had been arranged—two leather armchairs drawn up to make a triangle with the desk. So there was to be a third party to the meeting. Ross sat.

The file drawer slid shut like something in the morgue. Myerson brought a *Top Secret* folder to the desk, pulled his chair out, sat down and crossed his plump legs. He was twenty pounds overweight, a big-hipped man with the attitude of command. His pale tan suit nicely set off the mahogany sunlamp tan of his bald head. "We're waiting for Cutter."

"I thought he was in Kuwait?"

"Aden. I've pulled him out. He'll have landed at Dulles by now—he should have been here. It may be the traffic. While we're waiting for him have a look at this."

It was a copystat, something typed, fourteen double-spaced pages. *Conspiracy of Killers*, it was headed. *By Miles Kendig.* He looked up and Myerson was smiling, anger bubbling visibly beneath it. "Go ahead—read it."

He was on the fifth page when Cutter came into the office. Ross got to his feet. They'd never met but he'd heard a great deal; Cutter was a man who trailed legends.

Cutter's handshake was quick and dry. He would remember Ross's face twenty years from now. He had cunning eyes and a cynical mouth. He ran to a physical type: narrow and vain—dark, trim, long angular face, graceful. He had tiny teeth and beautiful dark womanly eyes: he looked the sort who'd race stock cars on dirt ovals in Appalachia. He was no rustic but he had that aura of raw primitive machismo.

Myerson wasn't a man for polite preambles. "Take your coat off, sit down, read this. Then we'll talk."

———

Cutter absorbed the fourteen pages in the time it took Ross to read the last nine. Then Cutter sailed it onto the desk. It indicated something about him: he wouldn't have to look at it again, he'd committed it to memory. "Where's the original?"

"I imagine Kendig's still got it."

"Then where'd this come from?" The chilly precision of Cutter's voice disquieted Ross.

Myerson reached for the big glass ashtray. It was the first time Ross had noticed the cigar. While they'd been reading Myerson had chewed it to shreds; he dumped the remains in the ashtray and licked his teeth distastefully. "It came from Bois Blanc in Paris."

Cutter said drily, "Well then he's picked the right publisher for it."

"Can we stop them from publishing it?" Ross asked.

"Wouldn't help," Myerson said. "He went hog-wild on the Xerox machine. At least fourteen publishers in as many countries have received copies of this thing. Or at least that's what Kendig claims in his covering letter to Desrosiers."

Desrosiers was the iconoclastic publisher of the Bois Blanc series. He'd published all the clandestine *samizdat* best sellers that were smuggled out of the Soviet Union. Myerson said, "We don't know who the other publishing houses are. We'll find out in time of course but I'm not sure what good it will do us. We can't burn them all to the ground."

"We might persuade them not to buy it."

"How?" Cutter shook his head. "They know it's a multiple submission. Damned few of them will turn it down and risk missing out on their cut of the pie. It'll sell of lot of copies."

"Can't we convince them he's a crazy?" Ross insisted.

"Desrosiers knows Kendig," Myerson said. "They've known each other for thirty years. Kendig brought him Medvedev's first manuscript."

Ross slapped the typed pages in his lap. "But this stuff—it's so wild. Who'd believe it?" He turned a page and read aloud, a sarcastic tone: " 'What was Richard Nixon doing in Dallas on the day John Kennedy was assassinated there?' I mean that's the cheapest kind of gossip-rag innuendo. It's nothing but an empty teaser. 'How many tons of counterfeit North Vietnamese currency has Air America dropped on North Vietnam since the truce was signed?' And the bit—I can't find it now—the bit about the assassination of Duvalier."

"Page eight," Cutter murmured.

It flustered Ross but he went on indignantly: "Or this thing about the Soviets assassinating Nasser with a spray of prussic acid. I mean how wild can you get? And it's all unsupported, he's given no details. All we've got to do is lean on them, show them how irresponsible it would be to publish unconfirmed rubbish like this. Make Kendig out to be a paranoid idiot who's gone around the bend. I mean that's what he is, isn't it? It's got to be that."

Myerson said, "He's a little crazy. But not that way. You're right about one thing—it's a teaser, nothing more."

"But he's got the goods to pay it off," Cutter said.

Myerson nodded. "That's the thing. It's all true, you know. And Kendig will cite chapter and verse."

———

It was hard to absorb. Ross said, "It's *true?*"

"Of course it is," Cutter said. "He's not an absolute fool."

"But he was a field agent. He'd never have had access to anything like this."

"After his convalescent leave he spent eight months working two doors down the hall from this office," Myerson said. "He didn't fit in, he couldn't stick it out—he never had the patience to sit at a desk. We offered to move him to NSA but he gave it the back of his hand. We had no choice but to retire him."

"And in those eight months he came across all this stuff?"

Cutter said, "He must have made a point of looking for it. To give him an arsenal against us in case he ever had to use it."

"That's a little fanciful."

"He was never a man to trust anybody. He always had to have an edge. That was what made him so good at the job. He never let anybody get him into a corner. He always had the escape route staked out in advance."

Ross stacked the pages neatly in his lap, evening up the corners. "I've never come across any of this stuff and I've worked here six years now."

"Not on the fourth floor you haven't," Cutter said. "This outfit's like the *Waffen SS*, it's got a compulsion to keep records of all its crimes in quintuplicate." He was talking to Myerson now: "I've bitched about that for years. Haven't I."

"When they move you to the fifth floor you can start making policy," Myerson replied, unruffled. "We'll get along faster if you stop dredging up I told-you-so's. Right now we've got a problem and I expect you to provide the solution."

Cuter only nodded; he was deep in thought. Ross said, "What am I doing here?"

Myerson blinked. "You'll have to ask Cutter."

Cutter said, "I asked for you."

"Me? Why?"

"Because you've got a reputation for doing what you're told without stopping to make waves."

Myerson said, "We can't assume anything; but we can hope he hasn't written the rest of the book yet. If that's the case your job is easy—just prevent him from finishing it."

"With extreme prejudice," Cutter said, very wryly. "Personally I prefer the word 'kill.' It's the goddamned euphemisms that'll do us all in." He snaked out his long brown hand to glance at his watch; shot his cuff and asked, "When did Desrosiers receive that?"

"Four days ago."

"Shit. Hand delivered?"

"In the mail. It had a Paris postmark."

"How did we get it?"

"We've got an editor in our pocket. Naturally. Kendig knew that—that's why he picked that publisher to send it to first. I suspect the Russians have someone there too, in view of the sort of thing Desrosiers publishes. Maybe it's even the same editor, who knows. In any event you can be sure there's a copy of this in Moscow by now—and I think you can be sure Kendig knows that too."

"And they won't like the thing any more than we do. So we'll be tripping over the Comrades."

Ross sat silent as if forgotten; the dialogue went on—Myerson said, "There'll be copies surfacing in Whitehall and Bonn and the Arab capitals and God knows where else. The way he's gone about it guarantees that. He's trying to make the biggest noise he can."

Ross said, "I don't understand that. Why?"

Myerson pointed at Cutter. "You know the man. What's your judgment?"

Cutter's index finger flicked toward the pages he'd tossed on

Myerson's desk. "'If the peoples of the nations concerned find out what has been done, and is being done, in their name. . . .'" He was quoting it verbatim after the cursory reading he'd given it; Ross looked it up to make sure and Cutter had got it letter perfect.

Cutter said, "It's got a phony ring to it. Kendig's never suffered from the obvious brands of moral rationalizing. He never went in for sterile liberal dogmas. The only time I ever heard him get near the subject was once when Nixon was running in 'sixty-eight. He said he figured people got the kind of government they deserved. Nothing surprises him. He's not the type to get indignant or bleat about injustice."

"And?"

"The last I heard he was having fits of Gothic melancholia. Severe depressions. Bored to death."

"So?"

Again Cutter pointed at the pages. "Maybe that's his suicide note. He's not the sleeping-pill type. He'd want to go down in flames. So he wants us to come and kill him."

"Then you'd better do it," Myerson said.

"He won't sit and wait for it. He won't make it easy."

"I have every confidence in you." Myerson turned a wholly fictitious smile toward Ross. "Cutter can find a man the way a dog can smell out a bitch in heat."

Cutter raised one hand a few inches to acknowledge the tribute. "Kendig's a professional. A professional is somebody who doesn't make stupid mistakes. He had this planned ten moves ahead before he put that thing in the mail."

"Don't be defeatist."

"I think we ought to ignore him," Cutter said. "Why play his silly game? I doubt he's got the patience to sit down and write the whole book. If he sees we're not going to play with him he'll give it up—he'll stand in a highway somewhere and wait for a truck to run him down."

Myerson said, "We're not the only ones involved. If we don't get to him somebody will. Most likely the Comrades. They'll realize when they read this that he knows a lot more than they ever thought he knew. They'll want him alive—at first. We don't really want them to have him, do we."

It was obvious Cutter didn't like it but he had to concede the point. "Then we'll get the son of a bitch. It's a grisly waste, though."

"Granted. Can't be helped."

"All right. The tedious details. Last known location?"

"He checked out of a hotel in Paris a week ago today. It's all in the file. Hasn't been seen since."

"Anything on the type face?"

"We ran it through analysis. It's a Smith-Corona portable. The type is called Presidential Pica. There must be a hundred thousand like it. He bought the paper and the manila mailing envelope—envelopes, actually—at a stationer in the boulevard Raspail. Three weeks ago."

"Most recent known associates?"

"It's all in the file. One interesting item—about a month ago Kendig had a meeting with Mikhail Yaskov in Paris. We keep tabs on Yaskov when we can."

"A month ago. That's before he bought the typing paper."

"Yes."

"Christ. There's a connection then."

"Maybe. Who knows. Follett interviewed him but he couldn't get anything out of him. At any rate he hasn't defected—we'd have known." Myerson picked up the papers Cutter had tossed on his desk; he straightened them and put them into the file folder along with the thick sheafs that were already in it. Then he proffered it and Cutter got up to take it. It was evident the interview had ended; Ross got to his feet.

Ross's office was a third-floor cubicle. They used it because Cutter, a field man, had no office of his own. Ross waited just inside the door, uncertain of his priorities. Cutter settled it for him by walking around behind the desk and occupying the position.

They shared out the contents of the file and read it. Ross felt useless in the knowledge that he wasn't absorbing a fifth as much as Cutter was taking in. And for the last forty-five minutes Cutter leaned back in the tilt chair steepling his fingers and inquiring of the ceiling while Ross finished reading it all.

Then Cutter said, "Notice anything interesting?"

"Sure. He's a hell of an odd bird."

"About the file itself, I mean."

"Oh that. You mean the absence of photographs and fingerprints."

Cutter nodded slowly and gave him a brief glance that might have been approval. "He's always had an allergy to cameras. We've got a few shots of the back of his head. That's one reason Myerson put your name forward—you've met Kendig."

"Only a few times—casual, around the building."

"But you remember what he looks like, don't you?"

"I'd know him if I saw him."

"There you are, then."

"I thought you said you were the one who asked for me."

"I asked for a gopher. Myerson suggested your name. I agreed with him."

"Am I supposed to be flattered?"

"No. I'll run your ass ragged."

"It'll be a change at least."

"Hold onto that thought when it gets dicey. Now you'd better know about the fingerprints. We haven't got Kendig's."

"At all?"

"At some point he got into his own file. Removed the mug shots and dental records and substituted a phony fingerprint card. We didn't get onto it until after he'd left us. Then I made a point of tracking it down—I'm not sure why. They belonged to a waiter in a dump out in Alexandria. Kendig paid him twenty dollars to put his fingerprints on the card."

"Why'd he do that?"

"He's never trusted anybody. He's pathological about it."

"Why?"

"You've read the backgrounding."

It was phrased in dry officialese and you had to have a talent for deciphering that sort of thing. It had left Ross with quick impressions: Kendig's search all through the 1940s for his father—trying to find out who his father had been. Gradually accruing a picture of a sad old man, a pessimist who'd tried to love everything, hated violence, had a kind word for the worst of men. Gentle, loving, a hapless hard-drinking drifter with a social worker's illogical faith in goodness: the need to trust everyone, yet the knowledge that savagery was the nature of man. Kendig evidently had spent important chunks of his youth trying to track down the old man. Then he'd caught up. On a nightmare binge one morning in the fall of 1949 the old man had leapt from bed screaming and fled in panic from the monsters that swooped in his alcohol-invested sleep: he had shut his eyes and lept past the ring of monsters through a window, nine stories to his death. Miles Kendig had met him for the first time at the morgue. According to the psychiatrist's report it had been the beginning of the great void in Kendig's life.

"I'm not sure I believe too much of that psychological horse shit," Ross said. "It's always too pat. Do you buy it?"

"Until a better explanation comes along." Cutter examined his fingertips. He seldom looked at the person he was talking to; Ross was learning that about him. Cutter's eyes fixed themselves on a third person—he'd stared at Ross half the time he'd been talking to Myerson upstairs—or on an inanimate object.

It was said Cutter had a wife and sent her money at regular intervals but hadn't seen her in years. It was said he was a loner, an old-fashioned derringdo type from the cloak-and-dagger tradition; but he couldn't be more than thirty-eight or forty at the outside. The dimmer wits on the third floor had nicknamed him 007.

Still looking at his fingers Cutter said, "It's something you learn when you're in the field. Whenever you pick up a drinking glass or a piece of paper, whatever, you twist your fingers to smudge the prints. Kendig hasn't left a clear print on anything he's touched in the past thirty years. It doesn't really matter. I don't think anybody's tracked down a man on the basis of fingerprints since Sherlock Holmes."

"Okay," Ross said. "We haven't got his prints and we haven't got a photograph and we don't know where he is. Where do we start?"

"Stop clutching that file as if there was something in it that might help—that's the first thing."

"It's the only record we've got on him, isn't it?"

"Except what's in our heads. But records won't do this job. You're one of those eager beavers, aren't you—the new breed that's weaned on the theory that if our computer keeps better records than the other side's then we're bound to win out. You're going to have to forget that shit for a while. Nobody's ever taped Kendig. For one thing when Kendig got into this business you still had to be a bit of an adolescent to want to do it in the first place—immature enough to be attracted by the risks. You understand? He was always the fastest driver I ever rode with. Sometimes he'd put himself in a position where he had to fall off. It was just to prove he could land on his feet."

Ross watched him bite the words off with his even white teeth and it occurred to him that Cutter might just as well have been talking about himself.

"Kendig was my Control for seven years," Cutter said. "He ran me in Laos and Indonesia and out in the Balkans."

"Then you were friends—that's why Myerson gave this one to you."

"No, we weren't friends. He was the teacher and I was the student. He knew I had the makings of a professional. But I don't think he liked me."

"Did you like him?"

"Not very often," Cutter said. "But I suppose I was jealous of him."

"I still don't really understand this. If you've figured it right it looks to me like a hell of a complicated way to commit suicide."

"It's the way he is. He could have been a grand master at chess."

"That's part and parcel of all this messing with the files, is it? I mean phonying up his own file. And stealing all that top secret material he's using in his book."

"He didn't steal the documents," Cutter said. "He memorized them. You'd better remember that."

"It's the same thing."

Cutter gave him a glance. "The hell it is."

"So what do we do?"

"Cast a fly."

"How?"

Cutter looked at his watch. "It's still business hours in Paris. Let's put through a phone call to Desrosiers. I have a feeling Kendig's waiting to hear from us."

| 4 |

It was a small postal exchange outside Lyons. There was a drizzle that gave the street a fogged *pointilliste* atmosphere. Kendig went inside unbuttoning his raincoat; he bought *jetons* and stood in the call box waiting for the interminable connections to be made. It took fourteen minutes and then all he had was Bois Blanc's switchboard; it used up two more *jetons* before they pulled Desrosiers out of a conference and Kendig had his voice on the line.

"It's rather insubstantial, isn't it?" Desrosiers said cautiously. "Not to say libelous."

"I shouldn't worry about libel if I were you," Kendig said, belaboring the obvious. "In the United States it's impossible for a public figure to sue for libel. And the Russian's can't take you to court, can they."

"That's all very well, Miles, but what you've given me is unsupported sensationalism."

"What do you think it is that sells books?"

"I have a reputation for integrity," Desrosiers said stuffily. The connection, as always in France, was poor; his voice crackled thinly on the line.

"Are they tracing your incoming calls yet?"

"I really don't know." And by implication he didn't care to. Desrosiers was very old-world.

Kendig said, "I've got chapter two finished. I'll have it in the mail to you today."

"I hope it's a bit more specific."

"It's got nothing in it but nuts and bolts. But it's the last material you'll see until I've got a contract for it. I'm not giving this stuff away—you can understand that, can't you?"

"I have spent a lifetime dealing with greedy artists, Miles."

"Then perhaps you'd like to start mentioning numbers?"

"Not until I've seen this new material. You must realize I've been handed what you Americans call a pig in a poke more than once. Clearly I cannot commit myself to publishing your work if the whole of it is as tenuously inferential as the sample you submitted last week."

"You know me better than that."

"I don't know you as a writer at all. Do I."

Kendig was neither angry nor impatient; he was going through the motions, that was all. "I'll be in touch next week perhaps."

"Please do. Oh Miles, there's one thing. I've had a transatlantic call from someone called Cutter. He urgently desires that you make contact with him."

"I'll just bet he does." Kendig smiled broadly in the privacy of the booth.

———

Marseilles was a city of criminal ferment and Kendig went right down into its rancid crotch. Streetwalkers drifted from doorway to doorway, bedraggled, wrung out, degraded, battered and hostile;

inquiring out of the sides of their mouths whether he was out for a little sport; loftily ignored by the strolling *gendarmes* who were the best police that money could buy. The city was as full of vendettas as a Sicilian mountain village and the sharp-featured Corsicans who hurried by were deadly and chronically frightened. It was a capital of international affairs—for smugglers, for businessmen who dealt in cocaine and heroin, for the *Union Corse*. For Kendig it was familiar turf.

He threaded the passages, moving alertly on the damp cobblestones. A windowless masonry wall was decorated with the tatters of old circus posters and Johnny Hallyday concerts. Rusty fire escapes zigzagged down the alley walls. Spherical black oil lanterns around an excavation looked like sputtering anarchists' bombs.

He made his way into a flyspecked building. The hall was painted in a dingy yellow that covered a multitude of years in which the turnover in tenants probably exceeded the turnover in wall calendars: the kind of office building whose occupants could be expected to be on the way up, down or out.

The occupant of *B, deuxieme étage* was unique: he had been there at least eleven years.

A. Saint-Breheret. The paint had faded. Kendig knocked on the panel and after a moment a beam of yellow light appeared at the Judas-hole, dimmed as an eye blocked it, brightened again and then went black; and a key rattled.

Saint-Breheret beamed. "My old friend—it has been such a long time!" He pumped Kendig's hand and they went inside.

Saint-Breheret was a twinkling little man, fat and half bald, baggy worsteds and a gold chain across his waistcoat; his cheerful smile concealed the chronic indiscriminate terror of a quivering Chihuahua dog.

Kendig said, "I'm only in town a short while."

"Yes?"

"I heard you'd got your hands on a mint 'seventy-nine peso."

The teeth flashed brilliantly—on and off, like a timed neon sign. "The news has traveled fast. I bought that estate only last week."

"I'd like to see it. I've still got that hole in my collection."

"I keep such valuable coins in the bank vault, of course. Would you prefer to wait here or come along to the bank with me?"

"I'll walk along," Kendig said drily and waited for Saint-Breheret to get his raincoat down off the rack. The office was as nondescript as its owner: a desk, chair, file cabinet, Oriental rug separated from the rest of the small room by a wooden railing with a gate in it; and a six-foot Mosler safe against one wall.

Saint-Breheret turned toward the door. "It was one of those fortunate strokes one cannot anticipate." He kept talking on the way down the hall; "The estate of Jean-Louis Arnauld—perhaps you'd heard of him? An amateur collector of course, but quite wealthy. His taste in coins was more eclectic than specialized—the heirs found they could not obtain a fair price for the whole, so there was an auction of individual pieces." They went down the stairs. "By the ordainment of fate I was able to obtain a few pieces at remarkably fair prices. You won't be disappointed." Saint-Breheret held the door for him and they went out into the street.

The firepots smudged the intersection. Saint-Breheret made a right turn and they walked unhurriedly past grimy shops and bistros. "What is it you need?"

"Three passports, three driver's licenses. At least one of each of them must be American. Blanks only. A couple of credit cards."

"There's no such thing as a blank credit card, you know that."

"As long as they're fresh. But the passports and licenses have got to be blank."

The nervous smile: "You have great experience hanging paper?"

"We'll manage," Kendig said. "Give me a price."

They turned the corner past a drunk who sat propped in a doorway. Saint-Breheret had stayed in business for many years because he was a cautious businessman who said nothing meaningful inside any four walls which might be bugged. "The price will be high."

"Russo stole a truckload of American passport blanks for you three years ago. You haven't unloaded all of them."

"They are getting scarce," Saint-Breheret said imperturbably. "If you prefer a wholesale price perhaps you'd do better to try your own government printing office."

"You stay in operation because it's convenient for us to know where you are. We appreciate your cooperation. But if you start dragging your heels maybe we'll have to re-evaluate your usefulness."

The tongue darted across the pale lips. "I have never turned you down."

"How much?"

"Five thousand francs for the passports. Two thousand for the license blanks. The credit cards you may have for five hundred."

Kendig said patiently, "My bureau is on a budget."

"*Oui*. So am I."

"Six thousand for the package."

"I must cover my overhead you know."

"You'll survive."

"Seven," Saint-Breheret said.

"I'd hate to turn in an uncooperative report on you."

Saint-Breheret threw up his hands. "You would have my blood!"

———

He worked a full day on the documents. First he penciled in each letter lightly in outline; then he forged carefully with a straight pen with several nibs. He could have had Saint-Breheret do the job— Saint-Breheret was far more accomplished at it—but in time they'd get onto it and question Saint-Breheret and he didn't want the Frenchman to be able to tell them what names he'd sold Kendig. Saint-Breheret knew the credit cards but that was part of the scheme.

The credit cards were in the name of James Butler and he prepared a passport and a driver's license in that name; Butler became fifty-four, a management consultant, born in Cincinnati, resident of Arlington. The French passport identified one Alexandre Vaneau, forty-nine, born in Saintes, resident of St. Ouen. The second American passport and license remained blank for the moment because he didn't want to spend another half day over them.

As James Butler he went over the border to Barcelona and then flew TAP to Lisbon. Butler lost three hundred French francs at the casino in Estoril, spent the night in the Hilton, paid with an American Express card and hired a Volkswagen from Avis in the morning with his BankAmericard. Before noon he left the rented car parked on a lot in Cascais. A man who didn't give his name— none was asked—took a taxi from Cascais back to Lisbon International and paid the driver fifteen dollars in American cash. At four o'clock, on American Express again, James Butler boarded a Pan Am flight for Dulles International Airport.

———

Ennui was not a cocoon to be broken out of in one grand flapping metamorphosis. He sat on the plane watching the sunset take shape very slowly while they chased it across the Atlantic. He felt dejected. But he reasoned it was inevitable. The game hadn't really begun yet; it had been announced but neither the stadium nor the time had been fixed.

Saint-Breheret could be relied on to be indiscreet; he would put them onto James Butler. In that respect the fun would be in deciding how long to keep Butler—how close to allow them to come. That was the key to his enjoyment of the game: and the enjoyment was chiefly his own; Cutter wouldn't share in it to nearly the same extent because Cutter could afford to blunder all he wanted to. The game was far more taut for Kendig because he needed to make only one mistake and it would be ended.

It was bound to be anticlimactic; that was one thing that troubled him. The game had to be more enjoyable than the endgame: the chase was what had meaning, not the kill. Victory was never as heady as its anticipation had been. In a very real sense it wasn't whether you won or lost; it was how you played to win.

For Cutter and his minions it would be a dreary business, wasteful and perhaps distasteful. Chickens would suspend their pecking order when there was a weak sick chicken in the coop: they'd all turn on it and peck it to death; but most likely they didn't take much pleasure in it. Kendig didn't see Cutter taking great glee from it; Cutter was a cold man but not a vindictive sort.

So Cutter must be primed. *Make him mad,* Kendig decided. *Flaunt yourself. Embarrass him—insult him.*

That was it then. Prolong the game. Stretch it until Cutter made a laughingstock of himself. Force it to the point where Cutter's career was on the line. Make a fool of him and it had to turn out that way.

He smiled a little and was aware of it; the realization made him smile even more. It was infectious. The stewardess smiled back. "Is everything all right, sir? May I get you a drink?"

"I think I'll go up to the lounge, thanks."

He went up the self-conscious little spiral stair. They were Americans, most of them; no one else paid to travel first class. Each of them would have some "business" excuse for the vacation to make the fare tax-deductible. One of them was pounding the piano with more ferocity than skill. There was a lot of drinking and a lot of talk: poses struck, laughter forced. It wasn't the sort of gaiety he could stand. He had one drink and went back down to his seat.

One of them had been a twin for Myerson, right down to the phony smile. He remembered the last summons to the office down the hall on the fourth floor. "I take it you don't like it much up here. Or are there personal problems perhaps?"

"Has the man on the fifth floor registered displeasure with my performance?"

"You've been lackadaisical, you've got to admit that."

"But not sloppy. I've done my job."

"With all the enthusiasm and initiative of a typist third-class."

"I wasn't cut out for shifting bureaucratic rubble from one office to another."

"We did offer you an alternative."

"Filling out my time decoding telegrams over at NSA?"

"Assistant Deputy Director for Eastern European Affairs. That's a responsible position, Miles."

"A ringing title and a big salary and they'd never let me within a mile of action or policy. A nice faceless assistant to an assistant."

"Miles, you're fifty years old and by all the medical prognoses we had a year ago, you should have been dead. You had a God damned bullet in your head."

"It hasn't affected my brain. I'm still the best field man you've got."

"We don't get much call for those kinds of skills any more. You're perfectly aware of that."

"Sure."

"Then what's your beef?"

"Christ I don't know. I'm just bored."

"We're all bored. It's just another challenge to meet, Miles. We've still got to do the job."

"Why?"

"Because—oh to hell with it."

"Look—use me for a decoy. Anything."

"Begging demeans you, Miles."

"Not as much as being junked like an old car."

"Damn it, I hate a man who doesn't know when the party's over. At least have the grace to know when to go home. If you can't fit in behind that desk then give me your resignation. You'll get a full early-retirement disability pension."

"Wonderful."

"Well?"

"You'll have my resignation this afternoon. With parsley."

"If that's the way you want it. . . . Let's have lunch soon, what do you say?"

———

Alexandria was a strip town. The long main drag was crowded with impatient kids driving their souped-up cars uselessly about. He walked past a theater that advertised mature adult films. Beyond that was a string of advertising boards along the waiting-bench wall of a bus depot. One of the ads told young men they could get job-training for high-paying skills if they joined the Army. Another begged businessmen to hire unemployed veterans.

He rented a Mustang under the name James Butler and booked himself into a motel near the Interstate. He slept from midnight to nine in the morning and after the rush-hour traffic had dissipated he drove up to Langley and went into a drugstore phone booth and rang the number.

"Farm labor division, may I help you?"

"My field number is four-three-three-eight," he said. "I'd like to speak with Joseph Cutter. I don't have his extension."

| 5 |

When the phone rang Ross was nearer so he picked up. "Seven six two."

"Who's this?"

"Leonard Ross. Who's calling?"

"Kendig. I'd like to speak with Joe Cutter."

Ross's jaw dropped. He turned and covered the mouthpiece. "It's him."

Cutter took the receiver and sat down on the edge of the desk. He held it at an angle against his ear so that Ross could listen in. "Miles. What a pleasant surprise."

"I'm glad they put you on it, Joe. I was afraid they might not throw in the first team. I'm flattered. They still respect my talent—and yours."

"And I got mine from you. I see what you mean. What can I do for you?"

"You've read my book?"

"The first chapter."

"Desrosiers ought to have chapter two by now. You'll probably hear from him today. I ought to mention there are a couple of pages missing from it. I withheld them on purpose. They contain the references to documentary sources and the names of the witnesses who are still alive."

"Interesting," Cutter said. Ross leaned closer to catch the tenor of Kendig's voice. Cutter said, "Have you thought of putting a price on the exclusive worldwide rights?"

"What am I offered?"

"It appears to be a seller's market, doesn't it."

"I'll give it some thought."

"Sure," Cutter said. He changed the subject abruptly: "You could waste a lot of our time and energy, Miles. What are you trying to prove?"

"All I want is revenge."

"I see. The spy who was thrown out in the cold wants to get even with the people who threw him out there. That what you mean?"

"That's why I'm writing the book, Joe."

"In a pig's eye."

Ross heard the chuckle on the phone. Cutter said, "That bullet in the head scrambled your brain. You can't hurt the Agency—it's like trying to knock down an elephant with a flyswatter."

"An elephant can choke to death on a flyswatter, Joe."

"You belong in a rubber room. What's the real point? What will it take to call you off?"

"It's too late for that. I'm just going to finish writing my book. I'll be sending it out to the publishers a chapter at a time. I'll be withholding a few evidential pages here and there—they'll be mailed in along with the final chapter. If you haven't nailed me yet, of course."

Ross saw a quick grin flick across Cutter's lips. "So it's like that. The longer it takes us to catch you, the more damage you'll do."

"You've got the picture."

"We'll have you on toast, Miles."

"Come off it. Don't go making any funeral arrangements until you're sure you've got my corpse."

"None of us wants that."

"Myerson would like nothing better."

"Hell, Miles, we've already arranged to sell your body to science. But you can still call it off."

"No point in that. You people need me like the axe needs the turkey. If I stopped writing now it wouldn't change that."

"You really want this fox hunt, don't you."

"It's a way to pass the time."

"Want to know what I think, Miles?"

"Avidly."

"I think you've picked this game because it's impossible. You'll have plenty of excuses for your failure. It's a hell of a cheap shot."

"You're talking into a dead phone, Joe. I'll see you sometime."

Click.

Ross leaned back. "Of all the—"

"Shut up." Cutter was jiggling the phone cradle; then he put the instrument back to his mouth. "This is extension seven six two. A call just came in on this line. I want the log on it."

Ross stood up and went back to his chair. The ashtray beside it was crowded with butts. They'd been waiting three days and every time he'd made a suggestion about taking some action or other Cutter had told him to go ahead if it would make him feel better. Cutter just sat by the phone and waited. It made Ross feel like an ass. He knew how Cutter regarded him: for Cutter people seemed to have glass heads. To Cutter he was a tall excitable kid, an overgrown precocious schoolboy. And the power of Cutter's personality was such that he'd half convinced Ross he was right in his judgment. Ross was a six-year veteran of the Agency and Cutter was making him feel like a green recruit.

Cutter grunted into the phone and hung it up. He swiveled on the corner of the desk and said, "The son of a bitch."

"What?"

"It was a local call," Cutter said. "The son of a bitch is right here in Langley."

———

"He must have the balls of a brass gorilla," Ross said.

"There never was anybody like him."

"No way to trace that call, is there. Well it's not such a big town. Shouldn't we scout around and see if we can spot him?"

"He'll be halfway to the West Virginia line by now."

"Then what the hell do you have in mind? Sit on our asses and diddle ourselves until he calls back?"

"He won't call back," Cutter said. "He's said everything he had to say."

"He didn't say much of anything."

"He's waving a red flag, that's all. All right, it's time we got started."

"Doing what?"

"Collect the composites from the second floor. Get us a conference room for eleven-thirty. And organize some transportation." Cutter had the phone again. "It's Cutter," he said into it, and covered the mouthpiece to talk to Ross again. "I'll be with Myerson. You chair the conference. You'll have twelve men. Take them into town and blanket the pay phones. Take the composites. Find out where he made the call from, what he was wearing, what kind of car he's driving, which way he went when he left."

"You think we'll find anybody who noticed?"

"Probably not. But we've got to cover it."

Ross started gathering things together and putting them into his briefcase. Cutter had gone back to the phone:

"Kendig's here somewhere. In Langley. I'll want a few more men on it. . . . Nuts, he's priority enough. He's mailed a second chapter out of those publishers. He's going to keep mailing chapters out until we get him. How long do you want it to take? . . . No. He says he wants revenge because he got canned but that's not it. He's like a bicycle, when it stops moving it falls down. He's rolling again, that's all. There's no point to it beyond the movement itself. As long as he keeps rolling he stays upright, you follow? . . . Hell I'm not wasting your time. You *asked* me. Now he's got to be traveling on phony papers. I'm going to need authority to call on some of the overseas stringers. We'll have to canvas the dealers. He must have bought papers from somebody, probably before he left Europe. . . ."

Cutter was still arguing with Myerson on the phone when Ross went out into the corridor.

| 6 |

He didn't use the superhighways. There wasn't any terrible rush and it was remotely possible they'd play the odds and cover the toll roads like the New Jersey Turnpike. The volume and concentration of traffic on those arteries was such that they might feel justified in using up manpower on stakeouts there. So he drove the old forgotten highways around the western suburbs of Philadelphia, up through New Hope and Lumberville, up the truck across the Delaware through Stockton and Flemington and Somerville, route U.S. 22 to Newark Airport. There as James Butler he turned in the rental car to the car agency. Then he took an airport bus into the West Side terminal in Manhattan.

A hunt built its own momentum. Later on they'd be close behind him with their noses to the ground and there wouldn't be time to sit down and write. The thing to do was to write the whole thing and carry it along with him and post the chapters one at a time; he'd let Cutter's actions dictate the intervals between mailings.

But it meant he had to go to ground for a period of weeks.

The book didn't have to be very long but certain things had to be covered in detail; he didn't want to leave them room to squirm out of anything. It had taken him five days to rough out the chapter and another four days to polish it until it satisfied him; the second chapter had taken a bit longer than that. Probably the whole book would run about two hundred pages of typescript, of which he'd already written thirty-five; if he could do forty a week he'd have it finished in four more weeks. That meant hard steady work but it could be done; he wasn't trying for any literary prizes.

The limit would be self-imposed because they weren't going to go away no matter how long he took; but if he wasted too much time on it there was a danger he'd relapse and maybe not finish writing it at all. He had to keep the tension on. So he set himself a thirty-day limit. It would be just about the right length of time to get Cutter into hot water too.

But before he went to ground he'd have to lay a false trail—something to keep them occupied and leave them looking silly.

———

Number 748 Third Avenue was a steel-and-glass office tower that had been architected in evident imitation of a sheet of graph paper: as functional as a bayonet and just as warm. He consulted the building directory in the lobby and found IVES, JOHN H., LITERARY AGENCY—3302. He found the proper bank of elevators and touched his thumb to the depressed plastic square; it lit up in response to the heat of his skin and he twisted his thumb slightly, out of habit.

Muzak and two delivery boys accompanied him to the thirty-third floor and he found his way to Ives's door. A chic receptionist asked him to wait; he sat while the girl talked into an interphone.

The desk and shelves were cluttered with an awful mess and the floor was a jumble of opened cartons of books.

A man came through the door. "Mr. Butler? I'm Jack Ives. Come into the office."

Ives was younger than he'd expected—very tall, glasses, beard, wavy brown hair cut and shaped by someone expensive. He didn't exactly look distinguished; he looked like a character-actor who specialized in playing distinguished roles, but he was too young for the part and his eyes were too bright and crafty.

The office was as littered as the anteroom. It had the studied elegant decor of a nineteenth-century gentleman's library but the frantic disorder dispelled that. Ives shut a door behind Kendig and waved him to a chair. "I don't ordinarily talk speculative books with unknown writers. But I've checked with Desrosiers and he tells me I'd better listen to you. Your name's not Butler, is it."

"Kendig. Miles Kendig."

Ives squinted as if trying to place the name.

"You've never heard it before. I'm a retired employee of a government agency. My last position there was Deputy Director of the Plans Division."

"You don't look the type."

"Which type?"

"E. Howard Hunt, that type."

"That's another breed. Those are the downstairs troops."

"Go on, Mr. . . . . Kending?"

"Kendig."

Ives reached for a notepad. "Spell it."

Kendig spelled it out. "The government will deny my existence. If you were thinking of checking with Washington."

"It won't be necessary. I've already got Desrosiers's recommendation. Let's talk business, Mr. Kendig."

———

Ives was a fast reader. He went through the two chapters and Kendig handed him an unfolded list. "Those are the publishers I've sent it to."

Ives glanced at it, set it aside and went back to the manuscript. "There are a couple of pages missing."

"They'll be supplied later on. Names of witnesses, documentary sources for confirmation of my facts, that kind of thing."

Ives had a shrewd smile. "Not to put too fine a point on it but have we got any way to make sure you're not bluffing?"

Kendig had pages 23 and 24 folded into an envelope in his pocket. He showed them to Ives. Ives's face changed. Then Kendig took the two pages back and put them away. "They'll be delivered with the final installment of the manuscript."

"And you want me to handle the contractual details."

"I need a middleman. I've got to finish writing it—undisturbed."

"I think I understand. Why'd you pick me?"

"Desrosiers recommended you. You handled the Harry Bristow book."

"Are you putting a floor price on it?"

"I'll take whatever the market will bear."

"Then it's not primarily a money thing with you."

"I won't be a patsy—I'm not giving it away."

"Do you need money right now?"

"I've got plenty of money. But I want them to have to pay for the book—I don't want it neglected for lack of big promotion."

Ives smiled again. "Don't count on publishers to act logically. I've seen them pay a fortune for a book and then drop it right down the gratings. They're in a mass business but they do no market research, they never test their packaging, they only advertise a book if it's already selling well—and even then they haven't the slightest idea how or where to get the most for their advertising dollar. They've got an archaic distribution system and haphazard retailing. Actually they have no idea at all what sells books and what doesn't. But this property looks as sure-fire to me as anything I've seen in the past five years. It could be the most explosive book of the year—and you've already done the groundwork with the publishers. I'd be an idiot not to handle it for you."

"It won't be the usual agent-client relationship."

"There's no such thing. Every client is a separate lunacy."

"I'll give you a power of attorney," Kendig said. "You'll have to conclude the arrangements in my name. You won't be able to communicate with me. I'll be sending copies of each chapter to each of those publishers at irregular intervals—and I'll be withholding evidential pages from each of them. It may be months before I've delivered the complete book."

"You could send it directly to me. I've got copying facilities."

"No. That would give the Agency a bottleneck to work with. I've got to be sure the material reaches every one of the publishers."

"Very well—if you feel the risk is that great. But send me a copy when you send it to the rest of them."

"Naturally."

"There'll probably be a matter of libel insurance. With a book of this kind the premiums may prove costly."

"The publishers will have to pay for that."

"I'll arrange that if I can."

Kendig said, "What's the usual procedure for paying commissions?"

"I take ten percent of the client's gross receipts off the top. When I receive a check from a publisher I deposit the check in my corporate account and draw my own check for ninety percent of that amount, payable to the client. Naturally the client is welcome to examine my accounts at all times. There's no written contract between me and any of my clients—it's a handshake arrangement. When a client's dissatisfied with my work he's free to go elsewhere."

Ives continued, "In your case since you say I won't be able to reach you the thing would be for me to open an account for you and make deposits as the money comes in."

"No good," Kendig said. "A bank account can be frozen by court order. I'll want cashier's checks, made out in my name, sent by airmail to this address in Switzerland." He wrote it down and tore the page out of his pocket notebook and tossed it onto the desk. Ives picked it up curiously.

Kendig said, "People from the government will be around to see you before very long."

Ives' grin made him even younger. "They won't learn anything from me. Not without a warrant."

"They won't use warrants. They don't work that way. You'd find yourself up to your ears in income tax audits. Your driver's license would be mysteriously revoked. Your credit rating would evaporate overnight. Maybe you'd find that certain publishers were no longer buying anything from you. You'd start to lose clients—they'd give some vague excuse for shifting to another agency. Your wife would find her charge accounts canceled. Your kids would be caught with narcotics planted in their pockets. I could give you a list of subtle persuasions ten pages long."

Ives's manicured index finger touched the piece of notepaper. "Then you want me to reveal this to them?"

"It won't do either of us any harm."

"But they'll trace the address."

"They already know it. Those are my brokers in Zurich. One of them has my power of attorney to make deposits in my bank. He doesn't have the account number. He takes the check and the power of attorney to the bank. The bank deposits the check in my numbered account without giving the number to the broker. It's a dead end for the Agency. He can't lead them to me. Neither can you. Just cooperate with them when they approach you."

"What if they insist I stop representing you?"

"Then do what they ask. Inform the publishers you're no longer representing me. Ask them to send the payments directly to that address."

———

At four o'clock he was ready to leave. Ives said, "I can only think of one thing more. Not to be gruesome but I gather there's a chance you could suffer a fatal accident. Have you made a will?"

"Yes. My Swiss brokers have it." On the way out he added, "I've left everything to the Flat Earth Society."

Cutter made a face when he stepped into the FBI building. Myerson beside him took off his hat, wiped the inside hatband and then his forehead where the hat had welted a red dent. Then he looked at the hat. "That's appropriate."

"What is?"

"I walk in with my hat in my hand." Myerson winced and blubbered his heavy lips around an exhalation. He patted his stomach. "I'm back on the cottage cheese and salad number. I envy you wiry bastards. Here we are."

The secretary kept them waiting a while and then they were granted their audience with the Assistant Director of the FBI, a trim sandy man named Tobin in the regulation seersucker.

There were the usual interdepartmental preambles—cautious courtesies—and then Myerson gave Cutter the floor. Cutter proffered one of the composites. "His name's Miles Kendig. Retired Agency official. . . ."

"I've met him a few times," Tobin said. "What'd he do, defect?"

"He may have. He's ramming around somewhere and we've got to get our hands on him. There are things we need to find out from him."

"What secrets did he steal?"

"That's what we want to find out from him," Cutter said smoothly. He didn't like the Bureau; he especially didn't like it when they had to kowtow to the Bureau. "He was in Virginia yesterday. God knows where he is by now. But if he's still in the United States it's your bailiwick, not ours. Anyhow we haven't got the domestic manpower for it."

"You're asking me to put up a dragnet for him?"

"I'm afraid we are," Myerson said. "It's that important."

"But you won't even tell us what he's charged with?"

Cutter said, "He hasn't been charged. We want him for questioning."

"Sure you do. *In connection with what?*"

Cutter contained his temper and deferred to Myerson because he didn't trust himself to speak calmly. Myerson said, "I'm afraid that's on a need-to-know basis."

"You guys are something else," Tobin said. Now Cutter was amused: this was the kind of treatment the Bureau habitually gave to local police departments and now the shoe was on the other foot.

Myerson said, "It's a matter of national security."

"That's a phrase that's lost a lot of meaning lately, Mr. Myerson."

———

On the curb Myerson put his hat on and scowled. "I'll have to take it upstairs. Tobin won't put any enthusiasm into it. It's going to have to come down from the top before he gets his ass in gear. But that'll take a day or two. In the meantime keep your people working around the clock—and keep them working afterwards too. I'd like to get to Kendig ahead of the Bureau if we can. Shove their noses in it. Smug bastards."

"I'll be surprised if anybody gets close to Kendig very fast. He's quick. All he ever needed was the smell of an opportunity."

Myerson shook his head. "He only needs to slip once and the ceiling comes down on top of him. You want to have some lunch?"

"No thanks. Ross will be reporting back at one."

"Cottage cheese and salad." Myerson left him.

Cutter caught a taxi to take him back to the Arlington lot where he'd left the motor-pool car. *He'll go to ground for a while*, he thought. *Now where would he hide?*

———

Ross was early—waiting for him. Ross looked too long for the chair he was in—absurdly tall with pink smooth baby-skin and the brown hair cropped close to the skull like fuzz on a tennis ball, incandescently eager and energetic. "We had a signal from Follett."

"Where's Follett?"

"Marseilles. Kendig bought his papers from Saint-Breheret."

Something twanged inside Cutter. This was the real start of the hunt.

"Three blank passports—two American, one French. Three blank driver's licenses, same distribution. But he bought a wallet full of credit cards in the name of James Butler."

"Okay," Cutter said. He smiled abruptly. "Okay. It's a con game but we'll play it his way. Maybe he'll tell us something he didn't mean to."

"What do you mean a con game?"

"We're supposed to waste a lot of energy tracking James Butler. It'll turn out to be a dead end when it suits Kendig's purpose. But he may leave us a trace or two he didn't count on leaving." He reached for the phone. "FBI headquarters, please. Mr. Tobin."

| 8 |

He spent two days combing the bars and employment offices and late-night eateries of Philadelphia and didn't find anybody who fit the physical requirements; on the third night he canvassed a dozen places in Camden and on the fourth he hit pay dirt in a jukebox-and-color-TV saloon on the west side of Trenton about six blocks inland from the river. The man had gone to seed but spruced up he'd look the part well enough. Kendig had searched thousands of faces to find this one and he made his sales pitch a strong one.

His name was Dwight Liddell; he was fifty and the calamities had befallen him like bricks tumbling one after another out of a dump truck. At forty-eight he'd lost his wife to a charming real estate broker he'd thought was his friend; at forty-nine he'd been laid off by the aerospace firm that employed him as an aeronautical engineer. He was candid about it: "I was one of the first ones they let go. I should have stayed a draftsman, I guess—I'm not what you'd call a world-beater, I'm no Theodore von Karmann. But I had fifteen years of incredible money. You know the kind of salaries they used to pay guys like me? It was all government contract work, cost-plus. But then the shit hit the fan."

"What happened to the money? Didn't you save any?"

"Enough to pay my way to joints like this. But I've got to pay alimony and child support and I haven't got a job. I can see plenty of tunnel all right but I don't see any light at the end of it." Liddell wasn't drunk but he was high enough to be loose and in any case he wasn't the secretive sort; he'd confide in anybody who looked interested—he'd tell the world his life was an open book.

Kendig bought a round. Liddell said, "Look at this suit—threadbare. You wouldn't believe this was a guy who used to travel twenty thousand miles on vacation every year. Hell we hit Japan one year and Tanzania the next. You asked where the money went—that's where it went. We figured we'd enjoy it while we were still young enough to. It was a good thing we did—otherwise my wife would've taken it anyway when she left. I wish she'd marry the son of a bitch."

Kendig said, "Any place around here where you can get a decent meal?"

"There's an inn up at Washington Crossing that used to be pretty good. You might try it."

"I'll treat us both," Kendig said. "I've got a business proposition for you."

———

The steaks weren't bad. Kendig did most of the talking during the meal. Afterward he tasted the coffee. Liddell said, "I'm sure to be arrested."

"Yes. Arrested and held for questioning. But after they've milked you they'll let you go. You won't have committed any crime."

"What about the phony credit cards?"

"You only use them for identification. You don't charge anything on them. Of course you can try if you want but I wouldn't recommend it. You know they're going to arrest you anyway and if you've used the credit cards they can have you up for fraud. Other than that you're clean and they've got to let you go."

"But what do I tell them when they start bringing out the rubber hoses?"

"Tell them the truth."

"What?"

"Tell them the absolute truth."

Liddell squinted at him. "Christ, they'd never believe it."

"They'll believe it all right. I promise you that."

"And then they'll let me go?"

"Yes."

"I don't get it."

"You're only a decoy, they'll understand that. They'll get mad but they'll be mad at me, not at you."

"What if they decide to shoot me first and ask questions afterward?"

"They won't. They're not that mad yet. They'll want to question you first. As soon as they do that they'll know they've got the wrong man. They won't have any reason to harm you."

"It's the craziest thing I ever heard," Liddell said, "but I swear to God I'm tempted to do it. I really am."

"What can you lose? It's a lot of money."

———

Writing the book was harder than he had dreamed it could be. Early on during training and apprenticeship he'd had to learn the patience of the stakeout but he had never developed the habit of it: he knew himself to be a neurotic man and because he couldn't afford to make careless mistakes he'd forced himself to be diligent but even so, after all the years, he still was thorough only by training, not by instinct. After the first two days' typing—sixteen pages rough—most of the fun drained out of it and it became sheer drudgery and he found any excuse to avoid the typewriter for five minutes or two hours.

The third day was Wednesday and on that September afternoon he gave up after the seventh typed page and went outside into the damp dazzling heat. The pine forest was thick with the smell of resin and faintly he could hear the rush of the dark river down below. The broken screen door slapped shut behind him.

The house was a Victorian ruin, a little remaining white paint peeling from its grey clapboards. The yard was high weeds across to the dilapidated barn with its inevitable accouterments: the rusty wreckages of a cultivator and a 1953 DeSoto, the flies buzzing, dragonflies beating from point to point, butterflies jazzing amid the wild azaleas and the aged chinaberry trees.

He got in the battered Pontiac and drove slowly, rutting down the overgrown track, bottoming a couple of times before he tipped it onto the county road scraping the tail pipe. He didn't push it past forty miles an hour because for one thing he wasn't sure the car would take it and for another there was a sheriff's cruiser that made a practice of lying in wait behind the Dr Pepper billboard a mile west of his turnoff.

The road two-laned through the pines, here and there a clearing with its lopsided grey shack and its tumbledown barn painted with the attractions of Coca-Cola and Jesus and Prince Albert tobacco. Every yard was an auto graveyard. The blacktop for a while went curling along the steep slope of the riverbank and he had glimpses of white water through the dusky boles. The occasional side road would lead back to a tumbledown cemetery or a sharecropper outfit or a moonshine still. Insects crashed into the windshield, leaving smears. He switched on the radio and got the tag end of Waylon Jennings singing "Not Comin' Home to You" and then the announcer came on cheerfully, stumbling over basic words. He twisted the dial, driving lefthanded, until he picked up the weak fringe signal of an Atlanta station and went on down the road accompanied by Tchaikovsky.

The edge of town grew uncertainly from weeds: eyeless shacks, cluttered lots, rusty corrugated lean-to roofs. Fat women in cotton and old men in dungarees sat on sagging porches.

He had to be in town today but he was two hours early and his weakness annoyed him; it had been a stupid lapse. But there was no point going back now; it would take forty minutes each way and that wouldn't leave time for any work before he'd have to make the trip again. He parked aslant in front of the country store, racking it between a dusty Cadillac and a dented Ford pickup.

The shade porch supported four hookwormed backwoods folk who stood around with their hands in their back pockets, their heads covered by old straw hats that had turned an uneven brown. They watched him with lizard eyes. When he got out of the car the sun drew the sweat out of him. He climbed the porch and gave them his grave nod—it was returned unblinkingly by all four—and tramped inside.

A huge ceiling fan revolved slowly, stirring the heat; the place was perfectly preserved, a relic of forty years ago, the few un-shelved patches of wall crowded with faded photos of forgotten pugilistic champions and rifle meets. There was even a sody-cracker barrel by the fountain. The proprietor went by the name of Leroy; he had the suspicious face of mountain inbreeding and his belly made a perilous arc over the waistband of his beltless Levi's. "How do, Mr. Hannaway."

"Sure is a hot one," Kendig said. "Draw me a beer."

He was representing himself to be a writer who'd come into the piney woods in search of solitude to finish a book. He'd let it drop that it was a book about fishing the Arkansas River—a topic he'd chosen because he'd once used up the better part of a two-week vacation flatboating and fishing out of Fort Smith at the insistence of Joe Cutter. It had taught him he despised fishing but it had also taught him the lingo and enough local color to bluff out any questions that might be asked. Not many were likely to be asked; he'd picked the deep South to go to ground because it was a country of close-mouthed xenophobia. But it was also the most cheerless land he'd ever entered and it was already on his nerves.

He drank his beer in silence; then he bought a newspaper and a magazine and sat at the counter over them and gnawed on a chicken-fried steak and cornbread. It had been a slow day for news; a school-bus wreck had made the headlines. He read the paper and the magazine from cover to cover and finally it was five minutes to five and he finished his third beer and went outside and hung around the phone booth pretending to look up a number in his pocket notebook until it was 4:59; then he stepped into the booth and made the call.

The number was that of a public phone in a booth in the lobby of the Pan Am Building in New York. It rang only once before it was picked up and the operator said, "Please deposit eighty-five cents for the first three minutes."

The coins bonged and pinged. Then Ives's voice said, "You're right on time."

"How's it going?"

"Desrosiers balked a bit but he finally went the price. And I think we've sewed it up with the New York publisher. When we've got that one signed the rest of them will fall in line. In London they're drooling over it—they can't wait to have the finished manuscript, they're planning a crash schedule to get it on the market as fast as they can. I'd say you're in fabulous shape."

"Have you been approached by government types?"

"I had a call this afternoon from someone named Ross. He

was pretty vague about his function but I gathered it was official. He wants to come up and meet with me tomorrow morning."

"All right. Tell him the truth—whatever he asks."

"Yes."

Kendig said, "You won't hear from me again for quite a while. I'm on my way out of the country tonight."

"Well—good luck to you then."

Kendig cradled it and went straight to the car and drove back into the pines.

| 9 |

Ross disliked John Ives immediately and it was reciprocated: he sensed the underlayer of distaste and it came to the surface before he had been in the office five minutes. Ives said, "I know why you're here. Let's not waste each other's time."

"That suits me. All right, you're representing Miles Kendig."

"Who told you that?"

"I thought we weren't going to fence. Claude Desrosiers's publishing company is negotiating a contract on Kendig's book through you, isn't that right?"

"When a contract's pending I don't make it a habit to give away information," Ives said. He was young and smooth but the brown beard made Ross think of porcupines. "This is a competitive business, Mr. Ross. And I regard the agent-client relationship as confidential."

"I don't represent a rival publishing house."

"I know. Miles Kendig warned me I'd be questioned by people from your agency. He instructed me to answer any questions with the whole truth. If you find me evasive it's my own doing.

You see I don't like dealing with people like you. I don't like what you stand for."

"I'm afraid I haven't got time to get sidetracked into a philosophical debate," Ross said. "But I'd advise you to obey your client's instructions. It would make things painless for both of us."

"And the alternatives?"

Ross couldn't help smiling a little. "I didn't come here to make any threats. Why, were you expecting me to? Are you by any chance recording this conversation?"

Ives made no answer but his expression revealed that Ross had scored a hit. Ross shook his head. "I'm only going to ask you to do your duty as a public-spirited citizen. I've got no power to force you to do anything against your will. But we're concerned with possible violations of the national security here. Kendig is threatening to publish material which is highly classified."

"No," Ives said flatly. "You can't take that tack."

"Why the hell not? It's perfectly true and you know it."

"I know it damn well, Mr. Ross, but it's something you can't take into court. If you accused Kendig of stealing legitimate government secrets you'd have to admit under oath that the material in Kendig's book is true." Then he grinned infuriatingly.

"It's not. He's a liar, obviously."

"I see. And his motive?"

"How much money do you suppose this sensationalist tract will earn him if it's published in fourteen countries, Mr. Ives? Isn't that motive enough?"

"Not for a man as wealthy as Kendig."

"Has it occurred to you that he may have lied to you about the extent of his wealth? Kendig was a salaried government employee for twenty-five years, Mr. Ives. I can assure you none of us has much opportunity to salt away a fortune on a civil service salary."

"I have reason to believe he's made quite a lot of money since he retired from government service."

"But you have no real evidence of that, have you. Still, even if it were true, he might be doing it for notoriety. Celebrity is quite a temptation to most people."

Ives said drily, "I doubt you people would permit him to appear on television programs."

"I'm suggesting to you the possibility that Kendig is merely trying to do Clifford Irving one better, Mr. Ives. You've got to admit it's possible."

"Anything's possible. But I notice you've made no effort to refute any of Kendig's charges."

"Would you believe me if I did?" Ross smiled again in an effort to be disarming. "I'm only asking you to grant us the benefit of the doubt."

Ives's shoulders lifted slightly, and dropped. "In any case I've told you what my instructions are. Ask your questions, Mr. Ross, and then get out of here."

———

The plane's vibration made concentric ripples lap at the rim of the coffee cup. He watched through the scratched Plexiglas port while the shuttle flight made its descent toward Washington National. He had rather enjoyed hectoring Ives because smug righteousness always annoyed him.

Cutter was waiting to collect him and he got into the car talking. "He was bugging it."

"Naturally."

"About all he got on the tape was his own opinionated claptrap. I hate moralizers."

"Do you?"

"They sit on the sidelines and carp. What have they got to lose? They never have to make the decisions."

"What did he say?"

"Hard stuff? Well the best bit is he heard from Kendig yesterday afternoon. A prearranged phone call to a booth in the Pan Am Building—Kendig probably expected we'd have Ives's phone tapped by now. Anyhow Kendig told him he was on his way out of the country. It was a long-distance call from a pay phone. The operator had a Southern accent and it cost Kendig eighty-five cents for three minutes. That was either just before or just after five o'clock."

"There's a difference in the rates."

"I know. I tried to pin Ives down but he really wasn't sure about it. He wasn't trying to fudge it."

"What else?"

"When money comes in for Kendig, Ives is supposed to send it to Switzerland in the form of a cashier's check. It's Kendig's brokers, I've got the address here."

"We've already got that in the file. It won't help us—they wouldn't know where he was."

"I got the names of the fourteen publishers."

"For all the good it'll do us."

Ross said, "We probably can discourage the New York publisher."

"What's the good of that if it's published all over the rest of the world? There's no way to keep it secret. We've still got to stop him from writing the rest of it."

Cutter parked in the Official Cars Only zone and they went into the FBI building.

Tobin was waiting for them. "We've got a line on your man." Ross disliked his complacency instantly.

Tobin was all but smirking. Cutter said, "Yes?"—withholding a great deal from his tone of voice.

Tobin sat back and ticked the items off on his fingers. "He entered the country a couple of weeks ago on a Pan Am flight from

Lisbon. P.O.E. Dulles. He rented a car there and turned it in twenty-four hours later at Newark Airport."

Cutter said, "Then he went into New York."

"Did he? Well anyhow. He shows up again two days later in Philadelphia—another rent-a-car. Then we lose him for a week. But he turned the car in."

You bastard, Ross thought. "Okay. Where?"

"Down South somewhere?" Cutter said.

Tobin gave him an irritated look. "That's right. Charleston, South Carolina."

Ross nodded. The Southern-accented operator.

Tobin said, "So we're a lot closer behind him now."

"Unless he stops using those credit cards," Cutter said. "All right, thanks for the update. Keep on it, will you?"

"We'll nail him cold for you, brother, don't give it another thought. Any time we can be of service." Tobin grinned at them.

Out on the sidewalk it was Cutter's turn to smile. "Those guys gloat too early. He's put one over on them."

"How?"

"We'll see. You don't suppose there's a phone booth in this neighborhood that the boys back there haven't bugged for practice, do you? No, why take the chance—we'll drive a few blocks." They went around to the car and Cutter said, "When we find a booth I want you to call Customs and Immigration. Check on all planes and ships that left Charleston in the past ninety-six hours. Find out if James Butler was on one of them."

They found a booth and Cutter double-parked and sat in the car until Ross came back from the phone. "Okay?"

"All set. Now what?"

"Back to the salt mines. We've got to catch up on the paperwork."

At four-fifteen the call came from Customs. Ross took it and wrote down the information and hung up. Then he swiveled to Cutter. "James Butler took passage on a steamer for Capetown three days ago. One of those freighters with accommodations for twelve passengers. The *Cape of Good Hope*, Panamanian registry. First port of call is Casablanca on the nineteenth."

Cutter nodded. "Sure. That's nearly two weeks away."

"I don't get it."

"Two weeks from now we'll nab him coming down the gangplank in Casablanca. He'll look like Kendig and he'll be carrying James Butler's credit cards and passport, but he won't be Kendig."

"Maybe that's what he wants us to think."

"No. Because he knows we'll be there on the pier to meet the guy whoever he is. Kendig wouldn't box himself into a trap like that. It's got to be a ringer."

Ross said, "It could be he's made some arrangements to transfer to another boat while they're at sea, you know. Then we'd never find him. Suppose they get to within half a day of Casablanca and a small boat comes out and takes him off?"

"No. He'd like us to worry about that but he won't play it that way. For one thing it would mean depending on a second party. Suppose the boatman chickened out or got appendicitis on the wrong day? No, Kendig's too independent—he never relies on anybody else to pull him out of anything. For another thing he's too restless to confine himself to a ship like that one. He'd get cabin fever. Kendig needs a lot of room around him—he needs several exit doors. He won't trap himself on any ship."

"You know him better than I do," Ross said, "but let's not ignore the fact that he may be using your knowledge of him. Maybe he knows how you'll figure it and he's acting accordingly—by doing exactly what you don't expect him to do."

Cutter gave him a slow nod. "I'll tell you what, Ross, if it'll make you feel better you can send a radiogram to the captain of the *Cape of Good Hope*—ask him to signal us immediately if James Butler leaves the ship."

"Hell they can't be that far out to sea yet. We could probably reach it by helicopter right now."

"And do what?"

"Well—apprehend him. That's what we're trying to do, isn't it?"

"On a Panamanian ship on the high seas? What would you use for a warrant, Ross, a stone tablet from God? Or would you prefer to go in shooting and mow him down in front of two dozen witnesses?"

Ross spread his hands. "At least we'd find out if it's Kendig or not."

"Take my word for it," Cutter said, "It's not Kendig."

| 10 |

By the end of the third week in the pines he'd written and blue-penciled one hundred and eighty pages of double-spaced material but for several days he'd realized there was no way to wrap it up in two hundred pages; it was likely to run at least half again as long before he got it all said.

He wasn't bored with it. But the steady work was getting to him. He was getting jaded; he had concentrated too intensely for too long without respite. It was like repeating a word so often that suddenly it lost its meaning. He'd lost his grasp of the thing. It wasn't irretrievable but he needed a day away from it.

He thought of packing and moving out: going to Mexico or Africa and getting back to work in new surroundings. It was a little unnerving to spend too long in one place. But in this stage it was best to stay inside the United States because it kept him out of Cutter's technical jurisdiction. It didn't mean Cutter wasn't hunting but it meant Cutter couldn't mobilize much manpower. They'd have to use the FBI. The Bureau had its talents—like establishing Communist cells so that its agents would have something to report on—but the FBI wasn't likely to track him down unless he stood in Constitution Avenue waving a Soviet flag. . . . And if he stayed in the States he might as well stay here because it would be hard to find a better place.

But he'd need certain things when he began his run and they weren't obtainable in the backwoods. The nearest cities were Atlanta and Birmingham and he decided on Birmingham because he knew its workings.

It was September seventeenth, a Tuesday. The drive took nearly seven hours. At two in the afternoon he saw the industrial smudge on the sky and at half-past three he was parking the car against the curb on a hill as steep as anything in San Francisco. He spent the next hour buying articles of clothing, luggage, cosmetics, automobile spray-paint, a leather-worker's sewing awl and a few other items. The city was acrid with coal fumes from the great steel furnaces. Its faces were predominantly black.

He bought a ream of bond paper, carbons, erasers, masking tape, a thick stack of nine-by-twelve manila envelopes; as with all his purchases he paid cash and asked for a receipt because if you did that it meant you had a legitimate business reason for buying things.

He had a meal in a mediocre restaurant and there was still time to kill; he walked back to the car and stored his purchases in the trunk and then he sat through the first hour of *The Outfit* in a theater redolent of stale buttered popcorn and unwashed feet. When the movie's climax began to build so that nobody was likely to leave his seat Kendig went into the men's room and made his few simple cosmetic preparations, darkening his hair with a mascara rinse and poking a few wads of cotton up into his cheeks to fatten his face. Ordinarily he wore his hair parted on the left and combed across his forehead; now he combed it straight back without a part. Then he knotted the tie he'd bought an hour ago and would throw away after this one use; he turned his reversible sports jacket inside out to show the plaid side which clashed stridently with the necktie and then he stood at the urinal until people started coming out of the movie house; he blended into the crowd and went up the street.

He could see the building from several blocks short of it—a fifteen-story office tower and the neon sign was still there, *Topknot Club*; there wasn't much chance it had changed hands in seven years, it was too profitable a front. He went through the heavy glass doors into the lobby and the doorman gave him an incurious glance before he got into the express elevator behind an expensively dressed couple who talked excitedly all the way to the top in accents so relentlessly thick he lost one word in four.

The elevator gave out into a wide foyer with judiciously spaced spots of colored indirect lighting. The carpet was as deep and silent as spring grass. The man at the desk was clean and well dressed but the muscles and the attitudes were there: not exactly a gorilla but not far from it in function.

Kendig waited for the Southern couple to show their membership cards and go through the door beyond the desk and then he said, "I'm from out of town. A friend brought me up here once a few years ago."

"You can buy a one-night membership. Cost you three dollars."

Alabama had local-option drinking laws and you had to be a member of the club to drink here but all it did in effect was give every bar the right to skim a cover charge off every customer. Kendig paid the three dollars and the man in the dinner jacket pressed an ultraviolet stamp against the back of his hand and waved him through.

A trio of haggard musicians played sedate cocktail music on a small bandstand bathed in whorehouse-red illumination. Businessmen sat at tables by twos and threes and there was a discreet sprinkling of high-class B-girl doxies but there was no bar as such. The dimension of the half-drawn curtains on either side of the orchestra indicated that the stage could be opened out for floor shows. ~~Three sides of the room were paneled in pane glass for floor shows.~~ Three sides of the room were paneled in pane glass with a southward view of the city's lamplit mountainsides. Beyond the doors on the fourth wall would be the bar, the kitchen, the managerial offices and a few smaller rooms for banquets and proms and lead-outs. Southerners were early diners and it was only nine o'clock but few of the patrons were eating; it was a place for convivial drinking more than dining out. And for a few people, the insiders who ran the faster tracks, it was something else entirely: a place where if you knew the right names and had the right amount of money you could buy anything at all.

The tables at the windows had been claimed and that was fine; he took a table close to the door marked *Private* and when the miniskirted waitress came he ordered bourbon in a hoarse prairie twang. "The best you got, honey." He gave the girl a wink.

When she brought the drink he touched his lips to it and said, "Now that's sippin' whisky. Honey I wonder if you'd do me the kindness to ask Mr. Maddox to drop by my table here? Just tell him it's old Jim Murdison, he'll most likely remember me."

"I'm not sure whether Mr. Maddox is in tonight, sir. I didn't see him come in. But I'll check for you."

"Thank you kindly."

She had other tables to serve and it was five minutes before he saw her slip through the *Private* door. He glimpsed a blonde girl behind a desk inside; then the door slid shut on a silent pneumatic closer.

After a while the waitress came out. "I'm sorry sir, Mr. Maddox hasn't come in yet."

"He likely to be in later on tonight?"

"I'm sure I couldn't tell you, sir. I'm terribly sorry." She gave a synthetic smile and glided away, hips oscillating.

But she'd been in the outer office too long; they'd had a little discussion and Mr. Maddox had decided he'd never heard of old Jim Murdison and maybe he'd had a peek out through a Judas-hole and hadn't been impressed by the look of Kendig. So Kendig had to force the impasse. There might be other ways to obtain what he wanted—even legitimate ways—but it was best to deal with an underworld type like Maddox because he wouldn't have any ties with the Bureau or with Cutter and because the Maddoxes were in it for profit, they were businessmen, you knew just where you stood with them: they weren't going to slit your throat or ask the wrong questions. With an ordinary good-citizen amateur run-ning a legit charter business you wouldn't have that assurance.

A little while later the waitress went into the kitchen and that was when Kendig stood up and walked to the *Private* door.

The blonde girl looked up from her typing. "Yes sir? May I help you?"

"It's all right, I know the way." He went straight across to the door of the private office. When the blonde made to get up he turned. "What's your name? Are you new? You don't know me, do you."

It flustered the girl; she was very young, hired for her orna-mental excellences, not her mind. "I—I'm very sorry, sir."

Kendig went in.

Maddox looked up, burly and muscular, thighs bulging against his trousers, a ledger in his lap. He was tough enough not to look alarmed. The tentative beginnings of a polite smile: "May I help you, friend?"

"Name of Jim Murdison, out of Topeka. Expect you don't re-member me but I was up here a few times seven, eight years back, with old Jim-Bob Fredericks from Dallas?" He went booming right across the carpet and pumped Maddox's hand.

Maddox suddenly beamed. "Why of course I remember. Now I'm real sorry about all that confusion. You have a seat, hear—tell me what-all I can do for you?"

Maddox didn't remember at all of course. But Kendig knew Jim-Bob Fredericks by sight—nobody who'd ever had anything to do with international oil machinations didn't know Fredericks—and once seven years ago he had in fact seen Fredericks in this club talking to Maddox.

"You said if I could ever use a little help on this little thing or that I should look you up. Well sir here I am." Kendig looked around the room with quick appreciative nods. Maddox had no desk; he worked in an easy chair by a coffee table. The middle-sized room had the grandiose pretension of an antebellum drawing room: high ceiling, brocaded furnishings, leather-laden bookshelves, a painting that might well be a real Stuart, living-room lamps that illumined without glare.

"I'd be pleased to help out, Mr. Murdison. What can I do for you?"

"I'd kind of like to charter a private plane."

Maddox gave him an outdoor squint. In another month he'd be out in the piney woods himself—he was the kind who'd like to prove his carnivorous superiority to a 140-pound whitetail buck. "I'm not exactly in the airplane binness, Mr. Murdison."

"Well this is for a little vacation I've got in mind. It wants to be a real private plane, you understand?"

Maddox dropped a piece of notepaper in the ledger to mark his place; closed it gently and set it aside. "Well now I expect you realize a binnessman like me can't go involving himself in extrale-gal activity."

"I'm not in the smuggling line, nothing like that. I have a lit-tle problem about these private detectives that sort of keep tabs on me, you follow? And it just might be I promised this little lady friend of mine a nice quiet vacation down there in the islands for two, three weeks?"

Maddox slid back in the chair, clasped his hands over his belly and grinned slowly. *We're both men of the world.* "From time to time I do pass on a contact or two in the right direction. How long a flight would this be that you had in mind?"

"This little girl sort of has her heart set on Saint Thomas down there in the Virgins."

"That's about eleven hundred air miles from Miami. You couldn't exactly do that in a puddle-jumper. You'd need a Bonanza, Twin Apache, something like that."

"That sounds about right, yes sir."

"A plane that size is likely to cost you a little money. You'd want service both ways, two or three weeks apart?"

"That would be just about exactly right, Mr. Maddox."

Maddox squinted at a point above and behind him. "We'd have to face the fact that private aviation fuel's a little hard to come by."

"Yes sir. Between you and me I think there's always ways to get around these little problems. If a man's willing to spend a little money here and there. I wouldn't be here talking to you if I didn't intend to spend a little money. I mean what else is the stuff for?"

Maddox smiled gently and watched him. Kendig took the flat wallet from his inside pocket and counted off ten one-hundred-dollar bills and placed them neatly on the arm of his chair. Then he put the wallet away. "I'm on my way down to Houston, a meeting tomorrow afternoon, and then I've got to be back in Topeka by Friday. I'd rather you didn't get in touch with me—I'd better get in touch with you."

"I'll tell you what. If you've got a few hours to spare right now why don't you wait around the club a while or come back later tonight. I might be able to help out. I happen to know a charter pilot here in town who's done a few discreet chores for me from time to time. Why don't you check back with me in about, say, two hours?"

Kendig stood up. "That's mighty kind of you." He shook hands—Maddox didn't get up—and went to the door; and hesitated with his hand on the knob. "My name's not Murdison of course."

"Didn't think it was, Mr. Murdison."

"Jim-Bob likely never heard of anybody called Murdison from Topeka. If you were thinking of checking me out with him."

"I don't guess that'll be necessary now, Mr. Murdison." Maddox smiled coolly and nodded and Kendig went out.

———

They were shooting straight pool on a nine-foot table in a paneled room off the kitchen and he watched the play with a glass of bourbon in his hand. He wasn't partial to bourbon but it went with the Murdison image. The two contestants were good, each trying to outhustle the other before the big money got laid down. Pool wasn't Kendig's game; it was too mathematical; but watching was a way to pass the time.

By half-past eleven the two hustlers had concluded their ritual courtship dance and by general consent everyone took a break before the commencement of the big game. Kendig went back to the clubroom with the rest. Both players retired into the men's room to spruce themselves like actresses before an opening curtain; the predictability of it amused him. He took a seat behind a lonely little table and a woman three tables away drew his attention because she was striking and because a curious defiance hung in an aura around her. One of the pocket billiard spectators was trying to join her and she wasn't having any; she didn't look at the man. Kendig saw the man's lips move: *Could I buy you a drink?*

I've got one.

But the man stayed where he was and kept his hand on the back of the empty chair until the woman lifted her eyes slowly and fixed him with a flat stare of contempt that sent him away shaking his head.

The waitress moved by, stopped at the woman's table and spoke; she was indicating Kendig with a dip of her head; and the woman got up from her table and came toward him. She had a supple spider-waisted little body and short dark hair modeled to the shape of her Modigliani face.

She let him have his look before she said, "You'll know me again." Her voice was cool, low in pitch—more smoky than husky. She pulled out the empty chair and sat down. He guessed she was thirty-five; she was attractively haggard. "You're Murdison?"

"Could be."

"Maddox said you want to hire a plane."

"Do you work for a charter outfit or are you just taking a survey?"

"Neither. I fly my own airplane."

That made him readjust his thinking. She'd taken him by surprise and he rather enjoyed that. It didn't happen to him very often.

"I'm Carla Fleming," she said. "It's Mrs. Fleming."

"Jim Murdison."

They shook hands across the table—rather like pugilists before the bell, he thought. "Did Maddox fill you in?"

"Round trip to Saint Thomas, two or three weeks between, and very private. When do you plan to go?"

"Early October, I think. I can't fix a date right now."

"If you expect me to hang around waiting my time comes pretty high, Mr. Murdison."

"All right," he said. "The way we'll do it, you'll fuel up and draw your overseas papers at Miami International. File a flight plan to Charlotte Amalie. You fly out at not more than four thousand feet until you're off the screen of their radar control. Then you swing down to the old landing field at Coral Key. You know it?"

"I know where it is. I imagine it's pretty overgrown."

"It's serviceable."

"Then I pick up you and a lady."

"And fly us to Charlotte Amalie. Your flight plan will check out—you'll be about an hour late, that's all."

"And the same number coming back?"

"That's right, ma'am."

She watched him with direct amusement. "It won't be cheap, Mr. Murdison—since I don't know what we'll be carrying."

"I'm not smuggling anything."

"I hear you saying it." She was poised, neat, confident; she knew how to sit and what to do with her hands and she was sitting there working out exactly how high she could bill him before he balked at the price. "I fly a Bonanza," she said. "Executive charters generally run fifty cents a linear mile—that's for the plane, not per passenger. But this will run you more than that."

"How much more?"

"Half again. Seventy-five cents a mile. And you're paying for the two trips I'll have to make empty. Two round trips, that's about forty-four hundred miles. Thirty-three hundred dollars, Mr. Murdison."

"I didn't say I wanted to buy your airplane."

She smiled. "If you want a better price why don't you try one of the commercial outfits down in Miami? Actually I think the airline fare to Saint Thomas is about sixty dollars."

"Three thousand," he said, "in cash."

"That's agreeable but I get two hundred a day for me and the plane while I'm waiting for you in Miami."

"All right," he said. "Be there on October third. Where do you usually lay over?"

"There's a motel called the Flamingo a few blocks from the airport gate."

"Fine. Check in with the desk every two hours after noon on the third."

He dipped the fingers of his left hand into the flat wallet inside his jacket, extracted the envelope from it and put the envelope on the table. "That's five hundred. I'll give you another fifteen hundred when you pick us up at Coral Key and the rest when you pick us up at Charlotte Amalie for the return flight."

"I guess that's fair enough. If you're making any deals with Maddox about papers you'll have to do that personally with him—I don't want to know anything about it."

"I didn't say anything about papers, Mrs. Fleming."

"So you didn't." She put the envelope in her handbag; snapped the clasp shut and put the bag on the floor by her feet. "Now you may buy me a drink. Scotch mist, with Dewar's."

———

At half-past one he was in her apartment without quite being sure why. "There was a Mr. Fleming," she said. "He's a nice guy. One day we just decided neither one of us would be worth looking at across a breakfast table for the next thirty years."

But she was vulnerable; it was evident in the way the apartment looked. It was a very personal place, she'd made it hers. The furniture looked Mexican: pale wood, very heavy with thick comfortable cushions. There were a couple of wicker armchairs with Indian patterns dyed into them. She had Navajo rugs on the walls and they looked as if she'd had them for a long time; the lower edges were frayed where cats had sharpened on them. The single painting was a limited-edition Georgia O'Keeffe reproduction. She had an air race trophy on an end table and the LP jackets by the stereo were thoroughly used clues to a taste in music which was catholic but not undiscriminating: she had Toscanini but not Fiedler, Ray Charles but not Bob Dylan, *Sgt. Pepper* but not the Stones, MJQ but not Brubeck.

The two cats were alley-bred grey tigers, aloof and athletic. They inspected Kendig. One chewed his finger. He let them prowl, not making a fuss over them. A little corner of his mind was pleased that there was a little flap cut into the screen at one of the windowsills so that the cats could come and go. And she didn't baby-talk them. "They do care whether you like them or not," she said, "but they're too dignified to let it show."

When he kissed her she drew back and smiled to show she was willing but not serious.

———

They were not touching but he could feel her warmth and the rhythm of her breathing. She got up from the bed, trailing her fingers along his arm, and he lay staring at the ceiling until she came back from the loo. Her dark eyes were heavy with sleep; she gave him a soft-lipped kiss and he felt a pang of weary sadness. She sat up then, hair tangled around her face; she offered him a cigarette but he shook his head, withdrawn.

"You're a feline sort of man. I don't mean that unkindly." She touched her lips to his hair and lay down against him. "I'm a feline sort of girl. But sometimes you just need somebody."

"Yes."

"Usually it's enough to be in the air. That's the only real freedom I know—being in motion in three dimensions." She switched off the light. He thought of leaving but hadn't the desire to, nor reason to. Then she said, "Two strangers rutting in bed. But it's not as sad as it might be."

"No."

"You just talk a blue streak sometimes, don't you."

———

She was fast asleep when he went down to his car. In the predawn half-light the furnace reddened and charred the sky: like a landscape out of Dickens. She lived on the steep side of the hill that led up toward Vestavia. In the shadows he stole the front license plate off a Buick; the owner probably wouldn't notice its absence for a long time and then he'd chalk it up to accident or vandalism and the likelihood of its being reported to the police was remote. He mailed a letter to Ives and threaded the streets; by breakfast time he was a hundred miles toward the Georgia line. He ate in a truckers' café. It was when he returned to the car that he saw the glint of metal in the back seat.

It was a woman's compact the color of brass, mottled finish, monogrammed CJF in an engraved scroll. He opened it and saw himself in its round mirror but he couldn't find anything particularly feline about the face. When he snapped it shut it left a little powder on his fingers. He twisted to smudge the prints and dropped it into his pocket. Impulse or calculation? He wondered which had made her leave it there. She hoped he'd bring it back to her. Well he'd see her in Miami.

He crossed the state line and toward midday he was in the pines. Heat trembled off the blacktop. The road was narrow, badly graded for the curves, an upward lip at each side. He felt nagged by an unease he could neither place nor comprehend. It made him think about obtaining a revolver. But a gun was always to be regarded as the last of all last resorts; he had not shot at anyone since 1944 in Italy and that had been in the lines, in uniform, shooting at helmeted *Wehrmacht* soldiers who were shooting back. The use of a gun was the admission of amateurism and the only thing Kendig had was his professionalism.

He drove slowly up the rutted track. Insects talked in the heat. When he switched off he could hear the hot engine ping with contractions and distantly the roughhousing of the river. He sat in the car scrutinizing the dappled shadows—the edge of the forest, the barn, the abandoned machinery, the disheveled house. He sensed the place was empty. When he felt sure of it he walked up to the porch.

There was no one around and no one had been there; the tell-tales he'd left had not been disturbed except for the string at the bottom of the screen door and that likely had been a squirrel or perhaps during the night a raccoon.

He brought his purchases inside and retrieved the boxed unfinished typescript from its hiding place in the rusted wreckage of the DeSoto. For the next two hours he sat still, reading what he'd written.

The book was a brusque account of facts assembled in chains. It struck him now for the first time that what he was writing was essentially a moral outcry and that impressed him as a curious thing because he hadn't had that in mind. Yet it was unquestionably an outraged narrative despite its matter-of-fact tone. When he made this discovery it caused him to realize that he must add something to the book that he had not intended including: there had to be a memoir, a self-history (however brief) to establish his boná-fides—not his credentials or sources but his motives.

The book had become more than a gambit; it had been born of him and now claimed its own existence. In no way did that negate the game itself; but he saw that in order to maintain the illusion of freedom he had to complete the book not as a means but as an end. Otherwise it was only a sham—toy money, counters on a game board. It had earned for itself the right to be much more than that; and if he failed in this new responsibility it made the game meaningless.

He put a new page in the typewriter.

| 11 |

They were ranked in three lines, the back row standing and the middle row kneeling and the front row sitting down with their arms around their calves. They were all grinning because they'd survived Basic Training. Three of the four corners had broken off the four-by-five print and it had faded with age.

The second print was a grainy enlargement of a small section of the first. It showed one young face and parts of the adjacent two.

Ross said, "Kendig all right. But you'd have to know him to tell. This was a nineteen-year-old kid."

"It's the only picture of him we've got, so far," Cutter said.

"Where'd it come from?"

"Myerson went through the Army personnel records division in Saint Louis. This belonged to some guy who went through boot camp with Kendig. Then they shipped out to different outfits. This guy never saw Kendig again."

Ross put the photographs down and went back to packing things into his attaché case. "Doesn't he have any friends? I mean everybody's got friends."

"With the possible exception of Kendig. Well there was me for a while. And there was a woman."

"Would he get in touch with her?"

"He might, if he knows a medium," Cutter said drily. "She's been dead for three years."

Ross looked at him sharply. "Three years. That was about the time he got his cover blown, wasn't it?"

"Around then, yes."

"One thing have anything to do with the other?"

"I don't know. You'd have to ask Kendig."

"I will."

"Sure," Cutter said. He was smiling but there were subtle vibrating signs of great controlled pressures in him. "Look, don't leave yourself absolutely wide open, will you?"

"I'll be careful."

"All the time I knew him I never saw him sleep more than four hours at a stretch. Kendig's got a consummate control of time. And he knows how to pace himself. If you ever get close to him you've got to intercept him, you can't chase him—he'll outrun you every time."

"You make him sound like some kind of four-minute-miler."

"He's fifty-three years old but I imagine he could run the shoe leather off you, Ross, if he had a hundred yards' head start."

"But he's no sprinter?"

"He doesn't let himself get caught in a position where he needs to sprint."

Ross picked up the attaché case and hung his jacket over his shoulder by one fingertip. "I guess that's everything. My bag's down in the car."

"Good hunting," Cutter told him. "I guess I ought to say something like that."

"You're just absolutely convinced it's a blind alley, aren't you."

"Sure. But it may give us a lead. Get it all on tape and we'll all go over it when you bring it back."

Ross swallowed that without a retort and went out. He threw the attaché case in the back seat and pulled out on the highway to Dulles.

On the plane he read the copystats of the fifty-one pages they now had of Kendig's exposé. The latest sixteen-page chapter had arrived at the French publisher's office four days ago, having been posted in Charleston on the day after James Butler had set sail from that port. The typescript was double-spaced, which made it easy to read between the lines. You had to give the bastard credit for effective understatement. Another few chapters like these and he'd blow the lid off every capital that counted.

It was cleverly conceived and executed; there was no innuendo, every statement was flat and factual. A government could deny it or confirm it but nobody could accuse Kendig of slanting it or getting things out of context. He simply didn't go in for interpretation.

The matter of the Hammarskjöld assassination—chapter three—was a raw exposition of meetings, decisions taken at specific hours on specific days by named individuals and then a day-by-day trace of itemized actions by individuals, again named, effecting the mechanics of the event. There were no suggestive interpolations, no sub-text. Pages 47 and 48 were missing, withheld by Kendig; page 46 ended with the line, "Documentary evidence to support these facts, and witnesses who took part or observed these events, are as fol-"

Of course it was unsupported testimony but there'd been so many people involved and once the thing was published they'd all be on the defensive, details would be demanded of them, sooner or later one of them would crack and spill his guts out of guilt or disgust or desperation.

In a fine sense it was history and didn't matter any more but to discount it on that basis would be absurd and specious. Kendig had them over a barrel and the barrel was headed right over the falls. Coming on the heels of the Nixon spectacle a book like this would wreak unimaginable damage because the structure of human faith was so weakened already; at least Ross saw it so, his own convictions having undergone severe questionings and doubts in the past few years. But in the end it came back to the same thing for him: there was still something worth preserving and worth fighting to preserve.

―――――

Casablanca was new to him but he'd been in Tangier and the ambience was the same—the startling juxtaposition of unspeakable poverty and first-class modernity. It was a resort city and a capital of commerce and there wasn't anything in common with the Warner Brothers sets of the old movie that everybody knew. A Mercedes diesel taxi took him to the Hilton and he ate a big dinner and slept the clock around, trying to overcome the glaze of jet lag. In the morning he paid his call on the Agency's stringer, a beefy sweating backslapper named Ilfeld who was Assistant to the Commercial Secretary at the consulate. Ilfeld brought along a couple of goons in wilted seersucker when they went down to meet the *Cape of Good Hope*. The port was shallow and not very big and there wasn't much nautical traffic; Rabat was only a little way up the coast and that was most ships' preferred port of call.

Ilfeld gave the customs people on the pier some double-talk and the four of them went aboard before anyone was allowed to disembark. The First Officer was a ruddy squat Englishman who told them the way to James Butler's cabin.

Ross was startled by the closeness of the resemblance when James Butler opened up. It wasn't Kendig but from a distance it might have been. The eyes were too close together, the hairline was a little wrong, the mouth too thick, the real Kendig was a little taller and less full in the hips and had longer legs.

Butler didn't seem surprised. "Well come on in, gents."

Ilfeld said, "You mind a whole lot if we search you for weapons, old buddy?"

"Go ahead. I'm not armed. But go ahead."

The two goons spread him out in the frisk position with his hands against the top bunk and his feet splayed well out. They went over him meticulously and Ross waited until the ritual had been observed. Then he said, "I suppose you know who we are and why we're here, don't you?"

"I know why you're here. I don't know who you are."

Ilfeld flashed an ID wallet and gave him time to read it. "I'm with the consulate staff here. This gentleman is from the State Department in Washington."

"Sure he is."

Ross said, "Here's my identification," but James Butler didn't give it more than a glance and Ross put it away feeling a little foolish.

Butler said, "You gentlemen are out of your jurisdiction here."

"A regular sea lawyer," Ilfeld said.

Ross said, "You want to come along with us, Mr. Butler?"

"Actually I'm rather enjoying the voyage. I wasn't planning to go ashore here at all."

"And if we insist?"

"Then I'll stand on my rights. You can't hijack me off this ship if I don't want to go. Not legally."

Ross said, "Perhaps you three gentlemen wouldn't mind waiting outside while I talk with Mr. Butler." In his pocket he had the recorder running.

Butler sat down patiently. Ilfeld ducked his way out behind the two goons and the bulkhead door rang when it closed. Ross walked two paces—the width of the stateroom—to the porthole and hooked his elbow in it. "Okay, let's cut the shit. What's your name?"

"James Butler."

"Traveling on a false passport is a serious offense."

"No. Not if I stay aboard this ship until it returns to the United States. I haven't tried to sneak into any foreign country on a false passport. And I haven't defrauded anybody out of anything. I paid for my passage in full, in cash. I'm clean—you can't touch me."

Ross looked out through the open port. A dark rainbow rippled in the patch of oil that drifted on the water thirty feet below him. A quarter of a mile down the waterfront a tanker was pumping its cargo into tank lorries drawn up in a row along the dock. The sun was bright, fierce; when he turned inward to look at James Butler he could hardly see him for a moment until his vision adjusted. "You're in a lot of trouble nevertheless."

"I don't see how. I haven't done anything wrong."

"Then you'll have no reason to refuse to cooperate with us, Mr.—Butler?"

"Go ahead, ask your questions."

"What's your name?"

"Dwight Liddell."

"Vital statistics, Mr. Liddell?"

"Fifty years old. Divorced. Unemployed. I was living in Bala Cynwyd for a while but my residence is in Trenton now. By profession I'm an aeronautical engineer. What else do you want to know?"

"Who gave you James Butler's papers?"

"James Butler."

"He said that was his name, did he?"

"He had the passport to prove it."

"Mind if I have a look at it, Mr. Liddell?"

And suddenly there was a ball of excitement in him because there had to be a photograph in that passport—and Kendig had used it to get into the States a month ago.

But Kendig had thought of it of course. The photograph was Liddell's.

"How much did he pay you to take us on this little wild goose chase, Mr. Liddell?"

"Call me Dwight," Liddell said. "I don't think it's any of your business how much money changed hands."

"But he did pay you."

"Sure he did. What else would have induced me to put up with this grilling?"

"I haven't even reached for a rubber hose, Mr. Liddell."

"You won't have to." Liddell spread his hands and smiled. "My life's an open book."

———

On the twentieth he flew back to Washington and Liddell went on his way aboard the *Cape of Good Hope*. Ross had been a little worried about that but Cutter set him at ease: "No point making waves when it doesn't prove anything. You did the right thing letting him go. Provided you milked him first."

"I've got six hours of tape. He was pretty dry by the time I finished with him. He didn't hold anything back except the size of the money Kendig paid him."

"The man doesn't want to have to pay taxes on it, does he. All right—I'll listen to the tape tonight but tell me what's significant on it in your estimation."

"Not a hell of a lot," Ross admitted. "Kendig dropped him off in Charleston by taxi in time to catch the boat. From what the FBI tells us Kendig turned the rental car in about an hour before the sailing. So we might get something from taxi companies or the airlines or whatever, but I'm sure the FBI's working on that."

Cutter nodded. "When it comes to that kind of drudgery they do as good a job as anybody."

"The taxi they took to the pier in Charleston was a Yellow Cab."

"Naturally."

"I just thought I'd mention it. I happened to ask Liddell and he happened to remember it. Yellow Cab, he thinks it was, and he remembers the driver was black but he couldn't tell me fat or thin, tall or short, bald or short hair or afro. He's not lying, he's just a typical witness."

"We'll pass it on to the Bureau. But either Kendig paid off the cab right there at the pier or he got himself dropped off downtown on a street corner. Didn't you get anything at all out of Liddell?"

"Nothing that looked interesting to me. Maybe you'll find something I missed."

"Maybe I will at that."

———

Q. Then you drove from Trenton to Charleston together in Butler's car on the twenty-seventh, is that right?

A. Yes.

Q. That's a long day's drive. Did Butler make any stops on the way?

A. Well sure, we stopped for gas several times. We had lunch in a service area, one of those Hot Shoppes or Howard Johnson's, whatever they are. We had dinner in a Chinese place in a shopping center outside of Norfolk. Oh, and he bought some typing paper in a discount store there.

Q. You remember the name of the store?

A. . . . No, I guess I don't. But I remember the paper all right. It was Southworth Bond.

Q. How come you remember that, Mr. Liddell?

A. Well he wanted a heavy grade of paper. He really wanted twenty-four-pound paper but the heaviest they had was twenty-weight. See, the reason I noticed was that my wife writes children's books. My ex-wife. She always buys twenty-four-pound paper because it duplicates better in copying machines. You know, it feeds easier, doesn't get rumpled up. And she always buys this Southworth Bond paper, so I recognized the package when he bought it.

Q. What was it he bought, a ream of it?

A. They only had it in one-hundred-sheet packets. That's what he bought. A pack of a hundred sheets and a pad of carbon paper.

Q. And this was ordinary letter-size? Eight and a half by eleven?

A. Well yes, sure. It wasn't legal size or anything like that, if that's what you mean.

Q. Okay. Then what happened?

A. After we left the shopping center? Well it was getting dark but we went right on, all the way to Charleston. It must have been after midnight when we got there. We put up in a motel.

Q. What motel?

A. I don't remember the name of it. It wasn't one of the big chains, I'd remember that. I mean you stop in a Holiday Inn or something, you sort of recognize the surroundings. This was just a motel, you know. It was just off Interstate Ninety-five but I couldn't tell you which interchange—there's four or five along there, exits for Charleston. We just got off the highway and stopped at the first motel we came to that had a vacancy sign.

Q. You stayed in the same room with him?

A. No. We had adjoining rooms. Not connecting, adjoining.

Q. So it was late and you went right to bed?

A. I did. He didn't.

Q. What did he do?

A. Well he had his portable typewriter along, you know. I heard him typing away in there.

Q. For how long?

A. I have no idea. I went to sleep, he was still banging the damn typewriter.

Q. How about when you woke up in the morning? Was he still typing?

A. No. He called me on the room phone, that's what woke me up. He was all dressed and ready to go when I came out. We got in the car and drove in toward the city. We stopped for breakfast in one of those pancake houses. Then he went over to a drugstore next door, it was one of those places that sold school supplies and paperback books and stuff—a big drugstore, a Rexall I think. He bought a whole bunch of those big manila envelopes with metal clasps. Then we drove on a ways and he stopped in a post office and bought a bunch of stamps.

Q. But he didn't mail anything there, did he?

A. No. How did you know that?

Q. Because we know what he mailed and it wasn't postmarked until the next day. He couldn't have mailed it in a post office that early that day. All right, Mr. Liddell, what happened after he bought the stamps?

A. Well we went downtown and he parked the car at a meter and he went into a bank. He got me a cashier's check and some cash.

Q. How much was the cashier's check for?

A. I don't think I can tell you that.

Q. All right. How much cash did he give you?

A. Let's skip that one too, all right?

Q. What did you do with the money?

A. Well I put some of it in my wallet and I put some of it in various pockets. The cashier's check and some of the cash I put in separate envelopes and I mailed them somewhere. I'm not going to tell you where.

Q. Okay, okay. You don't want to talk about the money, all right. What happened then? Did he do anything else in the bank?

A. I don't know. When he got the cash and the cashier's check he was with an officer in the back. I wasn't with him, I was waiting out front. I don't know what he said or did. Anyhow we left the bank and I mailed what I had to mail and then we got back in the car. He dropped me off at a coffee shop and I had lunch, and about a half hour later he picked me up again. He didn't have the car any more. We took a taxi down to the waterfront and I shook hands with him outside the customs door. That was the last I saw of him. He wished me good luck, I thanked him, the porter took my bags and went inside. Then I got on the boat and here I am.

Q. You didn't notice whether he hung around watching to make sure you actually sailed on the ship, did you?

A. No. I told you, I never saw him after we shook hands on the pier there. Look, how many times are we going to go over this?

Q. Well sometimes it helps to go over things several times, Mr. Liddell. Each time you tell it you remember something else you hadn't remembered the previous time. I mean like him staying up in his room typing after you went to bed, that sort of thing. Now suppose we just do it one more time. Let's take it from the night you met Butler in the bar in Trenton, okay?

————

Ross yawned helplessly and reached for the Styrofoam coffee cup. Cutter switched the tape deck off. "You don't find anything helpful there?"

"What's the use of finding out where he bought his typing paper or what motel they stayed in? He's long gone, he won't be back to those places. It was weeks ago."

"You're missing something then," Cutter said. "Look, I'm not being smug, I'm not trying to show off my muscles. But you've got to pay a little attention. Now stop yawning in my face and sit up and let's talk about it."

Ross shoved himself upright in the chair and sucked at the dregs of the coffee. "I can't handle time zones too well. I'm going to be a little bit of a zombie for a day or two—I can't help it, jet planes do that to me."

"You want more coffee?"

"I'm waterlogged already. No thanks."

Cutter said, "He bought a hundred sheets of twenty-pound Southworth Bond paper and a pad of carbon paper."

Ross shook his head. "You write a book, you need paper. What does it prove? It doesn't tell us where he is."

"It may."

"You're miles ahead of me, then."

"It's a little bit more expensive than most. You buy it by the ream; it runs seven or eight dollars for five hundred sheets."

"So?"

"One thing about Kendig—he's meticulous, he's orderly. If he started writing this book on Southworth paper he'll probably finish it on Southworth paper. Now he bought a hundred sheets and he bought carbon paper. That's enough to write fifty originals and make fifty carbons. Not enough to finish that book of his, is it. Not unless he had more of the stuff in his luggage. But if he had more of it why make a special stop just to buy it in Norfolk?"

Ross began to see. His eyes widened a little.

"He was low on paper," Cutter said, "so he bought a packet in Norfolk. But it wasn't enough to finish the book. So he's got to buy paper again."

Ross made a face. "I get what you mean now. But how many places are there in this country that sell typing paper?"

"We can rule out places that don't sell Southworth, can't we. So we start with Southworth. We find out who wholesales for them. We go through the wholesalers, find out which stores they supply with bond paper."

"That's still got to be thousands of stores."

"All right. It's a lot of phone calls. But that kind of mindless legwork—that's what the FBI has a talent for."

| 12 |

He was keyed up and rather enjoying it. They ought to be getting close by now. Kendig had dropped enough clues for them but if they'd allowed their brains to rust on the assumption that their computers would take care of everything then they wouldn't be within a thousand miles of him. But he didn't think Joe Cutter had it in him to succumb that way. They'd be a while yet because they wouldn't take the easy straightforward course even if one was available. Byzantium was in their blood: they would twist and contort, they would set snares within mazes. But they would be along.

For seven years, off and on, he had worked with Cutter and played poker with him. It was possible that no one knew anyone as well as he knew a regular poker opponent. The intimacy of his relationship with Cutter had been something far closer than family and perhaps closer than husband and wife: they knew each other's shadings, excellences, vulnerabilities—and differences.

Cutter was not so coldly mechanical as he pretended to be but nevertheless Cutter was logical in the procedures of his intellect: a percentage player. You could bluff him out of a good hand if he decided the pot odds weren't good enough; you could rely on him not to play a wild hunch; he bluffed often enough but he did it with calculation. Kendig relied more on instincts and talents and he had the advantage of flexibility but Cutter had qualities of relentless thoroughness. His ruthlessness included the ability to act with purposeful unpredictability; you couldn't count on him to plod along a prearranged path with his nose to the ground—Cutter was high-voltage; he had the spark to jump across gaps.

He could show up any time now.

Kendig made his preparations in the evenings after each day's typing hours. He had bought two identical suitcases in Birmingham and he cut one of them apart and used it to make a false bottom inside the other. Manuscript and part of his cash would go into the hiding place; the rest of the cash remained in wallet and canvas money belt.

He had a tripwire along the rutted driveway up from the road; if man or car approached it would break a thread and the old cowbell would fall to the porch.

But he needed a second exit. It could have been done in a number of ways; he took advantage of regional resources. It was white lightning country and the backhill bootleggers were numerous, their stills concealed everywhere in the piney woods. He'd spent part of every day in the pines along the county road, watching their comings and goings—mostly by night. There was one mountain-dew outfit that ran three tankers in and out: a '57 Oldsmobile, a '64 Chevy and a '59 Ford Fairlane. The still was a mile and a half back off the county road and he hadn't tried going up the driveway; they'd have it under surveillance twenty-four hours a day if not booby-trapped. But he'd had a look at the operation from the high country through 8x Zeiss glasses; it was about a four mile cross-country walk from his clapboard. They had at least three back-road exits that he could see from his vantage point; some of them probably went many miles before they gave out onto a main road somewhere. But the local law was indifferent and maybe the district federal office was in the moonshiners' pockets; at any rate the tankers had been using the front driveway in and out for as long as Kendig had been keeping tabs on them.

It would do; and the time for it was tonight.

At four in the afternoon he took page 243 out of the typewriter and hid the manuscript and drove down to the village. He bought groceries enough to last a solitary man two weeks. He bought a Vise-Grip wrench and then he put everything in the car and waited by the telephone booth until two minutes before five and dialed the New York number direct.

| 13 |

Both telephone booths had OUT OF ORDER placards on them. Ross motioned Ives into the first one at 4:55 and stepped into the adjoining booth. "Operator?"

"Yes sir. I'm all ready to institute your trace as soon as we get a ring on that line."

"Fine." Then he turned on the tape recorder and waited.

Ives obeyed instructions: he let it ring four times and then picked it up. Ross picked up simultaneously, watching Ives through the double glass.

"Hello?"

"Deposit eighty-five cents, please."

The money bonged distantly; then Ives spoke: "Kendig?"

"Did our publishers go the price, Mr. Ives?"

"Yes. I'm happy to say I've got a sweet batch of contracts for you. In fact I even managed to—"

"Never mind, I'm in a hurry. Just answer my questions yes or no. Did those people from Washington get back to you again?"

"Yes."

"Did you tell them the truth?"

"Yes."

"Have all the publishers received the fifty-one pages? No side-tracked manuscripts?"

"Yes."

"Good, Are they listening in on this call right now?"

"Yes."

Ross gritted his teeth.

Then he heard Kendig laugh. "That's fine, Mr. Ives. I'll be in touch again."

Click.

Ross tapped the cradle. "Operator? Operator?"

"Yes sir. We couldn't trace the individual phone I'm afraid—there wasn't time. But we've got the area code and we might have the town for you in a few minutes."

"What's the area code? Where was it?"

"Georgia, sir."

Ross grinned. It was all fitting together now.

| 14 |

He slipped the pump attendant ten dollars before the pump started running; the man grinned conspiratorially, topped Kendig's tank and filled the five-gallon jerrycan in the trunk. When Kendig drove out of the station the kid was watching him go; the kid would remember him well enough and that was part of his intention.

He drove half an hour up the asphalt; he stopped the car about a quarter mile short of the bootleggers' gate and hid the five-gallon can of gasoline in the trees. Then he drove on past the moonshinery to his own overgrown driveway; unhooked the trip-wire, drove in, reset the wire, drove up to the house and lugged the groceries inside.

He diced a steak and cut up a pepper and an onion and a ba-nana, threaded the pieces on skewers he fashioned of wire coat-hangers and marinated the kebab in a sauce he compounded of half a dozen ingredients; he boiled up some brown rice and then fried it while the kebab was broiling. He made a salad of spinach greens and sliced tomato and segments of mandarin orange. The only thing he didn't include was wine; he'd need a clear head tonight.

He put on Levi's and crepe-soled boots and a flannel work shirt. Over that he put a thick woven sweater and then his dark windbreaker; he needed padding and a smooth outer covering—he expected to get dragged on the gravel and he didn't want to lacerate his back. He put the Vise-Grip in his hip pocket and then spent ten minutes putting everything he'd need into the false-bottomed suitcase. When he tossed Carla Fleming's compact into the case he was ready. He put the suitcase in the barn and arranged the kerosene lamps where they needed to be; he didn't light them. He measured off the cleared floor space and made sure the barn door could be closed without obstruction. He left it wide open.

Then he walked down into the pines to make sure no tree had fallen across the pioneer road he'd spent two evenings cutting into the forest.

It was crude and not very long; it ran from the edge of his yard down a slope studded with second-growth pines and the remains of a fire that had gutted a few acres ten or twelve years ago. It had been the line of easiest resistance and he'd only had to cut down saplings; he'd sheared the stumps as close to the ground as he'd been able and then it appeared to leave sufficient clearance to get a car through although it was going to be a tight squeeze in two or three places.

Down in the bigger trees he'd had to hairpin it back and forth. Fortunately they were heavy old pines and there hadn't been much undergrowth to clear out; he'd blazed the trunks to give himself a guide because otherwise in the dark he'd likely make a wrong turn and get boxed in. It ended in the woods about twenty yards short of the county road and about a third of a mile south of the intersection of his driveway. There was only roadside brush and a few spindly young evergreens between the end of his pioneer track and the county road; gun a car out of there and it would crash right through breaking the bush, clearing its own path to the paved road. In the meantime he'd left that section untouched. You could conceal a Patton tank in there and nobody would see it from the road.

It felt all right, exploring it on foot; he couldn't take the chance of testing it with the old Pontiac because he'd designed it as a one-way escape route and it was unlikely the Pontiac or any other car could drive back up it. It was too steep, the pine needles too slick.

He was as ready as he was going to be; and it was past eight o'clock. It was time to go.

———

In three-quarter moonlight he had his look down across the slopes. The house was big but deliberately decrepit from the outside; the outbuildings looked tumbledown but most likely they were in splendid shape from the inside. The yard was cluttered with eight or nine ruined cars of which at least three were far more lively than they looked.

He watched the '59 Ford move out at nine o'clock but he didn't stir. The '64 Chevy took the Ford's place in the barn. They'd be filling its bootleg tank with eighty gallons of hundred-proof corn. He spotted one man with a rifle on the porch of the main house, another one up in what looked like a kids' treehouse on the edge of the yard. Probably there were two or three others scattered around on watch. He didn't go down any closer.

At nine-fifty the Chevy rolled out of the barn and went down out of Kendig's sight into the trees. He gave it a ten-minute start and then he walked circuitously down the hillsides to the county road and went along the edge of the trees to the moonshiners' gate.

It was a wooden cattle-gate sprung on a diagonal board, secured with heavy padlock and chain. The barbwire fence ran along to either side, six strands, five feet high. It wouldn't keep a determined prowler out but it would deter casual hikers. These were forest people; for security they relied not on fences but on their eyes and ears and instincts.

When the tanker cars drove in or out they had to go through a routine procedure: stop the car, get out, unlock the padlock, swing the gate wide open, get back in the car, drive through, stop again, get out, close the gate and fasten the padlock, get back in the car and drive on.

He climbed over the gate and posted himself prone in the shadows along the driveway just inside the gateway; it was a point parallel to where the rear of the car would be when it stopped.

They tended to run them out at forty-five-minute intervals; they were roughly on schedule tonight. He'd been in hiding a little short of ten minutes when he heard the Oldsmobile crunching down the gravel of the hill track. He gathered his muscles, tense as a runner in the starting chocks.

Stabbing headlight beams swayed wildly through the treetops and lanced downward; the car came over the last crest and made the bend and rolled forward without hurry. Kendig stayed put in the shrubbery and the front of the car went past within five feet of his nose. He was in motion before the car stopped.

He had the Vise-Grips in his right hand; he rolled behind the car, got a left-handed grip on the bumper and dragged himself sliding under the back of the car.

The driver's door opened. The car moved a little on its springs; he heard footsteps. He felt for the target with his left hand, running his fingers rapidly across the bottom of the gas tank; he found the hexagonal nut and squeezed the Vise-Grips onto it and heaved.

It was an awkward position, lying on his back with his arm cramped across his chest; he thought he might not get enough torque: the nut was probably a little rusted, likely it hadn't been unscrewed in years and it was covered with road grit, an uneven surface for the wrench. He heard the bottom of the gate scrape across its arc, the tinkle of the dangling chain. He locked both hands on the Vise-Grips and heaved again.

When it gave there was a rusty metallic groan. He froze.

The gate stopped and he heard the driver's footsteps approaching. But they were neither furtive nor determined; the driver hadn't heard. Kendig turned the nut. The car swayed with the driver's weight; the door clicked, shut to half-latch. Kendig reached up with his left hand and locked his fist on the outer cylinder of the shock absorber and tensed his biceps.

The engine gunned, the car dragged him forward, gravel ripping the back of his windbreaker. A stone hit his shoulderblade; he almost cried out, almost lost his grip but he hung on. His forehead glanced off the bottom of the gas tank; he'd have a lump there in the morning. Then the car kept moving and dragging him and for an awful moment he was afraid the driver wasn't going to stop but then the ride ended and Kendig jackknifed his legs so his feet wouldn't show.

The driver got out. Kendig rotated the Vise-Grips and now it turned easily; he unsnapped the wrench and turned the nut counterclockwise swiftly with finger pressure. When gasoline began to trickle down his wrist he pushed up against the nut, holding it shut, turning it another full turn to make sure it was free of its threads; he held it that way while he heard the padlock snap shut and the driver's boots crunch their way back to the car.

The door slammed. The Olds dropped into gear. He straightened his legs out and dropped his head back onto the ground. The car began to move, the tank inches above his nose; he held the drainplug in place as long as he could but then the car was away from him and he just stayed put, lying on his back; gasoline gushed over his extended arm, an overpowering stink of it, soaking his arm and his hair and his shoulder. He lay perfectly still and watched the inverted image of the taillights moving away down the county road.

He let it drive all the way out of sight before he got to his feet and wiped some of the stinking stuff off his face with his handkerchief. Then he started trotting after the car.

———

He gave it not more than a quarter mile before the high-powered V-8 would use up the fuel in its carburetor and fuel line; sure enough he was just reaching the bend when he heard it cough and die. It freewheeled a bit and he heard it stop. He cut into the woods and walked quickly on the pine-needle carpet, dropping the vital drainplug carefully into his pocket.

When he came in sight of the Olds the driver had the hood up and was playing a flashlight on the engine. Kendig moved down toward the edge of the road, picked up the five-gallon can of gasoline he'd cached there and waited in the trees, not moving, stinking of gasoline.

It took the driver a little while to figure it out. Finally he was down under the car feeling for the hole. He came out cursing audibly. Kendig watched him walk back up the road slowly exploring with the flashlight—looking for the drainplug. It must have been loose, he'd be thinking; vibration must have dislodged it; it's got to be somewhere around here. He'd walk on up to the yard, looking for the plug along the way; he'd tell the others—they'd have to bring one of the other vehicles down with a chain and tow the tanker back in.

It would take some time. Kendig carried the jerrycan down to the abandoned car, set it down and crawled underneath to put the drainplug back where it belonged. He tightened it in place with the Vise-Grips. He noticed for the first time the three-centimeter pipe that had been welded in place across the back of the car, concealed from above by the massive chrome bumper. It ran the width of the car and there were six jet-type nozzles sticking out of it, pointing down toward the road. That was useful to know about.

He crawled out from under and poured most of the jerrycan's contents into the tank; he opened the hood and disconnected the fuel line from the carburetor to pour some of the stuff down the hose to prime it. Then he splashed just a little bit into the carburetor—he didn't want to flood it—and reconnected the fuel line. He put the empty can in the back seat and glanced at the ignition lock but the driver hadn't favored him by leaving the keys. He had to get down under the dashboard, rip a wire off the clock and feel around for the tab-contacts on the back of the ignition switch. He was no expert at hot-wiring but he knew the drill well enough; he put it in neutral and made sure the emergency brake was set and then he gapped the contacts until the starter meshed.

The car started right up. He twisted the ends of the wire around the ignition tabs and sat up, pulled the door shut and went driving up the road less than six minutes after the driver had left the car.

————

Pretty soon they'd be down there with their tow car and they'd find the tanker missing. They'd figure out how it had been done but they'd have to conclude it had been a rival bootlegger outfit. They wouldn't report the theft to the law; they could hardly do that. They'd start banging around their neighbors' stills and the feudist mentality of the back hills would make things pretty wild for a while. It was what he wanted: the more confusion the better.

He drove the Olds into his barn and closed the barn doors and walked back down the track to repair the cowbell tripwire he'd broken when he'd driven in. Then he went up to the house and got out of his gasoline-soaked clothing, showered and scrubbed thoroughly, got into work clothes and returned to the barn to disguise the Olds.

He carefully applied masking tape to the chrome surfaces and edged the tape with razor-blade cuts. The car was a dark green hardtop with a white roof. He had a dozen aerosol cans of black automobile paint. He taped newspaper over the windshield and windows and went to work with the spray paint: two coats on the roof, one on the rest of the car. He wasn't an expert painter and the job looked mottled and amateurish but that was all right, it went with the age of the car. The paint wasn't thick enough to blacken the roof entirely; it ended up more grey than black but again that was good enough. He removed the license plates and threw them into the toolbox of the DeSoto in the yard, and bolted the plate he'd stolen in Birmingham onto the rear bracket of the Olds.

It was quick-drying paint. By dawn even the second coat on the roof was no longer tacky to the touch. He backed the Pontiac up to the Olds and siphoned off the Pontiac's tank, running fuel into the Olds until it was nearly full. It left him about a quarter of a tank in the Pontiac—enough, in case. He put the Pontiac back in its usual parking space in front of the house and then he went over to the wrecked DeSoto and disconnected the dome-light toggle switch from it. He wired the toggle to the ignition of the Olds and brought a pushbutton switch from the DeSoto to act as a starter switch; there wouldn't be time to fumble around under the dash trying to hot-wire it. When he had his wiring finished and everything screwed into place he tried it out and it worked fine: switch on the toggle, push the button and it started right up.

Then he inspected the spray pipe under the bumper. The faucet handles of the six spigots had heavy steel cables fixed to them; the cables disappeared through drilled holes into the body of the car. He found the control after a little searching. It was an old hand-brake lever they'd taken off some truck or tractor; it lay down against the floor between the door sill and the driver's seat.

He didn't touch it; you could only use a cable control once because you couldn't close it again without going around and closing each of the six faucets separately and by that time you'd have poured all the oil out onto the barn floor. But he did open one of the spigots a little and a hard stream of black oil sprayed out; he twisted the handle shut immediately.

They were guerrilla devices, the oil spigots on moonshiners' tankers; if you were being pursued by another car all you had to do was pick the right spot and yank the handle and you covered the road behind you with a murderous oil slick. Anybody pursuing you would slither helplessly on the stuff. Pour it out on a steep bend and you'd send pursuit to their deaths.

He didn't intend to hurt anybody; if he could help it he didn't even want anybody bruised. But it was a useful bonus—in case.

An hour after sunup he drove the Olds out of the barn and ran it very cautiously across the yard into the woods along the pioneer track he'd cut. He went down the steep grade in low gear standing on the brake, taking it as slow as he could; it bottomed a few times but not alarmingly. When he got into the bigger trees he had to do a great deal of backing and filling in places but after half an hour he'd got it down through the trees to the end. He parked it there and piled brush around it. Then he walked down to the county road and prowled for twenty minutes to make sure there was no piece of the Olds that might flash a telltale reflection to a passerby on the road.

He checked out the yard and closed in the top of the pioneer track with broken trees to conceal its existence. After that he went to bed.

———

Thirty-six hours later he finished the book. He put the manuscript in the false bottom of the suitcase and cached the case in the Olds together with a bottle of water, several cans of food and a can opener. Everything he'd need with him was either in the Olds or on his person. Now it was just a matter of finding out how quick they were—Cutter and the FBI.

He could leave now. Nothing kept him here. But it was time for the game to come alive and he wanted them to have the warm smell of him.

Now he hoped they wouldn't take long. If Cutter had been more of a gut player he'd worry about that; Cutter could see the clues he'd left and Cutter would realize their meaning. Kendig didn't leave clues unless he'd meant to. Cutter would have to recognize the invitation for what it was. A gut gambler might decide to pass it up; decline the invitation, take Kendig's neuroses into account, let him rot right where he was—anticipating entrapment but never seeing it happen. Time was Kendig's enemy: he couldn't sit and wait, he'd get bored with it and boredom was his essential weakness. Cutter knew that but Cutter had time pressures on him too and neither Cutter's own personality nor the circumstances would allow him to sit still even though it might have been the smartest way to handle it. No: Cutter would come after him.

The telephone rang.

———

It had rung a few times since he'd moved in. Did he want to subscribe? Did he want home milk delivery? Did he want a charge-a-plate? There hadn't been any of those in the past ten days. He'd made no calls out. He'd had the phone connected only as a convenience to Cutter.

Now on the fourth ring he picked it up. "Hello?"

Scratchy silence on the line and then a dull click. He cradled it and smiled. That had to be the FBI; if it had been Cutter he'd have played it better: sorry wrong number or would you care to contribute.

He put a short piece of pipe in his pocket and left the lights burning and walked out of the house.

| 15 |

The place was thirty miles out of town. Ross's odometer showed twenty-nine and a half when Cutter said, "This'll do. Pull over."

He slid it over against the wooded embankment and switched off. The two FBI cars parked in tandem behind them. Cutter stepped out and spread the topographical map across the trunk of the car and played his flashlight on it. The eight FBI agents walked forward and crowded around.

Cutter said, "Ross and I and four of you will walk it from here—sound travels in these hills, he'll hear the cars coming. You four give us forty minutes, then drive in. This car and your first cruiser you drive him into the farm. The second cruiser waits down at the foot of his driveway with two men in it." He put his finger on the map. "The Scudder farm. Pay attention to these contour lines—that driveway's damned steep."

Greiff said, "Any chance he'd have it booby-trapped?"

"No. He's not a killer. There may be telltales."

"He's not a killer—what is he then?"

"We want him. That's all you need to know."

Greiff wasn't used to being talked to that way; it showed on his middle-aged face. He was the District Director out of Atlanta and he had the habit of command.

A car came down the road, an old one jouncing on its springs. It slowed to a crawl and the three men inside it gave Cutter's party a xenophobic scrutiny. One of the FBI men slid his hand under his jacket. The old car moved on. Greiff said, "They'll figure us for revenuers—never mind."

Ross was looking at the map again. He saw how the farm tilted, how the driveway corkscrewed up from the road. If it was like the other places they'd passed it would be crowded pretty close by the forest.

Cutter said, "He's expecting us. All right, he won't be in the house. He'll be out in the woods watching." Cutter's finger moved along the lines of the map. "We won't walk all the way to the yard. We'll cut off the driveway and fan out through the trees. Three of us—I'll take you two—move left. Ross and these two move right. Everybody keeps his flare pistol charged and ready. We'll work our way through the woods and bracket the place. For God's sake don't go crashing around—keep your eye on where you're walking and don't blunder into any dead trees. Now if you spot him fire a flare. If you don't just settle down and wait."

Cutter turned to Greiff. "It'll take us about forty minutes to get positioned. Give us that long and then start up. The last car waits at the foot of the driveway on the main road. The other two go right up the driveway like you've got business there. Don't crawl but don't rush it. Keep your lights on bright. Drive right up into the yard and turn the cars around so you can pull out fast if you've got to. Then get out the bullhorn and challenge the house. Don't go charging it, just give him a shout—talk to him about tear gas, show your shotguns."

"Then what?"

"He'll have some diversion set up. A fire bomb in the barn or something. Don't stick your necks out and don't fall for it. Just yell at him. He'll make a move. It won't be from the house. One of us in the trees ought to be in earshot when he does—we'll light him up like Times Square with flares. Then we box him and throw down on him. Got it? All right—come on, let's walk."

———————

There was a good chance he'd be long gone. He'd had more than a half hour since Greiff had tested the phone. But Cutter had insisted he'd be there waiting for them. "He didn't set this up with all that care just to leave us with a cold trail. You've got to understand this is a game to him. He wants to see our faces."

"I wish I was as sure of that as you are. Those chapters I read didn't look like kiddy time to me."

"They're not. They had to be the genuine article, hot enough to scorch a lot of big people. Otherwise we wouldn't be playing his game."

They'd nailed him on the phone call to Ives actually but the Southworth Bond paper had brought them close and they'd have made him on that alone; the phone call had just speeded it up. He'd bought two hundred sheets of it in Chatsworth and then he'd bought a ream in Birmingham. Chatsworth was less than a hundred miles from here. But the phone call to Ives in New York had been placed from Adairsville and there were only nine phones in town, one in a pay booth between the gas station and the country store. The storekeeper knew Mr. Hannaway, recognized the composite Identikit portrait and said Mr. Hannaway had bought a big stock of groceries three days ago. The kid at the gas station described Mr. Hannaway's Pontiac and remembered filling it and the five-gallon jerrycan in the trunk. The kingpin in town was a back-porch country lawyer who owned the lumberyard and auto repair yard, and probably a distillery and half a dozen county politicians, and sidelined in real estate; he'd rented the Scudder farm to Mr. Hannaway and had received a second month's rent in advance just six days ago. Ross had been pleased with their detective work until Cutter told him Kendig had planned it that way.

———

They walked up the driveway slowly, spread out. Ross's ankle snagged something and he heard a distant tinkle—a cowbell, he thought; he listened for it again but it didn't repeat. They moved ever more slowly, keeping close to the trees on either side of the rutted drive. Lamplight winked vaguely through the trees. The moon was hazed with a thin cloud cover but there was light enough to see where you were going. The flare pistol in his hand was slippery with his sweat; he shifted it to his left hand and wiped his palm on his trousers.

Cutter stopped them and made hand motions. Ross took his two men into the forest and led the way with great caution, well back below the perimeter of the yard; only now and then could he catch a wink of the lamps. The footing was soft and quiet—a half-rotted carpet of needles. He touched one of the FBI men in the chest and pointed; the FBI man nodded and moved uphill and Ross waited until the man blended into the darkness. Then he took his remaining companion on with him, crossed another seventy-five yards and left the man posted in the trees and contin-ued alone. He keened the night with eyes and ears, breathing silently with his mouth open; he shifted the flare pistol again to his left hand, dried his right hand and brought out his .38 revolver.

He crossed into a stand of younger growth; there had been a fire here at some time, there were no big trees. Younger growth had sprouted and some of the saplings were ten or twelve feet high, no more. But they were close together and he had to move by inches to avoid sound. Above and to the left he could see the lamps of the house more clearly. Every two or three steps he stopped bolt still to scan the shadows. There was a racket of insects and he heard water running somewhere—a creek or a river.

He came to an opening that swathed irregularly from left to right. It began above him in a tangle of dead brush and it disappeared below him into heavier forest growth. He knelt and saw that some of the saplings had been sawed off close to the ground. Man-made then. For what purpose?

It was a puzzle he couldn't solve without more evidence and in any case it probably didn't matter. He studied it in both directions and then stepped across into the trees beyond and moved on, angling closer toward the house now. Cutter would be somewhere not far to his right, having come around the opposite way. This would be about right. He settled down to wait.

He was down on one knee sweeping the yard with his eyes when he heard or felt something but he didn't have time to move; a hand clutched his mouth and jaw, something rigid jabbed his spine and in his panic he heard a whisper:

"Freeze."

———

The man was behind him, it was probably a gun in his back and no amount of hand-to-hand instruction at the academy could prepare a man to counter that. Ross didn't stir; he hardly even breathed.

"I'm taking my hand off your mouth. Yell and you're dead. Understand me? Nod your head."

He nodded his head. The hand dropped away from his jaw and relieved him of his revolver.

He still had the flare pistol. The whisper anticipated him: "Don't even think about it. Drop it easy, right by your foot."

He let go. There was the slightest thud when it hit the pine needles.

"Hands behind you now."

He obeyed, felt something harsh against his wrists and judged it to be heavy wire of some kind—possibly coat-hanger wire. He drew breath but then something plunged into his mouth and he sucked for breath in panic before he realized the man was gagging him with a wad of cloth. He felt a strip of fabric go around his face and then the man was knotting it tight at the back. An abstract corner of his mind appreciated the economy with which it had been done.

He kept in mind what Cutter had said. *He's not a killer.* It would be an unfortunate time for Cutter to be wrong.

Then something dropped to the earth; the man stoped to pick up Ross's flare pistol. He saw two things: Kendig's profile and a short piece of half-inch galvanized pipe. He'd been bluffed—it hadn't been a gun at all.

There was the scrape and growl of cars coming up the drive. He felt the pressure of the gun—his own—against his back. The two cars rolled into sight, high beams jiggling across the porch; the cars swung wide and stopped nose-out in tandem and the drivers slid out and hunkered against the fenders; Ross saw Greiff lift the bullhorn. The metallic voice was magnified and unreal: "FBI. Come out of the house with your hands empty. You've got one minute."

The FBI man with Greiff lofted a shotgun and cocked its slide with a good deal of racket.

There was a whisper in Ross's ear: "Where's Joe Cutter?"

He shrugged his shoulders.

Greiff said on the bullhorn, "Thirty seconds. Then we fill the house with tear gas. Come on out—we've got you surrounded."

"Stay put," Kendig whispered and Ross thought of making a run for it when the gun pulled away from his back but Kendig was still right there; Ross saw the flare pistol rise past his shoulder. For a moment he thought Kendig was going to crown him with it and he flinched involuntarily but there was no blow. The flare pistol hung in the air above and behind his left shoulder.

"Ten seconds," Greiff roared.

Simultaneously there was a *whump* close in Ross's ear. It took him a moment to realize what it was: Kendig had fired the flare pistol, using Grieff's racket on the bullhorn to mask the sound of the discharge.

Then the flare ignited. High in the air above the woods across the yard—probably not far from where Cutter was posted. It bathed the trees in harsh brilliant white light and suddenly men were crashing through the forest and Ross heard voices calling across the night in harsh tones. . . . Then Kendig was spinning him with a hard grip on his arm: "Come on—*move*." And Ross was being propelled through the saplings, stumbling, yanked upright and pushed on by Kendig's powerful grip.

He skittered through the trees and suddenly they were out in the open swath he'd discovered before and Kendig was shoving him down the steep pathway; he slid and stumbled his way, eyes on the ground, avoiding stumps, trying to keep his balance with his wrists wired behind him. It was getting hard to breathe through his nose but Kendig kept shoving and yanking. He caromed down into the heavier forest and then Kendig slowed them down and they were walking, following a broad path among the trees, still hearing the hunters baying up at the far side of the yard; he heard Cutter's distinct voice, louder than the others, calling for order and after that the racket diminished.

Abruptly there was a heavier mass in front of him in the deep forest shadows. He didn't realize what it was until Kendig pulled the door open and shoved him into the passenger seat of the car. The door slammed against his right elbow and before he had time to react to it Kendig was behind the wheel flicking a switch and pushing a button. The engine roared and immediately they went bucketing forward, crashing through loose brush which he now saw had been piled there on purpose. It was a thin tangle of dead-wood and it gave way easily before the thrust of the powerful car; Kendig spun the car onto the blacktop and the rear wheels bounced from side to side before they dug in and propelled the car forward, pinning Ross back painfully against his trapped forearms.

When he twisted around to look back he saw a car pulling out, coming after them—the one Cutter had left at the foot of the driveway.

Then he looked at Kendig. It was the first real look he'd had at his captor.

Kendig was smiling—gently and happily.

———

The FBI car wasn't gaining but it was keeping up, maybe two-tenths of a mile behind them; he kept looking back for it and saw it intermittently on the straightaways. This was an old car but it must have had a souped-up mill and heavy-duty suspension for the bends; Kendig was treating it like a sports car and it was holding the road like one. It was all pretty damned neat, Ross conceded.

Kendig curled the car onto a straightaway and then his right hand came across the back of the seat and Ross ducked away but Kendig was only untying the gag and when he realized that he stopped flinching. He spat the gag out and Kendig said, "What are you, FBI or Agency?"

Ross didn't say anything and Kendig nodded. "Then you're Agency. A Bureau man would be proclaiming it to the sky, full of indignation. You're working with Cutter on this?" Kendig spared him a quick glance. "Sure. You're Ross, aren't you."

"Yeah." His voice was hoarse from the gag and he cleared his throat several times.

"You've come up in the world from the third floor."

"What are you trying to prove, Kendig?"

But Kendig didn't take the time to answer that. He had his eyes on the mirror and Ross twisted his head to look. The FBI car was still there, maybe a little closer. It was a long straightaway and farther back he could see the glow of headlights above a skyline.

Kendig said, "They've got three cars, haven't they. We'll have to lose those."

"You're bottled up on every road in this county, Kendig."

"You haven't got that kind of manpower. Don't try to bluff me, Ross, you haven't had enough practice."

They soared over a hilltop and then the road plunged into a series of tight bends on the downslope; they had to slow to twenty and even then the tires squealed and whimpered.

At the bottom there was a drain-off ditch beyond the outside of the curve, no guardrail. They went into the bend at about twenty-five and Ross saw Kendig yank something with his left hand, down beside the seat. Then Kendig gunned the engine and they gathered speed down the flats.

Kendig wasn't using a map but he knew what he was doing; either he'd explored the roads or memorized a map. He took a left turn at an intersection and they bumped along a dirt road that looked to Ross as if it ought to be a dead end but it let them onto another paved byway and Kendig only followed that a mile and a half before he cut to the left again into the pines and went up a narrow chuckholed track past a cluster of farms. Chickens cackled in the night from the disturbance. They came into yet another blacktop road, made a gravel detour and emerged onto a wider concrete highway. Kendig had fled southeast from his farm but now if Ross's sense of direction hadn't packed up they were rolling almost due west.

Then Kendig pulled over onto the verge. He stopped the car and patted Ross's jacket and lifted his wallet and ID folder.

"Now you add that to your sins," Ross said.

Kendig ignored it and pocketed Ross's wallets. "I want you to

give Joe Cutter a message. Tell him I've finished writing the book.
I'll be carrying it with me. Every now and then I'll stop somewhere
and mail off another chapter. I'll keep a crucial page here and
there, just as I did with the first ones. I'm playing fair—I haven't
hidden the manuscript with a lawyer to be opened in the event I
don't check in or anything like that. If you and Joe can catch me
you'll catch the manuscript with me. But the longer you take, the
more pages they'll be receiving at the publishers. And I'm likely to
start mailing out those evidential pages any time. Tell him that for
me—he ought to enjoy the news."

"You're a madman, you know that?"

"I'm having fun and so are you."

Ross couldn't help it: he said acidly, "You have any suggestions
where we might start looking for you next time?"

"I wouldn't want to spoil your fun." Kendig reached across
Ross's lap and pushed the door open. "Go on."

"What about my hands?"

"Use your ingenuity."

"Thanks."

"Somebody will pick you up sooner or later. Go on, Ross."

He clambered from the car, obscurely torn by anger and grat-
itude. The car bolted away, its momentum slamming the door he'd
left open. His own revolver bounced on the shoulder and dropped
to rest. Ross tried to read the plate but its light had been extin-
guished. It probably didn't matter—Kendig would have to ditch
that car soon.

He retrieved his revolver awkwardly and stood along the roadside quite a while, waiting. It amazed him how gently Kendig had
treated him. But then nothing made much sense on this assignment. All of them seemed to be reveling in an exercise in nostalgia.
Even Cutter in his cool way seemed to be facing the job as if
Kendig were a rival whitescarfed aviator in an open biplane—the
sort of man you saluted after you'd shot him down. The anachro-

nism made it hard to come to terms with the assignment: Ross saw what kind of game he was supposed to be playing but he'd never played it before and wasn't sure he had the capacities for it. Yet comprehension tantalized him; he almost had it—in spite of the absurd embarrassment of his position he felt something that wasn't exactly admiration or respect for Kendig; it was more like pride.

It was a long time before he realized the FBI cars weren't coming. He had a feeling that was oil Kendig had dumped back on the bend. They'd have been traveling very slowly there, not fast enough to do the passengers much damage but the cars must have tangled up in that drain-off ditch and it would be a foul-mouthed crowd there.

He began to work out ways to get the wire off his wrists.

| 16 |

At one time the Cubans had used the field for training; now it was wild with weeds. The ocean threw a redolent breeze across the flats, roughing up the trees. The shadows seemed to be inhabited by the ghosts of short brown guerrillas with obsolete weapons and quixotic ambitions.

Kendig had paid one hundred dollars cash for the gas-burning 1955 Buick; he left it parked on its bald tires in the trees with the key in the ignition—somebody would boost it within a week and joyride it until it died or ran out of gas and that would destroy the evidence for him. He carried his big suitcase to the verge of the overgrown strip and sat down with his back against the bole of a palm. The sun was two hours up, very bright in a pale ocean sky. He listened to the cry of the gulls.

The plane approached on the wind, preceded by its sound; he watched it descend, wingtips teetering in the uncertain air currents above the mild surf. It made a half-circle inland and made its final approach into the wind, nosing down over the trees and

settling gingerly on its tricycle gear at a very low stalling speed—
evidently out of respect for the tangled weeds on the surface. She
kept the tail down after touchdown and rolled forward on two
wheels, nose in the air; twice the tailskid bounced. She used up a
good deal of runway before the speed was down sufficiently to
make the U-turn and taxi back toward him. Kendig picked up his
suitcase.

She cut the port engine and opened the door. He climbed
onto the step and passed the suitcase inside, stepped onto the root
of the wing and ducked to enter the cabin.

The sun was behind him; he saw her Modigliani face twinned
in the mirror of the opposite window. She wore Levi's and a
denim jacket over a blouse that looked like yellow satin. He
pushed the suitcase across one of the rear seats and moved forward to settle into the right-hand seat beside her—the copilot's
position.

"Where's my other passenger?"

"Been a change in plan. I'm flying out alone."

"The price is the same."

"Naturally."

She said, "You picked a hell of a field. I hope we don't snag
something."

He only smiled and she fixed the door shut behind her; then
she pushed the starter switch to mesh the port engine. The props
ran up and there was too much noise for talk; she pointed toward
his lap and he fastened the safety belt.

It was a bumpy ride but nothing grabbed the wheels; she had
them airborne a quarter mile short of the beach. The sun hit them
square in the eyes. Kendig said, "Turn around now. Make your
course two-sixty-five magnetic."

"What?"

"We're going to Mexico."

"I think you're a little crazy, you know?" The plane came out of its bank; the sun was behind them now. They were still in a steady climb but they had airspeed now and the wind took the engine noise with it; she could talk without shouting. "I filed for Saint Thomas. If I don't show up they'll organize a search."

"Call Miami control. Tell them your charter passenger changed his mind. Request clearance for Corpus Christi. And remember you're still on the flight plan to Saint Thomas right now—give them a position report a couple of hours east of here. That'll add a couple of hours to your ETA. You'll have time to drop me in Mexico and get into Corpus Christi on schedule."

She gave him a sudden smile. "Hey that's pretty good."

Then he opened his pocketknife.

Her face whitened.

"It gets you off the hook," he said. "The man held a knife on you."

"That's hijacking."

"No," he said. "It's my charter. A man can't hijack his own plane. But you'll be making an illegal entry into Mexico and this covers you for that." He folded the knife and put it back in his pocket.

He took the oval compact from the same pocket. "You left this in my car."

"I know."

He remembered the cats, the O'Keeffe painting, the bed. But there was reserve between them now, they were talking like strangers—as if they ought to be calling each other Mr. Murdison and Mrs. Fleming.

"What happened to your lady friend?"

"There never was one."

"Then Mexico was the destination all the time?"

"That's right."

"What did you do? Hold up a bank? What's in that suitcase?"

"It doesn't matter."

"I've never driven a getaway car before," she said. "It's sort of fun."

———

She was good. They were just north of the Tropic of Cancer and they crossed a patch of turbulent air; she didn't buck it, she rode with it. Her fingers never whitened on the half-wheel. She made the corrections without hurry or tension; when they were through it they were cruising at nine thousand feet with a patchwork of fluffy clouds beneath them, sectors of choppy sea visible through the holes. She had the twin engines nicely in synch and there wasn't much vibration; it was a well-cared-for plane. Kendig said, "Mind if I steer for a while?"

"Help self." Then after a while she said, "You're not bad. You don't clench up when she pockets."

"I took flying lessons for a while. Though I wanted to do air races."

"What happened?"

"I found out my talents were pretty rudimentary. I didn't stick it out—didn't take the license." He locked the autopilot in. "How'd you get the money to buy it?"

"My ex settled a lump sum on me in lieu of alimony. That was the down payment. People like you are buying the rest of it for me."

"It does something for you, being up here. Doesn't it."

"That's why I'm up here." She looked at peace. "Van wasn't a bad guy. But we got into a triangle—Van, me and the *hausfrau* he wanted me to be. I'm not a fanatic libber, you know. But I'm nobody's ornament. I like to fly. I mean I *really* like it. It's my life."

"You're not a Southerner. Why do you live in Alabama?"

"Flying weather. I don't like winter. I worked charters around the islands for a year but it was too chancy—I've got to keep up the payments on the albatross here. It had to be an industrial city, that's where the business charters are. I don't like Houston at all. Atlanta's too self-conscious and I just can't stand California plastic. They're hypocrites and bastards in Birmingham but I'm sort of tuned into them—they don't disappoint me. What about you? You don't really live in Topeka."

"No."

"You don't volunteer much about yourself."

"People may ask you questions about me."

"So the less I know the better off you are, is that it?"

"Yes."

She said, "I don't believe that's all there is to it, Jim. Is that your name? Jim?"

"It'll do."

"You really don't want anybody digging into you, do you. Not even yourself." She had a blinding smile when she chose to use it. "You're a lovely man, you know that? The night I took you home—I don't do that with just anybody. You've got something rare. I don't know exactly what it is—you seem to be *alive*, that's what it amounts to."

She couldn't know how much it pleased him to hear that.

———

The descent began to clog his ears. The sun was in their faces again: it had moved across the sky faster than they had. Carla Fleming said, "I'm a little scared. It's the first time I've ever done anything like this."

"You'd be just as scared the second time, and the third."

"Good." That smile again. "I like it a little."

They mushed down through heavy cloud. Underneath there was a faint drizzle of rain and the afternoon light was poor but her navigation had been right on the button and the dusty reddish strip was right there ahead, ringed with scrub brush and rock-craggy mountains sprouting tufts of cactus and weeds. "How did you find out about this place?"

"It used to be a training area for exiled Haitian guerrillas. I expect it's used for narcotics flights."

"What did you have to do with the Haitians?"

"No comment."

"Off limits. Okay. You don't mind my asking, though?"

"No."

Then she had her attention on procedures. She was judging the wind, adjusting for the barometric pressure, making her preparations. She made one low pass over the runway before she made a 360-degree turn and came in low on final and when she touched down it was feather light. They threw up a great deal of dust but the surface was quite smooth and the Bonanza came to rest with plenty of runway left over.

She cut both engines and the propellers hiccuped a little before they stopped. The silence was a sudden tangible absence.

"What do you do from here? Walk?"

"It's not far to where I'm going."

He crawled back between the empty seats, gathered his suitcase and climbed out the door. She was already outside, standing by the wing in the drizzle, not minding the wet. He jumped down and dropped the suitcase and got the envelope out of his pocket. She opened it without bashful pretense and counted it.

"It's too much," she said. "I'm not picking you up after two weeks, am I."

"No."

"Then you've paid twice the rate."

"Three thousand. It's what we agreed on."

"That was for two trips."

"Call it hazardous duty pay," he said. "Thanks for the ride. You'd better be going."

She put the envelope in the pocket of her jacket. She had a little trouble fitting it in; her hand came out holding the compact. She looked at it as if it were a completely unfamiliar object, turning it over in her hands, opening it, snapping it shut. "I guess I won't see you again."

"Who knows."

"Well that's all right. I've got a cauliflower heart." But her hand tightened into a quivering little fist around the compact. Her face, suddenly, was flaming. "I'm not going to get on the radio and start screaming the minute I take off. I'm not going to tell them anything in Corpus Christi—just that I dropped off a passenger from Miami there, name of Jim Murdison from Topeka Kansas."

"All right. But if anybody asks questions you'd better tell them the truth."

"Nobody will," she said. "Nobody's going to know. Not from me."

He knew it was an unwise thing but he folded her against him and when she tipped her face up he kissed her long and hard. The drizzle misted their skin. There was nothing extraordinary about any of it but it was one of those moments he'd never forget—a spark that would grow brighter whenever it was touched by its associations: the smell of the desert drizzle and of airplane oil, the pale impressionism of the afternoon's color, the loneliness of the solitary aircraft asleep on dusty ground.

He stood beside his suitcase with his jacket billowing in the wind of the plane's passage when it roared by him and lifted, steeply banking, wings waggling in farewell; then he picked up the valise and walked away toward the narrow highway beyond the hill.

| 17 |

The room stank of yesterday's tobacco. The silence was such that Ross could hear Myerson's ballpoint pen scrape across the pad. Cutter merely sat in a placenta of patience. Ross kept looking at the door and finally it opened and Glenn Follett entered, burly and freckled and as dewlappy as a Basset hound. "Greetings."

Myerson looked up. He held the ballpoint upright, bouncing it on the desk. "Now that Mr. Follett has graced the room with his presence perhaps we can get started."

Follett sat down. "There was a traffic jam. I'm sorry."

Ross recalled Cutter's comment on the way up twenty minutes ago in the elevator: *If it was up to me I wouldn't hire Follett to carry out my garbage.* Follett was definitely cast against type. He seemed always desperate to reassure himself that he was lovable, that he had buddies like other people. His face in repose looked eagerly ready at an instant's notice to burst into tears. Perhaps to counter his appearance he had a lexicon of mannerisms designed to accentuate a sort of forced bonhomie. His voice was always too loud, he spoke with great heaves and lunges of his arms: his emotions were ebulliently on the surface, there for anyone to read.

"All right," Myerson said. "Let's have a rough Sit Rep. What's the score as of this morning?"

Cutter said, "Score? We're not even sure we know who the players are."

"You're talking about other countries now, Joe?"

"We don't know where he is, do we."

Follett said, "Hell let's don't get sour this early in the morning, Joe. So he's gone under again. People have gone to ground before. They always turn up sooner or later, right?"

"Later in this case could be too late," Myerson said. "Let's have the Sit Rep."

The situation report was Ross's department and he cleared his throat. "All right. Here's what we know." He consulted his notes. "On the twenty-fifth a man who was probably our subject spent half a day in an office-copying shop in Mobile, Alabama. He paid extra to run the machine himself so that nobody else could get a look at what he was running off, but according to Tobin's reports the general appearance conforms with our estimate of Kendig's needs. The man ran off thirty-three hundred copies and collated the sheets into approximately fifteen stacks. That works out to two hundred and twenty pages per stack. If his entire manuscript runs two hundred and seventy-odd pages and we subtract the fifty pages or so that he's already delivered, it works out just about right. He's got fourteen publishers and the fifteenth copy would be for his agent in New York. He retains the original and the carbon."

"Interesting to speculate on what use he's got in mind for the carbon," Myerson said. "All right—go on, Ross."

"Right. On the twenty-seventh he bought a 'fifty-five Buick in Pensacola for a hundred dollars cash." He felt the blood rise to his cheeks. "He had to use a driver's license and other identification of course—automobile insurance card, that kind of thing. He used mine—the wallet he took off me in Georgia."

"Cute," Cutter remarked. Ross was surprised to see him smile.

Ross went on: "He spent the night of the twenty-sixth in Tampa, a motel. Leonard Ross, but it's Kendig's handwriting on the registry card. All this stuff is from Tobin's people over at the Bureau."

Follett said, "Jesus. They must have put a ton of guys on the canvassing job."

"They've blanketed the South," Myerson said grudgingly. "They're pretty good at that."

"We had one piece of blind luck," Ross continued. "On the twenty-seventh a Florida state trooper issued him a warning because the car was throwing smoke. Safety check, you know. But he was still being Leonard Ross—the cop got it down in his book. That was near Plant City—it's roughly due east of Clearwater, maybe halfway down the Florida peninsula. So he was definitely headed south. Tobin sent his people into south Florida on the twenty-ninth to drag the net. They found out Leonard Ross had spent the night of the twenty-seventh in a motel near Sarasota."

"He wasn't in any hurry," Cutter said. "It's not that far from Tampa to Sarasota. Even in an old oil-burner he could have gone three times as far in a day's drive if he'd wanted to."

Ross said, "Well of course he was staying off the Interstates, that would slow him down. There've been FBI spotters along the big highways but he never showed on any of them. He's using back roads."

"Or was," Cutter said. "This was a week ago. He could be in Hong Kong by now."

Ross felt heat in his face again. "He stopped using my ID at that point. He mailed the wallet and the badge back to me on the twenty-eighth from Sarasota. I received them two days ago."

"He's very funny," Myerson said.

Glenn Follett shot his arm into the air. "Did you check them out for fingerprints?"

"Naturally," Cutter said.

"And?"

Cutter only shook his head in disgust: disgust with Follett, not with the predictable results of the lab tests.

Follett was oblivious. "I still don't understand how he could have used Ross's driver's license to buy a car and fool a state trooper. How old are you, Ross? Twenty-five?"

"Twenty-eight."

"Hell Kendig's nearly twice your age. How'd he get by with it?"

Ross said, "The cop described him as thirtyish."

"He used to be pretty good with makeup," Cutter said. "He could be an Arab one day, a Swede the next."

Ross went back to his notes. "On the thirtieth that bootleg-ger's Oldsmobile turned up in Mobile—he left it on a pay lot there. That was the car he used to bust out of our trap."

"The one you had a little ride in," Cutter said.

"Yeah." He hurried on. "But that didn't help—we already knew he'd been in Mobile. Okay, the last item is this—my wallet wasn't the only thing he mailed from Sarasota on the twenty-eighth. He shipped out fifteen copies of chapter four as well. Ives got his copy yesterday. Desrosiers hasn't reported yet. They'll be showing up in the next day or two, I expect."

"What's it about?" Myerson asked.

"It's the one about Duvalier being assassinated on White House orders."

"Wonderful," Myerson said. It was close to a groan. "Why doesn't he pick on the other side for a change?"

"That comes next. The Nasser chapter."

Cutter said, "On the twenty-eighth he dropped out of sight.

Sarasota was the last fix we had on him. That was a week ago to-day. He's taken cover."

Follett said, "I don't get it, Joe. If the bastard's still in south Florida what am I doing here? Florida's not my bailiwick."

Myerson said, "Joe thinks he may turn up in Europe next. That's why I called you in from Marseilles."

"What the hell makes you think that?"

Cutter smiled, not friendly. "He's playing cat-and-mouse with us. He's not trying to disappear into a hole. He only goes to ground when he needs time to do this or that. He hid out on that Georgia farm to finish writing the tract. Well he's got that done now, he doesn't need to hide in one place any more. He's on the run—but he needed a head start. That's why he dropped out of sight. Now he could turn up anywhere but it's most likely he'll show himself on familiar turf—someplace where he knows the workings. Europe, the Near East or southeast Asia. Unless he proves me wrong I'm going to rule out southeast Asia for the time being. Kendig's too tall, too Caucasian—he's too noticeable out there. He can't disguise himself as a Cambode or a Thai. He was all right working there when he was Second Secretary and not pre-tending to be anything but an American, but this is something else. He's going to be somewhere between Scandinavia and the Med—somewhere where he can stir up the Russians and some of our other opposite numbers. He wants to watch a whole gang of us trip all over each other trying to run him down. That's his idea of fun."

"You're awfully sure of that, aren't you, Joe? What if he heads for Latin America instead?"

"He won't. Not for long anyway."

Myerson said, "I think we've got to go with Joe's judgment for the time being. He knows Kendig better than you do, Glenn."

Follett shook his head. "I know Kendig this well—I know you can't depend on him to conform to a pattern."

Cutter made a face.

Myerson said, "Let's not get disputatious at this point. Right now we need all the cooperation among ourselves we can get. All of you are booked on a flight this evening to Paris. Joe Cutter will be running the operation, Glenn, and you're to give him complete cooperation in all your departments over there. This thing takes priority over every operation you've got in motion. If Joe tells you to pull people off other jobs then you'll have to do it immediately and not complain about it. Understood?"

"I understand your intent. But I've got people working on sensitive jobs that are in process. Some of them can't be yanked out just like that." Follett was miffed because he ranked Cutter in seniority and the regular chain-of-command. "You can't just disrupt the priority operations of my whole department to go chasing after one man. You know as well as I do what kind of jobs we're working on over there."

"Joe's not going to tap you for anything more than he needs, isn't that right Joe?"

Cutter grunted.

Ross thought, *This is not going to be fun.*

| 18 |

The train was due at nine in the morning and he didn't arrive at the depot until half-past ten but even so he was among the first; even the station-master hadn't arrived yet. If the train had been on time nobody would have caught it but this was Mexico and the passengers began to drift in by bus, taxi and foot around eleven o'clock and the train wheezed in with a scrape of sighing brake-shoes at eleven-twenty. Kendig went aboard in the midst of a crowd of mestizos carrying chickens, goats, a small pig, a goose and various baskets of produce for the market town three stops hence. Kendig's second-class ticket did not entitle him to a seat on the long bench; he stood against a window, resting his elbow on it, trying to breathe while the train lurched into the mountains. But the air was like coarse wool, too hot for relief even at forty miles an hour. Children and animals made a din; the faces were as stoic as those of Auschwitz.

He had no liking for Latin America and he had said as much at least once in Cutter's hearing; in part that was why he was here.

But he'd kept moving for three days and he'd be out of Mexico by tonight.

Sometimes it surprised him a little that everything south of the Rio Grande hadn't gone Communist by now. It was only because the Cubans had set such an inept example and because Ché had been such a visible idiot. They had the temperament for it, though. Tyranny suited them. You could be put up against a wall for nothing more than having a smudged passport or a suspicious face. Cynicism and defeat were their religions. It was not accident that the fugitive Nazis had found their best refuge in Spanish America. They believed only in macho—not courage but merely the surface appearance of courage: like the Oriental concept of face, the value of which also had always eluded him. He was a prisoner of his belief in realities rather than appearances. He had never cared what anyone thought of him, only what he thought of himself.

He was thinking better of himself now. For a time he'd fallen into the trap of conceding the validity of the Agency's judgment on him: from their point of view he'd been of no further use to them. It had not occurred to him before that he could prove them wrong. He was proving it now. It was possible his actions might save the career of the next middle-aged expert who began to look obsolete to them. Perhaps even Cutter. The thought amused him. He didn't dwell on it; it was also possible they'd carry their innate nihilism to its logical extreme and neutralize the next one rather than risk another Kendig on the loose. But the most likely probability was that he wouldn't change anything at all. They'd regard him as a fluke and it would have no bearing on their future decisions. They were not the sort of people who learned from history. No: the game had to be played on its own terms, not the terms of its speculative consequences.

Zacatecas at five-fifteen; he made it by taxi to the little airport by six and was on the evening flight to Mexico City. He was traveling light, just the one suitcase, not carrying the fifteen heavy copies of the manuscript. At the big modern terminal he booked onto the morning Aeronaves 707 to Madrid and paid for the ticket with travelers' checks he'd bought for cash in Miami under the name Jules Parker. He'd spent nine hours on October second in a Coral Gables motel forging Parker's passport and driver's license, the last blanks he'd had from Saint-Breheret. He still had the French passport, unused, which he'd made out in the name of Alexandre Vaneau.

He boarded the flight in the morning and was in Madrid at half-past eight that night, European time.

————

The next day was Monday, October the seventh. He ticketed Jules Parker onto the afternoon flight to Copenhagen by way of Paris. During the morning in Madrid he went to the huge central post office and identified himself as Parker and collected the airmail parcel from Miami at the general delivery window. He took the parcel to his hotel, opened it on the bed and separated seven stacks, each containing fifteen copies of a single chapter of the book.

He slid the copies of chapter five into fifteen of the manila envelopes he'd bought in Birmingham and addressed the first to Ives, the second to Desrosiers and the rest to his publishers in New York, London, Tokyo, Rome, Ottawa, Rio de Janeiro, Buenos Aires, Stockholm, Tel Aviv, West Berlin, Melbourne, Johannesburg and Leningrad.

Of the six remaining stacks none was more than an inch and a half thick; the longest chapter, the last one, ran 23 pages in length and made a 345-page stack. He doubled the stacks and laid them three abreast into his suitcase—a flat padding of paper; it took half an hour to stitch the false bottom into place above them.

Then he carried the fifteen envelopes back to the post office and airmailed them.

The stop at Orly gave him a three-hour layover between planes. He took a taxi into Paris, paid the driver at the Pont St. Michel and walked across the quai into the medieval narrowness of the rue Seguier. Sooner or later they'd find out he'd withdrawn money from the bank in Zurich; they'd put that together with the fact that he'd begun the operation in Paris and returned to Paris on his way from Madrid to Copenhagen. They'd conclude he had cached his money in Paris and at that point they'd begin to cover the commercial and savings banks. That was why he hadn't put the money in a bank.

The proprietor of the diamond exchange was heavier than he'd been when he'd bought his blue pinstriped suit; it stretched over rolls of fat. The blond hair was stretched over his pale scalp in thin strands. "Ah, *M'sieur* Vaneau!" With marvelously feigned pleasure he escorted Kendig to the basement vault. Two subtly armed men sat guard on the chamber. It was as impregnable as anything in a bank. Only M. Strauss and his partner M. Losserand had the combinations.

The vault was vaster than it needed to be. Diamonds did not take up much space. The walk-in interior was sectioned into compartments and each was a small safe in itself with its own lock; when you rented a compartment you set your own combination into it so that no one—not even Strauss or Losserand—could get into it. There was a great demand for such safe-deposit services among businessmen and politicians who were willing to pay high for discretion.

M. Strauss opened the vault for him. Kendig unlocked his compartment and slid the heavy black metal box out of it; carried it into the private cubicle, shut himself in and opened the box.

He'd withdrawn substantial funds from Zurich two weeks before he'd started the game with Desrosiers; he'd made a dent in it but when he refilled his money belt now it still left more than two hundred thousand dollars in American, English and French currency in the box. He wasn't going to have to forfeit the game on account of poverty.

He took the Alexandre Vaneau passport from his coat and placed it in the black box with the hoard. It would be a risk traveling without it but it wasn't wise to carry all your weapons on your person. If he needed it he'd come back for it.

He carried the box back to the compartment, locked it in and went upstairs with Strauss, who understood him to be an arms merchant who dealt in cash purchases. He walked out past the display cabinets of glittering stones, flagged a taxi in the boulevard St. Germain and returned to Orly in time to make his second flight of the day.

A chill drizzle muffled the purported gaiety of Copenhagen. It had never been a favorite of Kendig's; beneath the Hans Christian Anderson image of Tivoli and frivolity it was as grimly brooding a city as Hamburg and the phony cheer only made it more depressing. He thawed himself with an aquavit in the hotel bar before he retired.

In the morning he made the call from a telephone kiosk in the cavernous railway station; he kept the door of the booth ajar so that the phone would pick up the sounds of the trains and announcements.

It took a while for the international operator to place the call. When it rang back he picked up quickly.

"Ja bitte?"

"Herr Dortmund, bitte? Ich bin Kendig."

"Dankeschön, mein herr. . . ."

A scratching silence, then a click when the extension went up. "Mr. Kendig?"

"I wanted Michael."

"He is not in Berlin at the moment. My name is Brucher, may I help you?"

He didn't recognize the voice but *Herr* Brucher was being most solicitous and that meant *Herr* Brucher knew who Kendig was. "I'll want to talk with Michael. Will he be at this number at this hour tomorrow?"

"Zis can be arranged, I sink."

"Then I'll call back tomorrow."

"Perhaps Michael can reach you, *Herr* Kendig?"

"No, I think not."

"Very well. Senk you for calling, *Herr* Kendig."

———

He took the boat-train to Stockholm and put up in a small hotel he'd never visited before; it was on one of the outer islands and had a good view of the botanical gardens and the shipping beyond. He wrote a postcard to Joe Cutter and addressed it in care of the Paris office, chuckled aloud when he dropped it in a street-corner postbox and then took the ferry across to the main island in search of a night's entertainment.

———

He made the morning call to Berlin from a phone in the airport. It was the same ritual as before—the request to speak with *Herr* Dortmund, the click of the extension, the voice of *Herr* Brucher; then Mikhail Yaskov came on the line. "Miles, old friend. How good to hear your voice." Yaskov contrived to sound both surprised and artless.

"I've been writing a book," Kendig said.

"Yes, I've been following it with great interest."

"I thought you might have done."

"You're calling perhaps because the remainder of the book is for sale?"

"No, it's already been sold. I just wanted to let you know I've taken your advice—I've brought myself back to life. I've got back into the game. Those were your words, I think."

"I'm so happy," Yaskov said drily, "to know that you value my sage counsel so highly, old friend. Now what may I do for you?"

A disembodied announcement resonated through the terminal: "Mr. William Scott, Mr. William Scott, please come to the SAS passenger service counter."

Kendig said into the phone, "I just thought you might like to know that I'm visiting your territory at the moment. Just sightseeing, of course—you know how it is."

"Are you enjoying the trip?"

"Keenly."

"I'm so glad," Yaskov said. "Perhaps we shall cross paths, since as you say you are traveling in my area."

"That depends on whether you're still as good at your job as you used to be."

"You're giving me an opportunity to find that out, are you?"

"Yes. I thought you'd appreciate that, Mikhail."

"As a matter of fact I do—very much. Does that surprise you?"

"No," Kendig said. "I haven't forgotten what you said about the hunting way of life."

"Yes, of course."

"I'll be forwarding chapters of my book to the publishers at odd intervals. I thought you might like to know."

"So I understood from the samples you have delivered. Miles, I rather doubt your book will be published in its entirety by the Leningrad press you chose to submit it to. Of course they may see fit to publish certain selected passages from it, perhaps in *Isvestia* or some such suitable organ."

"Naturally. Tell them not to forget to pay me for it. You've joined the International Copyright Convention now, remember."

"To whom should such payment be made?"

"My literary agent is John Ives in New York. He has my power of attorney."

"I'm sure your estate will receive the money in due course, my capitalist friend."

Kendig let him have the last word; he rang off and went to the counter to check his bag through on the Finnair flight to Helsinki.

| 1 9 |

The office was less than two blocks from the Champs Elysees; autumn leaves rattled against the high old windows. Ross was sorting the signals from Washington—the courier still waited beyond the desk with the briefcase chained to his wrist—when Cutter came in. Obviously he had left his emotions in his hotel room. "Anything we can use?"

"A stringer for the SDECE spotted him in Madrid. Recognized him but didn't tail him—didn't know he was on the wanted list until he mentioned he'd seen Kendig, back in the office."

Cutter said, "That's hardly newsworthy, Ross. We already know he was in Madrid. Anything else?"

"No. Did Desrosiers—"

Cutter waved him off; his eyes went beyond Ross to the courier. "We don't need to keep you. I'm sure you've got important things to do."

The courier took the hint and left. Cutter asked, "Where's Follett?"

"I don't know."

"He was supposed to be here."

"Was he? He didn't tell me that. He went out about an hour ago."

Cutter picked up the phone. "Is Follett in the building?"

Ross heard the reply—the caustic voice of the dried-up woman at the front desk. "Do you think this is a hotel? I don't keep a register."

"This is Joseph Cutter."

"Oh—I'm very sorry, sir."

"When he shows up tell him to get his ass in here. And find out where he is and call me back." He cradled the receiver very gently and said to Ross, "It occurs to me that this office is making a deliberate effort to corner the market on stupid blunderers." He snapped a look at his watch and shot his cuff and sat down. Cutter was a little rattled; it was unusual and Ross marked it. Cutter was always so coolly controlled. But he didn't seem to have lost his un-canny talent for being punctual without hurry, for carrying a thousand things in his head without ever losing the balance of them, for always knowing the exact time—it was nearly the first time Ross had ever seen him look at his watch.

Then the phone rang. It was the wasp-faced woman; Cutter had dubbed her The Lemon Taster two days ago. Ross picked it up. "Mr. Follett is on his way up, sir."

"Thank you."

"Don't mention it." Was everything she said sarcastic or did it just sound that way?

Ross hung up. Cutter said, "Trying to work with this guy is like trying to mate a chimpanzee with a porcupine. I wonder where he finds the five coats of whitewash he must be using on this operation."

"You shouldn't underestimate him just because you don't like him." Ross was surprised by his own temerity; but it only elicited a brief smile from Cutter, cool with insincerity. Nevertheless Ross felt he had been reproved. He kept shifting the letter opener and pencils on the blotter, lining them up along various parallels.

Follett came in, hearty and beaming; Cutter deflated him before he'd had a chance to speak: "I'd better hang a bell on you so I'll know where you are."

Follett reared back. "You sound like you're a little peeved, Joe."

"Uh-huh. You can put that in the bank."

Conciliatory but not really giving an inch, Follett said slowly, "Joe, you won't have any trouble with me."

"You bet your ass I won't." The smile, again, was a forced sliver. "Seat thyself, Glenn, and let's program this thing."

Follett threw off his topcoat and lunged into a chair. His freckled face was ruddy from the October wind. "I had a vague conversation with my opposite number in French security just now. That's why I'm a little late. He's willing to—"

The phone rang again. Ross was at the desk; he answered it.

"Mr. Cutter? There's a—"

"This is Ross. Can it wait?"

"The caller says it's urgent, sir."

"Who is he?"

"He claims to be Mikhail Yaskov."

———

Cutter took the call and held it flat against his ear so that Ross couldn't overhear anything; Cutter's end of the conversation was monosyllabic and after less than two minutes he said, "Agreed," and hung it up and went back to his chair but didn't seat himself; he stood with one hand on the back of the chair and scowled.

Follett said, "Well?"

"He wants a meet."

"About Kendig?"

"Apparently."

Ross said, "Maybe they want to make a deal."

Follett said, "What kind of deal? Do you mean they've got Kendig?"

Cutter said, "No."

Follett began to bluster but Cutter, maddeningly, had lost interest and turned away. Follett flapped his arms. "Are you sure that was really Yaskov?"

"It's my business to be sure."

Follett began shaking his head back and forth. "I just don't understand any of this, I'll be the first to admit it. I don't understand Kendig most of all."

"Of course you don't. You couldn't in a hundred years understand a man like Kendig."

Ross said, "I don't see where any of us does. So far he hasn't made any mistakes at all."

"He's made one," Cutter said. "He's made me mad at him."

Follett tugged his earlobe. "You may be making a rash assumption, Joe. You're not brighter than he is—you're just younger."

Ross considered that in surprise; it had come out of the blue. But Follett was grinning slyly, knowing he'd scored a point; he'd been waiting for the chance. He got to his feet. "I presume you'll want to handle Yaskov without me."

"Correct."

"Then we'd better hold off the strategy conference until you've had your meet with him. How soon's it to be?"

"This afternoon."

"He's in Paris? He must think it's damned important."

"Of course he does," Cutter said in disgust. "All right, be back here at six tonight—we'll go over it then."

"Six? I was planning to—"

"I really don't much care what you were planning, Glenn."

Ross was happy to see Follett's back. He didn't dislike the man with Cutter's intensity but Follett's departure lowered the room temperature to something bearable.

Cutter had straight hair that wouldn't stick down; another man would have been continuously raking it back from his forehead. Cutter never paid it any attention. He said, "We're meeting him in the Louvre gardens in forty-five minutes."

"We?"

"I'll want a witness. So will he. Neither of us wants some third party accusing us of double-agenting."

"Cozy," Ross observed.

"The question is, what's the best way to approach it?"

"What do you think he wants?"

"I expect he wants a pooling of resources. Kendig's a threat to all of us—it makes a kind of sense. But it's more attractive to him than it is to me. I know Kendig better than he does—that gives us the edge. So what's he going to bargain with? We'll be better armed if we can figure that out before he springs it on us."

Ross ran it through his mind and shook his head. "Beats hell out of me what it might be."

"You're a big help, you are."

"Well I haven't been much of a help anywhere along the line that I can see. I let him make an ass of me down in Georgia—that phony gun stunt. I was convinced you'd tie a can to my tail after that. Why didn't you?"

"He made asses of all of us, Ross. I don't go in for scapegoating."

"That's mighty kind of you but it still doesn't explain why you've kept me on."

"I've been running a string of agents out of Beirut and Ankara."

"So?"

"You get used to having somebody to yell at," Cutter said.

"Sure—sure."

"You're green, Ross. You make mistakes—but you haven't made excuses. I like that. You're also flexible, you've got a good brain, you're a good learner and you've got something that seems to pass for a conscience, which is all but unique around here. I like that too."

"And?"

"I guess what it boils down to," Cutter said, "maybe I've been seeing intimations of my own mortality. A man wants a protégé."

Ross nodded slowly but he couldn't resist the riposte: "Like Kendig had you."

"Yes." Cutter was neither surprised nor angered. "Like that."

"Well I guess I ought to be flattered."

"But you aren't."

"Maybe I am. I can't tell yet. I'm not sure I like this business much."

"That's what makes you so valuable in it," Cutter said. "Come on, we might as well walk—it's a nice day for it."

———

Ross had worked for the Agency for quite a few years but it was the first time he'd seen an enemy agent in the flesh.

Yaskov had got there first and was standing in the path studying a linden tree as if he had a genuine interest in it. He appeared to be alone; Cutter pointed him out to Ross when they were still a hundred feet away. Ross said, "I must say he doesn't look the part. He looks more like he should have been a czarist spy."

"He would have been."

Yaskov was elegant, no other word for him.

They were fifty feet short of touching Yaskov when a little man bumped into Ross. It could have been an accident but the little man's feminine mouth smiled coyly and he fell in step with them. "My name is Ivanovitch."

"I'm Cutter. This is Mr. Smith."

Ivanovitch, whatever his name was, had the air of a man perpetually in a hurry. His manner was peremptory, his mannerisms impatient. The jostling he'd given Ross had been designed to find out whether Ross had a gun under his coat; he realized that now. Ivanovitch had cruel black little eyes—a glance intended to be silken, calculated to inspire fear. He was too ferrety to bring it off.

Ivanovitch walked along with choppy little strides but Cutter wasn't going to be hurried and Ivanovitch reached Yaskov ten paces ahead of them and turned. Cutter happened to be reaching into his shirt pocket at the moment and Ivanovitch moved abruptly, changing stance and bearing, and it was evident he knew the responses of unarmed combat. How expert he was was open to question in Ross's mind but it was not the time for adolescent contest with the Russian; Ross only shook his head and refrained from ambiguous motion and after a moment Yaskov laughed and Ivanovitch straightened up.

It was a toothpick Cutter produced. Now Ross saw what its purpose had been if Ivanovitch had gone inside his coat it would have indicated he was armed.

Cutter stopped six feet distant and said immediately, "Either let's move out of sight of those windows or let's meet somewhere else."

Yaskov glanced up. Two of the museum's windows overlooked the path. Anyone could be there—zoom lens, lip-reader, parabolic microphone, anything.

Yaskov bowed his head and turned; they walked back between the trees of the arbor. "Will this satisfy?"

"It'll do."

"We haven't met but of course we know each other."

"I've been looking forward to meeting you for a long time."

"Yes," Yaskov said. He ignored both Ivanovitch and Ross; so did Cutter.

"Our mutual friend Kendig"—Cutter seemed to savor the phrase with sardonic relish—"always had great admiration for you."

"Kendig and I are among the last of the old wolves," Yaskov said, "but perhaps there's still hope. I'm told you conform to the breed more than most of our colleagues."

They were under a tree; Cutter reached out one hand at shoulder height, put his palm against the trunk and leaned against it. "Can that suffice for the amenities, Yaskov?"

"Certainly, if you like."

Cutter's face turned slightly, half of it going into shadow. "Well? You're the one who asked for this meeting."

"Yesterday morning he telephoned me in Berlin."

"He was in Berlin?" Cutter straightened.

"No. It was a trunk call. I'm prepared to tell you where he called from, and where I think he may have gone from there."

Ross was sensitive to the pound of his own pulse. He glanced at Ivanovitch but the little Russian was looking away as if bored.

"And in exchange?" Cutter asked.

Yaskov smiled very slowly in private amusement; it came to Ross that behind his lofty pretense of man-of-the-world professionalism Yaskov was taking pleasure in Cutter's discomfiture. A far cry, this man, from the technocrats the KGB was known ordinarily to spawn.

"You know his haunts far better than I do," Yaskov replied.

"That doesn't mean anything. He'd avoid the old places."

"If you knew him to be in a certain city, you'd be more likely to know where to look for him in that city, *n'est-ce pas?*"

"It's possible," Cutter conceded. "It might depend on the city."

"I am suggesting we search together for him."

"It's an interesting thought."

"Yes, isn't it. A new high in *détente*."

"I'd have to clear it with my superiors of course."

"Naturally. So would I."

"How'd you expect to handle it?"

"Joint teams, Mr. Cutter."

"Like Vienna and Berlin in the old days."

Yaskov nodded slightly. "It is important to us all that he be—discouraged from carrying on. I rather suspect it is a bit more important to your side than to mine, but let's grant he's capable of embarrassing all of us, even if the embarrassment is in varying degrees."

Cutter said, "Before we go on with this I'd like to have Ivanovitch's camera."

Ivanovitch jerked as if stricken by an electrode; Ross stood up straight; Yaskov only shrugged and held out his hand, palm up, and a little camera came out of Ivanovitch's pocket. Yaskov gave it to Cutter. Cutter opened it, removed the film and gave it back, and it disappeared back into Ivanovitch's pocket.

"Thank you."

"May we be assured Mr. Smith is not similarly equipped?"

Ross pulled his hands out of his pockets, empty. Cutter said, "We didn't bring a camera. Or a microphone."

"Then none of us is wired for sound," Yaskov said.

Ross murmured, "Are we just going to take his word for that?"

"Why not?" Cutter said offhandedly; then he went back to Yaskov: "You weren't in earshot when I introduced Smith to Ivanovitch."

"It might have been Jones, mightn't it."

Both of them laughed a little and then Cutter said, "There's a little problem about all this."

"I wish you Americans didn't always think of things in terms of problems and solutions."

"I'd call this a problem, quite specifically. It's got more than one solution. That's where you and I have trouble. You want him alive—you want to milk him. We don't particularly want that to happen."

"As a matter of policy it is more important to my government that Kendig be neutralized than that he be brought home for questioning. I hope that clarifies my position?"

"You'd rather have half a loaf than none?"

"Precisely."

"My, you folks are getting flexible this year."

"I'm happy you appreciate that. Do we have a basis for cooperation, Mr. Cutter?"

"I'll put it to my superiors."

"And your own recommendation to them will be?"

"It will be negative."

"I'm sorry to hear that."

"I hope you are," Cutter said.

Yaskov inspected a fingernail. "I do hope nothing's happened to him."

"Yes. You'd be embarrassed if some third-rate power reached him ahead of you."

"So would you, Mr. Cutter."

"I don't think you need worry that anything's happened to him. Things don't happen to Miles Kendig. He happens to them."

Yaskov nodded as if on consideration he agreed. Then he said, "I fear your superiors will honor your negative recommendation."

"I imagine they will."

Yaskov's sigh was gentle. "A word in private, then." He took Cutter away a little distance. Ross saw him lean forward, intending Cutter to listen to him, staring straight into Cutter's face. The icy ruthlessness of the eyes unnerved Ross; it was a point-blank stare that destroyed the barriers of ordinary defense and pretense.

Yaskov spoke, Cutter nodded; then Yaskov crooked his finger and
Ivanovitch stirred. Yaskov bobbed his cane toward Ross and went
away, Ivanovitch hurrying after.

Ross said, "What did he say?"

"Kendig called him from Stockholm. Yaskov believes he went
on to Helsinki from there."

————

"A lot of this is going by too fast for me," Ross said as they turned
off the Champs. "Why'd he give it to us for free?"

"Because it's true he'd prefer half a loaf to none. He'd rather
we nail Kendig than not see him nailed at all. He tried to bargain,
we called his bluff and he had no choice but to give in to us for
nothing."

"You've got to be a Machiavelli in this business."

"You'll pick it up as you go along, Ross."

"What was all that about Ivanovitch's camera?"

"They haven't got you taped. They don't know who you are. I
didn't see any point making it easy for them—we might want to
use you in the field after this. Ivanovitch didn't matter, he's on
tape everywhere west of Warsaw—his name's Kirovoi, he's an er-
rand boy. One look at him and you know what he is and what he
does."

"But you brought me along instead of somebody like him."

"I wanted you to meet Yaskov," Cutter said.

"I'm glad you did. It was an education."

"There aren't many left like him," Cutter told him. They
turned in at the door and The Lemon Taster gave them an acidu-
lous glance. Cutter said to her, "I'll want six field men upstairs at
half-past six. The best you've got. Clear it through Follett. And
book us eight seats on the first flight to Helsinki after nine tonight."

"Yes sir. This came for you."

It was a postcard from Stockholm. Cutter let Ross read it over his shoulder.

Having wonderful time. Wish you were here. M.K.

Cutter's bark of laughter startled The Lemon Taster.

| 20 |

From a kiosk in *Stockmann* in Helsinki he made one call to London and then he rode a taxi to the airport and made it onto the British Airways Boeing with only a few minutes to spare. Snowflakes drifted past in the night when they lifted off. He catnapped most of the way to Heathrow and walked through customs with only a routine glance at the Jules Parker passport. He rode the bus in from the airport to the terminal in Kensington and then did a little charade designed to disclose a tail, transferring from tube-train to red bus to taxi; he left the taxi in Regent Street and backtracked by bus into Kensington and walked down to the Kingston Close Hotel in its mewsish seclusion behind the boutique that used to be Derry & Toms.

He told the hall porter he was in London on business from Bradford in the north; he put on a broad Yorkshire accent and therefore wasn't asked for a passport. He signed in as Reginald Davies and let a porter carry his bag up to the room.

The hotel was comfortable but neither grandiose nor luxurious; it attracted commercial travelers from New Zealand and Scotland, dowager aunts from South Africa. He'd met a contact here once but he'd never booked into the hotel; it wasn't a place where they'd start looking for him.

He sent down for a pint of Dewar's. Afterward he had to think a moment why he'd done that—it wasn't his usual Scotch but it would not have been prudent to order Haig. Then he remembered who it was that drank Dewar's.

He had a shower and found the bottle in the room; he poured two fingers into a tumbler and sat in the easy chair to think out the moves—his and theirs.

Yaskov knew three things he hadn't known before. One: he'd seen the manuscript so he realized Kendig knew far more than anyone had thought he knew. Two: Kendig had been in Stockholm fourteen hours ago. Three: Kendig was traveling as Jules Parker and had flown from Stockholm to Helsinki under that name.

Cutter would have him out of Madrid by now; he'd have traced Kendig through Orly at least as far as Copenhagen by now and he too would know the Jules Parker ID. That was because Cutter and Yaskov had their stringers out—they'd have to have them out by now—and it would have been no great trick for them to canvass the airports in the guise of national or Interpol officers; they'd have sifted descriptions and names, eliminated the genuine travelers and narrowed the suspect list to not more than three or four, of whom the only repeat would be Jules Parker.

The teaser phone call he'd made from Helsinki would bring the British into it as well. Yaskov might be a few hours ahead of the Americans, a few hours behind the British; but quite likely they'd all collide at Heathrow. The odds were that within twelve hours both Cutter and Yaskov would bring their physical presences into London.

Anticipating the hunter's moves was always dicey. You might be too slow, too stupid; there was also the chance of being too clever—expecting them to move faster than they actually moved. That could be equally dangerous.

The British would put Chartermain on it. About a thousand RAF pilots—the few to whom so many owed so much—had won the Battle of Britain; half of them had been killed; among the surviving Spitfire pilots had been Chartermain but he'd lost his left leg to a Messerschmidt in September 1940 and they'd transferred him into Intelligence. He'd run some of the Double-Cross agents until the end of the war and then he'd moved over to MI6. Kendig was now in the jurisdiction of MI5 but that wouldn't take it out of Chartermain's control any more than the FBI business had taken it out of Cutter's control in Georgia.

So he was dealing with Cutter, Yaskov, Chartermain and indeterminate lesser fry from the French SDECE, the ex-Abwehr West Germans, the East German BND and whatever peanut agencies felt too vain to delegate the responsibility to the big boys. It made for an obvious question: to what extent would they reinforce one another and to what extent would they get in one another's way?

In keeping with that would be the internal abrasions in the American operation. Cutter would be using Follett's personnel because there was no other source. Cutter had despised Glenn Follett for years. Myerson wisely had seen to it that the two men worked in separate districts but now that safety device had been neutralized. Follett spent his life playing the role of bumbleheaded loudmouth and Cutter never had been willing to see past that defensive screen; actually while Follett ran a loose ship he had a good talent and his achievements were commendable. But Cutter wasn't comfortable with people who acted as if they didn't know what they were doing; he had a few blind spots and one of them was a tendency to refuse to credit professionalism to those who lacked the appearance of professionalism.

Yaskov was a different artifact; he had the difficulties of bureaucracy but no one in his organization disputed his leadership. There was a temptation in nearly every human being to imitate that which he hated: men often displayed the very characteristics they most loathed in their fathers. Philosophically Yaskov was a dedicated Marxist, according to his lights; he believed honestly in the sort of society that encouraged five-year plans for the proletariat; but he was the son of a czarist officer and preferred elegance to efficiency, *noblesse oblige* to democraticization. In the elitist hierarchy of the Soviet KGB he enjoyed the privileged position of a Richelieu. He was a romantic and vanity dominated him; he would run the hunt with all his brilliant skill and energy because Kendig's freedom would be a personal challenge to his pride.

Chartermain was yet another factor: Chartermain was an imperial colonialist. He surrounded himself with staff who possessed ultra-English names like Colin and Derek. Most of the world was inhabited by poor ruddy bastards or bloody wogs. Chartermain's wife was "the memsahib." His operations displayed a genteel and sophisticated casualness that took civil service bureaucracy into account and assumed that they should muddle through anyhow. In his chortling fashion Chartermain probably had found and blown the whistle on more Soviet plants than had any other counterespionage chief in the West.

Kendig had invited only the very best people to the ball.

————

They would run the usual drill: question airline counter people at Heathrow, taxi drivers, rent-a-car girls. They'd put people on the taxi stand outside the West End terminal. They'd keep bumping into one another and the people interviewed would let their questioners know that they'd been interviewed more than once. Gradually each agency would accrete a picture of its opponents'

operations. Either they'd begin to confer or they'd proceed independently with the jealous pretense that the others didn't exist.

In any case they'd achieve facts which were mainly negative
but no less important on that account. They'd find out he hadn't
flown on from Heathrow. Cutter, with the advantage of knowing
through Saint-Breheret that Kendig had a blank French passport,
might treat with Chartermain to have all ports of embarkation
watched for both Jules Parker and a French emigrant who fitted
Kendig's description. The fact was that Kendig didn't have the
French passport—he'd left it in the safe in Paris.

They'd find out he hadn't taken a taxi from the airport or
from the West End terminal. They might find out he'd taken the
limo bus from Heathrow to the terminal but in any event they'd
lose the trail there; he'd covered his tracks between terminal and
hotel. They'd canvass hotels for Jules Parker, not for Reginald
Davies.

They'd know quite positively that he was in England. But that
was like looking for a needle in Nebraska. Knowing he was on the
island but not knowing where, they'd get snappish. Irritably they'd
blame one another. They'd get into a hell of a flap. It was fun to
contemplate.

But it wasn't enough. He couldn't sit cooped up and satisfy
himself with visualizations of their confusion. Passivity wasn't the
object of the game.

He'd have to come out in the open. Sting them.

———

Six years ago he'd spent months in the Middle East pulling the
camouflage off the Soviet-sponsored arms traffic in heavy arms to
Al Fatah. They were getting armored vehicles, field guns, long-
range mortars, even ground-to-air missiles. These came from various sources—Arab governments, Czechs, arms merchants in the

West—but the job was to determine how the stuff found its way to the secluded desert camps of the Palestinian liberation armies. It had become evident the smugglers' route was as neatly laid out and maintained as the Ho Chi Minh Trail. It had befallen Kendig to find and close it.

The job had required liaison with MI6 because Aden, which was British-occupied, was a key distribution point on the arms route. Local *apparatchiks* kept kicking the buck upstairs until Kendig had been obliged to fly out to London, meet with the top man and smooth out the arrangements.

The top man had been Chartermain and the meeting had taken place on a Sunday—not in Whitehall but in Chartermain's home in Knightsbridge, a detached Victorian manse in a mews: too large for practical living but then Chartermain and his mem-sahib were given to lavish entertaining. Chartermain used his study there as a second office; it was a good deal more than the usual gentleman's library.

An excellent way to enrage a lion was to disturb its den.

———

Luck could run bad; there was always the danger of the unhappy coincidence; there'd be scores or hundreds of them searching for him and if he spent a lot of time in public places there was the risk of someone's fortuitously spotting him. Pure accident like that accounted for a large number of man-hunting coups; pure accident like that was not accident at all but a mere mathematical long shot—if they kept enough people searching long enough then the chances of their finding him increased geometrically with the passage of time and the accretion of clues.

When he went out of the hotel he avoided using the lift which could be a trap; he used the stairs. When he set out for the first time he did it during the morning rush and melted into crowds.

Impulse made him cache the manuscript: he removed the pages from the false-bottomed suitcase, crept to the basement with them and found the domestic supply cupboard, a fair-sized room filled with mops and dustcloths and bedding fresh from the laundry, hampers on wheels for the daily room changings, cartons of loo paper and hotel-size bars of soap, brooms, vacuum cleaners, spray polishes and the like. He opened a bar-soap carton and counted the contents and multiplied that figure by the three dozen cartons stacked against the wall and concluded it would be at least seven weeks before they got down to the last carton in the stack, if they didn't cover it again with fresh supplies; he emptied the carton he'd opened, put the manuscript in it, filled the rest with soap bars and rearranged the stack with the manuscript carton at the back and bottom of everything. He marked it with a little pencil cross that nobody would notice unless he was looking for it and knew what it meant. He carried the excess bars of soap out of the hotel in an ordinary paper bag and disposed of them miles away in a sidewalk dustbin.

When he made his first evening reconnaissance he went out at dusk when the light was poorest. He used the underground a bit but mostly buses; never taxis.

Chartermain's garden was a horseshoe around the house, well tended but drab this late in the year. On the fourth side—the left—a paved lane ran past the kitchen door, made a little dogleg at the rear corner of the house and ran on through the back garden to a coach house that had been converted into a garage with servants' quarters upstairs—a remodeling job that had been done in the 1920s when occupants of such a house could afford a large staff. Goosenecked streetlamps bathed the front garden and the porte-cochere but the lane went back through a patch of shadow beyond the kitchen; the illumination at the rear was poor, thrown by a single lamp high on the side of the coach house at the head of an outside stair that clung to the ivied wall.

Past the garage the lane continued in a gentle bend, going on between two five-story Georgian monoliths into a street beyond. But there was a gate across the front of the lane and at its other end a chain hung across it to prevent traffic; it was no thoroughfare out of the mews.

It took him several days to work out the population and routines of the household. There were two servants; they looked like husband and wife; they lived in the quarters above the coach house. Presumably the maids' and butler's quarters in the main house were unoccupied—perhaps closed off to conserve heat. The wife evidently performed as housekeeper and cook, the husband as butler, chauffeur, gardener and handyman. On the second night of his surveillance there was a gathering of eight couples among whom Kendig recognized a member of Parliament and a man who had been, and perhaps still was, the Deputy F. O. Secretary to whom Chartermain's department reported through the Chief of M16. On that occasion two additional servants worked in the house but they went home afterward and presumably had been supplied by some agency on a temporary basis.

Each morning a Humber saloon piloted by a liveried driver—a government employee—collected Chartermain and drove him away to his duties. The garage housed two automobiles—an Austin Mini which the servant husband used for errands and the wife for shopping, and a Jaguar 3.8 saloon which the memsahib used twice in the four days, both times for afternoon excursions lasting several hours (shopping? hairdresser? liaison with lover?); she drove herself. When she returned she let herself into the house with a single key, indicating there was no burglar alarm system. That conformed with what he knew of Chartermain; the man was as old-fashioned as Yaskov, he probably had contempt for gadgets and gimmicks and the electronics of modern espionage.

He performed his surveillance from stolen cars. He would boost a car, park it somewhere in the mews and watch the house;

he would drive the car to another part of London and abandon it within a few hours before the description could have got onto the hot-sheets.

His break came on the Thursday evening. The servant husband emerged from the kitchen door carrying two valises; the memsahib, who was quite trim and attractive in her lean fifties, came along a moment later tugging on her gloves with brisk little jerks. She wore a topcoat and a little pincushion hat—a traveling outfit. The servant fed the luggage into the boot of the Jaguar and the memsahib smiled and spoke, got into the car and backed it out into the mews and drove away. Chartermain had private means and a country estate; quite likely she was going down to Kent for the weekend.

He'd had the Cortina since morning and it would be heating up by now. He drove out of the mews ten minutes behind the memsahib.

———

After dinner and a movie he purloined a Rover from the car park of a block of high-priced flats near Victoria Station. He chose it for three reasons: it was expensive enough to be in keeping with Chartermain's quarter; it had a Spanish plate and diplomatic tags which meant it wouldn't be disturbed by traffic patrols for illegal parking; and the keys had been left in it.

By the time its operator discovered the theft in the morning Kendig would have abandoned it like the others; in time it would be returned to its owner with the apologies of the Foreign Office and a shrug of the shoulders and a word of advice about leaving keys in the ignition.

He drove into the mews at half-past ten and made a three-point U-turn at the end of it and drove out again. It happened five times a day, drivers losing their bearings and not knowing they were going down a dead end. He drove slowly out of the mews again, scrutinizing the house. Two windows were alight upstairs; and a light burned in the bedroom of the apartment above the garage.

Both servants would be in the coach house by this hour. The two lights in the house were at the head of the main stair and in the memsahib's room—some sort of reading or sewing chamber where she seemed to spend part of each evening when they weren't entertaining. It didn't seem a room to which Chartermain repaired. The conclusion to be drawn was that there was no one in the house; the lights had been left on purposefully by the servants. Chartermain might have gone from his office straight down to Kent but it was more likely he was working late trying to collate the clues to Kendig's whereabouts.

He made three successive left-hand turns and parked the Rover in a no-parking space within fifty feet of the gap between the two Georgian blocks where the rear of Chartermain's lane emerged, chained off at the pavement. The Watney's pub at the corner was getting ready to close but he squeezed in and used the pay phone. He let it ring seven times; there was no answer. He went back to the lane and stepped over the chain and walked into deep shadow between the two five-story buildings, guiding on the weak lamp at the head of the servants' stair.

He stopped under the stair and studied the rear of the main house. There was a light burning in the cupola over the kitchen door, illuminating the steps down to the lane. Beyond at the head of the lane was a streetlamp. But the back of the house was dark; upstairs the middle window showed a vague glow from the stairhead chandelier at the far end of the corridor. He'd been up the main staircase, along that corridor and inside Chartermain's study which was at the rear of the house on that floor.

He wasn't a second-story human fly and that sort of ivy probably wouldn't hold his weight. An expert might do it but Kendig's expertise didn't run in that direction. He'd have to enter at the ground floor and go upstairs inside the house.

He crossed the lane, stepped over a cultivated bed that had held annuals in the summer, crossed the back lawn and stood in the shrubbery examining one window. It was a casement affair, latched on the inside with a heavy brass fitting. The only way to get at it would be to cut or smash a pane, reach inside and undo the latch. He had no glass cutter and he couldn't risk breaking a pane because the servants' bedroom window looked out on the house and they'd hear the glass shatter.

He tried four windows—all there were. They were latched firmly. He had no better luck with windows on both sides of the house toward the rear and he couldn't try the ones nearer the front because he'd be exposed to the mews there.

It left only the kitchen door. It could be seen from a small area in the end of the mews but he didn't see anyone there; it also would be plainly visible to the servants if they happened to look out their bedroom window but their curtains were drawn.

He had with him the only tools he'd bothered to improvise— a coiled length of coat-hanger wire and one of the hotel's plastic pocket calendars. The latch was a modern spring-loaded affair and the plastic sheet unlocked it easily and without sound but when he pushed the door open it creaked a bit on an unoiled hinge. He made a face, slipped inside and slowly pushed the door shut behind him, twisting the knob to prevent the latch from clicking when it closed. Then he turned to the window and looked out toward the coach house.

Did the servants' curtain stir? He couldn't be sure; he watched it but it didn't move.

Well the uncertainty put a little spice into it. He moved very slowly through the unfamiliar room, feeling his way with the backs of his fingertips: if the fingernail touched an object it would flinch away rather than toward and there was less likelihood of knocking anything over.

The door to the hallway was open; once he'd passed through it there was some light—it filtered along the hall from the foyer which was lit from above by the chandelier at the head of the stairs. He could see his way now and he moved rapidly to the foot of the steps. The staircase was a sweeping carpeted affair with a handsomely carved hardwood bannister. There was a bust of Churchill on a marble side table, a filigreed mirror beside the cloakroom and a portrait that probably was a likeness of the mem-sahib's father or grandfather.

Going up the stairs with the chandelier in his eyes made him uneasy; he passed beneath it quickly and retreated along the up-stairs corridor before he stopped to double-check his bearings. The study would be the third of the three doors on the left. He went along opening doors and looking into the rooms on both sides; that was elementary caution—better to be surprised while he was in the open corridor than to be trapped in the study. But he didn't really expect the house to be crawling with agents waiting to nail him. They hadn't enough evidence to lay that sort of trap. He hadn't confided his wild-hair scheme to anyone and it wasn't the sort of thing any of them could have anticipated.

The door to the study was locked and that pleased him be-cause it meant there was something beyond the door that Charter-main wanted to protect.

Just as he was not an accomplished cat burglar, so he was not an expert lockpick; but he'd had rudimentary training in the art and he was not pressed for time and after several minutes with the coat-hanger wire he had the old throw-bolt lock whipped and he was ready to open the door. But first he reached up and unscrewed the bulbs in the wall fixtures. They weren't burning but if there was a trap set up he didn't want them to throw a switch and silhouette him in the doorway like a cardboard shooting-range dummy.

He took several very deep breaths. If he was jumped it would help to have his lungs full of air. Then he went in.

He was alone in the room. He left the door open behind him; he wanted an available exit in case of trouble and besides he didn't want to light a lamp because that could be seen from the servants' window and he wasn't sure the drapes here would be opaque. The indirect illumination from the distant chandelier made the room dim but it would be enough to work by.

Something creaked. He froze until he was satisfied it had been natural settling; it was an old house.

He commenced his search, not sure what he might find, keenly hoping for one thing but not counting on it. If Chartermain wasn't carrying his passport it would be in his office in Whitehall or it would be here. With luck it would be here.

———

There was a wall safe; he didn't examine it—it would be impregnable to him, its contents largely composed of documents in binders with stern warnings from the Official Secrets Act on the jackets. He wasn't interested in stealing state secrets. He went through the desk drawer by drawer and had his piece of good luck: it was an old wallet, very thin pliable expensive pigskin of the old-fashioned diplomatic style, containing Chartermain's official red passport, the memsahib's civilian black-bound one an assortment of documents and foreign currencies.

Kendig took everything out of the wallet; he left the currency, the memsahib's papers and the rest of the things on the desk. Then he tore his photo out of his own passport; he put that back in his pocket along with Chartermain's VIP passport. He put the Jules Parker passport into Chartermain's wallet and placed the wallet on top of the other things in the middle of the desk blotter.

He wrote a little note in Chartermain's pad and propped the note against the wallet; and left the room.

The house creaked again but he went right along the corridor and retraced his path to the kitchen. He paused by the door before opening it and had a glance through the window at the coach house. The servants' light still burned upstairs; the curtains remained as they had been before.

He opened the door silently and slipped outside, unable to eliminate the click when he pulled it shut behind him; he went down the steps and then paused and turned his head, and wondered why he had hesitated; then he had it—a trace of tobacco smoke on the air.

They jumped him from either side of the steps. One of them pinioned his arms; the other whipped around in front of him and he saw the billy club.

"Red-handed, mate," said the one behind him with relish.

————

They were London police, not Chartermain's agents. He had to do it very quickly: he said, "Cor stone the crows, you give me such a fright!"

"Give you a heart attack mate, if I had my way."

At the head of the coach-house stair the door opened and the butler-chauffeur came hurrying down. "Good work, officers!"

In his Cockney rasp Kendig said, "'Ow'd you get onto me then?"

"Mr. Musgrove saw you in the act of breaking and entering."

The old man bobbed his head vehemently. "Heard something,

looked out my window, saw the door just closing behind the thief. Called you right the instant."

The policeman still had his arms in a vise lock and his partner was frisking Kendig for weapons, sliding around like a contortionist to keep out of range of any kicking Kendig might have in mind to do. The man holding his arms had the exact positioning of long practice; both wrists high under the shoulderblades, twisting him forward in a half-bow; there was no way out of that hold. Then the partner locked the handcuffs on him.

"You've a keen eye, Mr. Musgrove. You'll want to come down in the morning, I'm afraid, to give us a statement."

"Glad to do my duty," the old man said, rearing back on his dignity.

"I imagine the governor'll give you a rise for this, old boy."

Musgrove smiled. His wife stood at the head of the outside stair, watching with suspicion. The policeman hustled Kendig along the lane into the mews. Their car was a Morris 1100 with a globe light on the roof; he went into the back with the muscular officer who'd pinioned him. "Bloody crackers," Kendig mumbled.

"What's that, mate?"

"Crackers I said. Old fool ought've been fast asleep, this hour. Tell you I never had nothin' but hard luck my whole life."

"Ruddy well asked for every bit of it, didn't you," said the second policeman; he started the car and they rolled out of the mews.

———

It was a small police station, casual and Edwardian; a dozen police officers roamed in and out. His captors delivered him to a sergeant in a partitioned office. The sergeant said, "Give a squeal to in the morning to find out if he has any form. Good work, you two."

"It was the butler did it," the first policeman said and they all laughed at the little joke, all except Kendig who sat deep in a feigned gloom of self-pity, his senses cataloging everything and his mind racing with calculation.

The two arresting officers retrieved their handcuffs and left the room. A youth in the dark uniform passed them on his way in; he had a stenographic note pad. The sergeant said, "Very well now. Your name?"

". . . Alfred Booker." He said it as if with heavy reluctance; he kept shifting his baleful guilty stare from one patch of floor to another.

"How's it spelled?"

He snarled. "Spell it yourself, copper."

The sergeant's weary eyes sought inspiration and patience from the ceiling. "Come on now Alfie."

"Booker. Bee double-oh kay ee are."

The young cop wrote it down; the sergeant said, "Vite stats now, Alfie."

His whine got more resentful. "I'm forty-six, right? No permanent address."

"Got a job, Alfie?"

"No."

"Got a wife? A mother, a dad, anybody we should notify?"

"No. Let's get this over with."

"Solicitor?"

"Don't they give you one?"

"If you haven't got your own the court will appoint one for you. What's this, Alfie, you new at this game?"

"I got no bleeding record if that's what you mean. I'm clean as her ladyship's fingernails, copper."

"Not after tonight you're not. All right, come over here and empty out the pockets, that's a good lad—let's see what you made off with."

There was no helping it. Physical reluctance would only make them treat him with greater caution and he didn't want that. He emptied everything out onto the desk. He managed to turn while he was doing it so that he had a good view through the sergeant's open door—the back of the officer on the desk, the counter, the small squad room, the outside door beyond. A hell of a gamut to run but he had one thing in his favor: none of them was armed, they didn't carry sidearms.

The sergeant watched him with shrewd cop's eyes. Kendig passed his jacket to the sergeant and turned his pants pockets inside out to show he'd emptied everything. The sergeant went through the jacket meticulously. "Swank stuff for a Soho tramp. Paris label. Where'd you steal the threads, Alfie?"

"I paid good money."

"Whose?"

"You got me on nothing, copper. I stand on me rights."

"Rights? It's dead to rights for you, Alfie. But have it your own way. Now there's a money belt under your shirt. You can take it off or we can take it off for you. Which'll it be?"

He pulled his shirttails out and undid the canvas belt and dropped it on the desk. The sergeant gave his jacket back to him. He thrust his shirt back into his waistband and put the jacket on. He had a reason for doing that but it didn't arouse the sergeant's suspicion.

The sergeant intoned, "One length wire, heavy gauge, coiled. Probably coat hanger. One pocket calendar, plastic, Kensington Close Hotel. One knife, pocket clasp, two blades, one awl."

"That ain't no switchblade," Kendig snapped. "Just you make it clear, copper."

"Not a switchblade," the sergeant drawled wryly. "Pocket coins—let's see, fifteen, seventeen, shilling, hate this bloody coinage mess—make that thirty-five new pence. Pounds sterling, loose"—the eyebrows went up as the sergeant counted it like a bank teller, moistening his thumb and flipping up the corners of the notes—"blimey. I make it three hundred forty-six quid. Hit yourself a jackpot, didn't you Alfie."

"I didn't lift that money. Nobody can prove I did." In the outer office the cops were milling to and fro. The telephones rang now and then; two men laughed easily at something one of them said.

"Stole the governor's pasport, I see," the sergeant observed. "Know whose house that was you chose to break and enter, Alfie?"

"Boffin or something, in't he? But what's it matter anyhow."

"Hardly a boffin, mate." The sergeant chuckled. "Bit of a laugh, old Chartermain getting invaded by a common thief."

"I ain't no common thief," Kendig said loudly. "I was just—"

"You were just what?"

"Nemmind. I talk to my solicitor."

"Do that," the sergeant said. "One passport, diplomatic, property of William David Chartermain, Esquire. One wallet-size photograph of suspect identified by himself as Alfred Booker. One money belt, canvas. One ring of car keys to fit a Rover automobile. Rover, Alfie? Traveling in style, aren't we."

"I just happened to find those keys."

The sergeant glanced at the youth who was copying down the items. "Those aren't Chartermain's keys—I think it's a Jaguar he drives."

"And a Mini. No Rover—I know the house, sir."

"Right. Let's have a look for a stolen Rover in the neighborhood. Just getting in deeper every minute, aren't we Alfie."

"You can go right to bloody hell, copper."

"Let's have a look at the inside of this belt now. . . . Well well well! Seems our friend the master spy must keep a devil of a cash fund in his library—and American dollars at that. . . . Let me make the count. . . . mmmhm . . . Roll me over, laddie, this would dent the bloody Westminster Bank. . . . five one, five one fifty, five two . . . Mark this now, seven thousand one hundred fifty dollars in notes of fifty and one hundred denominations.

We'll run a list of serial numbers but you'd best keep it to a single original, no copies. Chartermain may prefer there be no record. We'll have to clear it with him."

"Aye Sergeant."

The sergeant hit his intercom key. "Are you chaps ready to fingerprint our boy?" He released the key and said to the youth, "Ought to find a proper way to hint to the old boy he ought to put first-class locks and alarms on his house if he means to keep this sort of lot on hand—"

Kendig scooped up the little photograph from the desk and made his break. He went out like a projectile: vaulted the phone desk, rammed shoulder-first into a policeman and hurled the man against his partner, dodged among the desk, caught glimpses of their faces agape, elbowed a third in the ribs, slithered past a belatedly swinging club, stiff-armed the last cop off his feet, wheeled through the door and sprinted into the night.

He had a forty-yard jump on them before they came boiling out into the street. There was the shrill silly bleat of their whistles, the clamor of their voices, the rattle of their feet; he ran around the corner and pushed along as fast as his legs could pump, aiming straight for the traffic light at the intersection. That was his only prayer of reprieve, the traffic light. Cars flowed through it along the high street; it was changing as he ran and they were stopping in their neat obedient column. He flung a glance over his shoulder— some of them were a lot younger than he was, some of them had longer legs and better wind; the pack was dissipating but the leaders were gaining on him frighteningly fast.

He heard himself gasping when he shot across the curb. The light held; the cars hadn't started to roll. He aimed for the front car of the row. If that door was locked . . .

He jerked it open. The man stared at him open-mouthed. Kendig gripped the man's arm and yanked him bodily out of the driver's seat. Crammed himself into the car and searched for the gearshift with his left hand. It had been in gear and when the original driver's foot came off the clutch it had stalled out and now he had to find the key and the pack was just into the intersection now and the driver was lurching to his feet shouting.

Kendig punched the door-lock button and the driver heaved helplessly on the outside handle. The key turned, the ignition meshed. Behind him a burly fool was emerging threateningly from a van. Kendig popped the clutch and roared away through the red light.

They'd be in cars within ninety seconds. He'd ditch this one within five minutes. The escape had worked but he had nothing now, nothing but his wits and the clothes on his back—no money, no papers, not a single possession except the two-inch-square photograph of himself that had been the most important object on the sergeant's desk.

Now they had him naked and running and when he left the car in a dark passage and dogtrotted away into the night he was breathing deep and grinning from ear to ear.

| 21 |

The telephone brought Ross awake and he fumbled for it in the darkness.

"Up and out, Ross. Meet me in the lobby in five minutes. Our man's broken surface."

"The hell time's it?"

But Cutter had hung up on him. He found the lamp switch and threw the sheet back and plunged into his clothes. He slid his expansion-banded watch on—it was just past two o'clock in the morning.

Cutter was irritatingly natty in a dark blue suit, tie knotted properly; how much advance warning had he had? Or hadn't he been to bed yet? The lobby was empty except for the hall porter. Cutter said, "Car's picking us up," and led the way out onto the curb of Park Lane. A few taxis whizzed by. A faint drizzle misted the air but there was no real fog. Ross buttoned up his topcoat against the chill and raked fingers through the mess of his hair. "What's happened?"

"He broke into Chartermain's house and the cops intercepted him." Cutter laughed. "Think of that."

"They've arrested him?"

"He was arrested. He made a break from the station house. He's on the loose again but they've stripped him down to nothing. Here we go—this must be Chartermain."

The chauffeured Humber slid in and the rear door popped open; Chartermain was leaning forward bulkily in the backseat. "Didn't expect to see you chaps again quite so soon."

Cutter climbed across Chartermain's knees and Ross took the jump-seat and reached for the strap when the car lurched forward. "Flabbergasted me, truth to tell," Chartermain said. "The cheek!"

"It's not far, is it?"

"Just round the park in Knightsbridge. Four minutes' drive this time of night. I say, I'm sorry to knock you out of bed at such a beastly hour."

"Don't be ridiculous," Cutter said. Ross couldn't stifle a yawn.

Chartermain took an envelope from his pocket. He had a pair of tweezers; he extracted the envelope's contents with them. "Don't touch it—it hasn't been dusted yet. I never knew him to have such a sense of humor."

Ross couldn't make it out. "What is it?"

Cutter was leafing through it with the point of his mechanical pencil. "Jules Parker's passport. I see he removed the photograph."

Chartermain said, "Found it on my desk with a note. Dear William, I do hope you're enjoying the game—something like that. It's in here." He tapped the envelope. "*Bloody* cheek."

"Did he cop anything?"

"My passport. The police retrieved everything. They seem to think he took a great amount of money from the house but that couldn't have been mine. We don't keep loose money about."

"Was it dollars or sterling?"

"Some of each. Total value near three thousand quid."

"That'd be his own money," Cutter said.

Chartermain was a short sandy man, square-faced and amiable in appearance; he was a little heavy but not grossly overweight. He had a false leg—the left one—but he didn't use a cane.

"Here we are."

They went inside. There were only two policemen in the squad room. (Was it called a squad room over here?) A bulky man in shirt-sleeves hurried out of a doorway in a rear partition. "Captain Chartermain? I'm Sergeant Twomey."

They went back into the partitioned office and Twomey made a gesture that encompassed the litter on his desk. "That's what he had on him."

"And this is what he left in exchange." Chartermain brought out the envelope. "I wonder if you'd be so kind as to have these things fingerprinted, Sergeant?"

Cutter was poking through the things on the desk. Ross watched him pick up a small plastic calendar. Cutter said, "Kingston Close Hotel," in a musing voice.

———

The hall porter was sleepy but anxious to help. "Right, Sergeant, I'd say that's Mr. Davies right enough."

He handed the IdentiKit composite back to Twomey and Twomey gave it back to Cutter but Cutter stayed his hand. "You'll want to keep that, I think. Scotland Yard will want to run off copies of it."

Chartermain said to the hall porter, "You haven't seen Mr. Davies this evening, then."

"I've been on duty since eight o'clock, sir. Haven't seen him tonight, no sir."

Cutter said, "Then we'll want your passkey."

Sergeant Twomey nodded to the hall porter and the key was

produced. The four of them went up to the room and made the search. Ross said, "False bottom in this thing. But there's nothing in it."

"For the manuscript," Cutter said. "All right—so he's stashed it. Damn."

They combed the room but Cutter was right; the manuscript wasn't there. Ross said, "No French passport either. Maybe he hid it with the manuscript?"

"Possibly," Cutter said.

Ross said slowly, "Look Joe, he's got to retrieve that manuscript, right? It's only a suggestion but haven't they got things like bus-station lockers over here? Wouldn't it be a good idea to put surveillance on places like that?"

"It's a damned good idea," Cutter said; and it galvanized Chartermain—the Englishman went directly to the phone. His limp was hardly perceptible.

Ross said, "He's had to abandon his clothes, even his razor and toothbrush. He hasn't got a dime on him. Joe, if he's ever going to need help from a friend it'll be now. Shouldn't we put coverage on every known contact of Kendig's in England?"

"It's worth a try." Cutter smiled a little. "We might make a pro out of you yet, Ross."

"Knock on wood but I think maybe there's a chance, Joe. We've got the London Police and half of Scotland Yard on it now and a lot of our own people and MI5—"

"And don't forget the Comrades," Cutter said drily. "But hold onto that thought, Ross."

Chartermain finished his call. "We'll have men on every rental locker in London within the hour. Good thinking, young man." He turned to the police sergeant. "It would be best if you trotted straight over to the Yard with that composite drawing, Sergeant. This is an important manhunt—it's a matter of the highest security priority. I've impressed that on the Superintendent just now.

I've told him to expect you. Our fugitive has been kind enough to commit a rather spectacular violation of the criminal laws and of course this places him within the Yard's jurisdiction. Now if you don't mind?"

"I'm on my way, Captain." Twomey backed out of the room with the obsequiousness of a well-mannered bellhop.

"It looks as if our friend's making every possible effort to multiply the odds against him," Chartermain said. "The man must be stark bonkers."

"I don't think he counted on being arrested at your house," Cutter said. "But he'll enjoy the additional challenge."

"I don't have the foggiest understanding of the man's purpose. He's behaving quite irrationally. Do you still seriously maintain that he's got every last copy of that idiotic manuscript in one single parcel?"

"I suspect he has," Cutter said. "He may have stashed the carbon copy somewhere but he'll be the only party who knows where it is."

"A sensible man would have given instructions to have it opened in event of his death."

"Not in this case."

"I fail to understand that, Mr. Cutter."

Ross watched for Cutter's reply but Cutter didn't make one; Ross stepped into it then because it occurred to him that Chartermain had to be given every chance to understand what they were dealing with. Ross said, "If he'd meant to make an exposure by publication he'd have written the whole book and mailed it out without telling us about it in advance. Kendig's playing a game, that's what we're involved in. Every game I know of is defined in terms of rules and the rules are always arbitrary. Kendig wants to prove his gamesmanship's better than ours. He defined the rules himself and he's playing strictly within them—they may be artificial and irrational as you say, but so are the rules of any game. Kendig wants to prove he can win without cheating. It's the only way to prove he's the best player. Does that make any sense?"

Chartermain nodded slowly, understanding what Ross had said but baffled nonetheless. But Cutter was looking at Ross with surprise and unconcealed admiration.

———

They ran a debriefing on the police sergeant and Chartermain's butler early in the morning and then Chartermain and Cutter called a joint evaluation meeting at nine o'clock; the fugitive was still at large. Ross had grabbed two hours of sleep which made him feel even groggier than before but at least he'd had a chance to shave and get into clean clothes. Riding up to Chartermain's floor in the lift he had Glenn Follett for company; he hadn't realized before how big Follett was but in the confined cage their eyes were on a level and Follett outweighed him by sixty pounds, his bulk emphasized by his camel's hair coat with its dark fur lapels. Follett's brown eyes looked excessively stupid in his sagging freckled face.

There were several maps on the walls of the conference room and each had its tray of colored pins—situation maps of the British Isles, London, Belfast, some of the other cities. There was no point trying to plot Kendig on a map like that, Ross thought; the man moved much too fast.

The room held a dozen people and a few more drifted in behind Ross and Follett—subordinates of Chartermain's and Follett's, a CID official representing the Scotland Yard Superintendent, two or three who were introduced to Ross by name only, no rank. One of them was American and had the rumpled look of a man who'd just stepped off a plane; it became clear in the milling confusion that the man was from some shadowy office in the White House.

There was a flurry of finding seats around the table. Follett sat down beside Ross and yawned in his face; Follett's breath made him turn away.

Cutter had been padding around the room like an intense hungry panther; he took the seat at Chartermain's right hand. Then someone's hard heels echoed on the floor outside and it was Myerson; he came in unsmiling, nodded to Cutter and Follett and Ross, shook hands with Chartermain, acknowledged the man from the White House, was introduced to the Britishers and took the chair that Cutter relinquished to him. Myerson looked dyspeptic as if he'd had too much cottage cheese and salad. He leaned over to say something to Cutter but Cutter didn't answer; he was chasing a line of thought. Myerson tapped Cutter's arm and repeated the question and Ross heard the mutter of the reply but not its content.

Chartermain took the floor and brought things to order. "I think we all know the outlines of the situation. The fugitive is American of course but he's on British soil. It's equally imperative to both nations that this man be brought to earth in the shortest possible time. I've spoken with the Prime Minister and I must assure all of you quite bluntly that neither Downing Street nor the White House will tolerate the slightest foot-dragging or chauvinism in this matter. It demands a full and frank pooling of resources and I personally shall accept nothing less. No information is to be withheld by anyone for any reason. I trust I've made that quite clear. Now I'd like to call upon Chief Inspector Merritt to bring us up to date on Kendig's last known movements."

Merritt was bald and had a thick brutal chin but his voice was pleasantly modulated and he didn't crutch himself on officialese. "Our man was last seen at approximately twenty past eleven last night, escaping west along Kensington Road in a car which was found this morning abandoned in a passage leading out of the Old Brompton Road. The car was dusted for fingerprints and then returned to its owner. The only prints we found were the owner's and a number of smudges. We've concentrated the foot-patrol search in the Chelsea area where the car was abandoned, but we're spreading the net wider as we go. And of course the composite photograph supplied by the Americans has been issued to every officer on duty in London and environs. Every man's been told it's a grave matter and I can assure you gentlemen there's not a policeman in London who isn't comparing every passing face with the drawing in his hand." Merritt's teeth clicked and he sat down as abruptly as he'd stood.

Chartermain reclaimed their attention. "I should remind all of you that the Soviets have a keen interest in finding our man. He possesses information they'd find quite useful. In concert with the Americans we've agreed to obstruct the Russians' efforts wherever possible. If any of them proves to be in your men's way, he should be arrested on the spot. We shall worry about the specific charges later as time permits; for the moment the purpose is to harass them and deny them whatever we can. The Soviet operation is being run personally by Mikhail Yaskov, who is a high senior member of KGB staff. The order to arrest Russian agents does not exclude Comrade Yaskov if he should happen to turn up. But let me emphasize that no effort is to be deleted from the hunt for Kendig for the purpose of throwing spanners in the Russian works. No one's to go out of his way in search of Communist spies." He said the last with dry sarcasm, poked a stubby finger at Cutter and sat down.

Cutter didn't stand but he had enough magnetism to command undistracted attention from every pair of eyes in the room. "He won't make it easy for us. It'll be a fluke if he falls into our hands very fast. The purpose of this maximum effort is to wear him down, deny him escape routes, push him as inexorably as we can into a box. Every airport has to be under massive surveillance until further notice. The same for boat marinas, private airfields, shipping docks, boat-trains, ferry landings, helicopter pads. Our first objective is to be certain we've got him bottled up on this island. It's a huge effort and a complicated one." Cutter smiled coolly. "In any case our departments are obliged to spend their budget allocations before the end of the fiscal year because otherwise our budgets might be reduced next year. So never mind the expense. Pour everything into it. Don't let your people get discouraged when every gambit seems to lead into a cul-de-sac. And for God's sake make sure everybody tells us exactly what he knows, not what he thinks we want to hear.

"Now then," Cutter continued, "we'll want special emphasis on the surveillance of rental lockers. We know Kendig didn't have his manuscript when he was arrested last night. It wasn't in his hotel room. It's hidden somewhere, and in due course he's going to have to collect it."

Glenn Follett stirred. Ross thought he'd been dozing but Follett said mildly, without his usual ebullience of gestures, "You mind if I toss out a little suggestion there?"

Cutter's teeth formed an accidental smile; the interruption—and Follett—annoyed him. In a visible effort to be patient and reasonable he said, "Fire away, Glenn."

"Well I may be on the wrong track." Follett rocked his hand, fingers splayed. "But it kind of seems to me his whole modus operandi involves harassing us. He's thumbing his nose, toying with us, right? He sends notes and postcards to people, he makes funny phone calls. And he slaps us in the face every now and then with another one of those Xeroxed chapters. I'm trying to pin down a pattern, Joe. Tell me if I've gone wrong so far."

"You haven't. But I don't see what you're getting at."

But Ross saw it, just a split second before Follett spoke; and he was beginning to grin before the words were out of Follett's mouth.

Follett put on a broad smile but his eyes lay unblinking against Cutter. He flapped his hands. "Well Joe let's just assume we don't nail him to some railroad locker. Let's assume he hid his manuscript where we won't find it. Seems to me he's going to drop another chapter in the mail sooner or later. Now as long as we're spending half the national debt and committing all this manpower to the job anyway, my little suggestion would be this: Let's put surveillance on the Goddamned post offices."

| 22 |

He'd been looking for a parked car to steal when an *Evening Standard* van had stopped for the light at the corner; its bed had been empty, evidently it was returning to the printery from its last delivery, and he'd hopped up into the dark open back just as it started moving so that the driver wouldn't notice the shift of weight.

When it slowed to make its turn into Fleet Street he'd jumped off and walked along the Embankment into the tangle of busy activity in the Black-friars area—the wholesale lorries banging in and out of warehouses. It was no great trick to hop onto a slow-moving staked produce truck; the driver never knew he was there.

Somewhere along the Archway Road, not quite sure of his bearings, he dropped off the truck and made his way afoot off the lighted thoroughfare into a dreary lane of grim Victorian brick—identical attached row houses of Dickensian bleakness. Cars were jammed together along both curbs but it wasn't transport he needed just now.

He went the length of the lane—two hundred yards, not

much more. It ended against a parapet; a steep slope fed down into a railway cut. He saw no signal lights along the tracks; perhaps it was an abandoned line. Garden allotments were terraced into the slope, each with its little padlocked tool shed, a few with greenhouses.

He'd worn no topcoat because he hadn't wanted the clumsiness of flapping skirts in his burglary; he was chilled to the bone in shirt and jacket but what mattered was that they knew the clothes he was wearing and they knew he had no money to buy different garb. He couldn't very well go back to his hotel for a change of clothes; they'd have that sealed off first thing because one or another of them was bound to be inspired by that plastic calendar with the hotel's advertisement on it.

He got up on the stone retaining wall and made his way around behind the row of houses. The back gardens had their degrees of individuality and some of them were fenced but none of the fences was too high to scale. He began to explore.

Each house appeared to have been subdivided into flats, one apartment to each floor; the three ground-floor windows at the rear of a house represented kitchen, bathroom and bedroom. Toward the front he surmised there'd be a sitting room and a stair hall. They weren't tenements but neither were they upper-middle-class digs; these were workingmen's flats.

The windows were of two kinds: casements on the baths and kitchens, old-fashioned bay windows on the bedrooms. These were vertically hinged-in panels and could be held open at specific apertures by ratchet-holed interior levers that lay at angles across metal pins on the sills. The Englishman was a creature who had a mystical faith in the curative powers of fresh air irrespective of chill, humidity or pollution. Nearly every bedroom window in the row was open at least one notch.

He judged it near three in the morning; they were as sound asleep as they'd ever be. He went along the row exploring. It was only a matter of reaching the fingertips inside, lifting each lever off its pin and swinging the window gently wider; then quietly press a curtain aside far enough to see inside.

They weren't people of uniform habits. Some were married, some slept alone; some were pin-neat and must have hung their clothes in the cupboards while others had left jackets and trousers strewn across chairs or dressing tables. One flat was postered with psychedelic colors and ban-the-bomb slogans and the bed seemed to be occupied by at least three people. It was the only iconoclast; the other bedrooms he investigated were sedate.

He retraced his way to the stone wall, climbed over and went carefully down the allotment paths. He broke into a splintered tool shed and picked the longest-handled tool he could find, a garden rake, and worked the rake head off the handle. It gave him a pole the length of a short fishing rod. He scrounged in the bins, found an old nail that would do and banged the nail at a right angle into one end of the pole, using the head of the rake for a hammer. He was thinking: if they'd found the manuscript he'd cached in the hotel basement than he'd have to grant them the victory and call off the game. The carbon copy was still safe in Florida but it would stay there untouched; he'd hidden it there for use only in the event some blind accident should destroy the original. But if Cutter's minions found it in the soap carton that wouldn't be blind accident; he'd have to concede Cutter the game.

But he didn't think they'd look for it there. They'd be more clever than that. They'd stake out terminal lockers and they might canvass the banks to find out if a man answering Kendig's description had rented a safe-deposit box. Probably it wouldn't occur to them to search the rest of the hotel if they didn't find the script in his room. And even if they did think of it they'd have to make it no more than a cursory search and the odds against their looking in that particular carton among many were pretty good.

He carried the hooked rod back up to the wall, went over it

and started to work through the bedroom window of the second house. He used the pole to reach in through the narrow window, hook the trousers off the chair and pull them out through the window. He did it with a great deal of stealth. The pockets were empty. He hung the trousers back on the hook and pushed them back inside onto the chair. The configuration wasn't the same as it had been but the man would never notice the difference and even if he did he'd be no more than mildly puzzled; nothing had been removed from him.

The third window was useless; he passed it up. The fourth yielded the first prize of the night: a tweed jacket with a wallet in the inside pocket. There were sixteen pounds in five- and one-pound notes. He took ten pounds, left six, and returned the jacket to the bedroom, hanging it carefully over the back of the chair as it had been before. Then he closed the window back to its original aperture. The man would have to conclude he'd miscounted the contents of his wallet.

The next window was latched shut; the one beyond was the ban-the-bomb hippies; the seventh yielded up a pair of dungarees with only two and a half quid in the wallet. He didn't touch the cash but he lifted half the loose change from the front pocket and he liberated a Barclay Bank plastic credit card from among three cards in the wallet pocket. He replaced the dungarees on the floor whence he'd hooked them and moved on down the row.

There were twenty houses in all; he hit seven of them with his fishing rod and stole not more than one or two small items from each—never enough to induce the victim to report the theft. When he was finished he had a threadbare topcoat, a trilby hat, an umbrella and a pocketful of mismatched identification, credit cards and money. He hadn't lifted any wallets because that would be noticed; but a wallet was easy enough to buy.

After a counter breakfast in Highgate he bought a shave and a short haircut in a barbershop. In a drugstore he bought an essential kit—toothbrush, paste, razor and a cosmetic tinting kit for people who wanted to cover grey hair. He rode a bus into the King's Cross district, bought a few items of clothing and chose a small unpretentious commercial-travelers' hotel and walked straight in across the lobby as though he had business there. No one challenged him; he went upstairs and searched the corridor until he found the bathroom for use by those whose rooms did not have private bath. It was past rush hour and the chamber was not in use. He locked himself in and took his time bathing, darkening his hair and getting into the new clothes—underwear, socks, dark blue slacks that fit well enough, an ordinary round-collar white shirt, a Navy four-in-hand, an imitation-suede sport jacket for which he'd laid out five pounds twenty. He brushed off the topcoat and trilby and put them on; wrapped his old clothes in the parcel from which he'd taken the new ones; and sat down to examine the night's haul of credit cards and money.

He'd taken three driver's licenses and now he chose the one that came closest to his own age and description; he tore the others into pieces and flushed them away. He had a bit over fourteen pounds remaining in notes and coin. It would do for the moment.

He carried the parcel of old clothes out with him and deposited it in a dustbin two blocks from the hotel; went down the King's Cross station and rode the tubes to Covent Garden. He had the hat down around his ears—he'd stuffed the bands with newspaper and it was still a fraction too large but that was all right. With the umbrella in hand he knew he was well camouflaged; nevertheless every stranger's face might be an enemy's and as he threaded the crowds he felt sweat break out like needles, prickling his scalp.

In a passage off Drury Lane there was a philatelists' shop run by a man who dealt not only in rare postage stamps but also in stolen documents and passports. The shop was on the Agency's list of sources but Kendig had never been inside it. There was a chance they'd be watching it; there was a chance they wouldn't be.

He stopped at the corner and went into a leather and luggage shop; bought a cheap wallet and a large cheap briefcase of the sort college students sometimes used to carry school books. It was a small valise, really; the manuscript would fit easily.

He carried the empty case up to Drury Lane and went down as far as the passage; he hadn't known the philatelist's exact address but the passage was only a hundred feet long and he saw the place as soon as he'd turned the corner. He stopped there to survey it.

The cardboard sign in the door said CLOSED. A few pedestrians moved through the passage but none of them was a stakeout; there was nobody sitting in a parked car, nobody holding up a lamppost. A uniformed traffic warden walked across the far end of the passage but didn't even glance down its length. Kendig crossed to the opposite curb and made another search from that angle but nothing showed up.

Then the philatelist's door opened and a squat man emerged, reaching behind him to flip the sign over. Now it read OPEN. The squat man went down the passage away from Kendig and turned the far corner.

Kendig put his back to the place and walked away. His steps were leisurely but his pulse raced.

It had taken only a glance to know what the squat man was. Kendig hadn't seen him before but the serge, the Slavic scowl and the clumsy shoes had been dead giveaways.

They'd set something up for him there; it was in readiness now and the shop had reopened. Ten minutes later and he'd have walked right into it.

It meant Yaskov had his people out in force. There were at

least three other passport dealers in London but if Yaskov had set a trap in this one it meant he'd set traps in all four. It meant, further, that Yaskov had been briefed by the British or had found out on his own hook through some English contact that they'd flushed Kendig and had him on the run without papers.

Coolly and relentlessly they were inscribing the pattern of his annihilation.

———

It began to rain again in the early afternoon. Discreetly he checked out an Avis car-hire office; there was a man in a doorway opposite it trying not to look like a policeman. He didn't need to know any more than that. He went into an oak-dark restaurant and sat at a small table over a mixed grill watching through the window beside him while cars moved by, their tires hissing on the wet paving.

Jaws and mind ruminated. They were handling it properly—the way it had to be done. Once they'd taken the decision to treat him as a security crisis they'd had no alternative. He'd given them an advantage by issuing the big challenge here in London: he was isolating himself on an island. It was a big island with an enormous population but it was finite and had a limited number of routes of escape; knowing that fact made it possible for them to commit great forces to the job. He'd chosen England for that reason—he wanted to make it as costly as he could, that was part of the game, and by giving them the opportunity here he'd made it possible for them to concentrate far more effort and manpower than they'd have been willing to spare on him if he'd picked a porous playing field like the Continent or South America.

The Soviets were in it in strength as he'd hoped they'd be. That fellow watching the Avis office had all the earmarks of copper; so Chartermain had brought the Yard into it and Kendig's likeness would be folded into every bobby's pocket south of Inverness. Cutter and Follett would be spreading the word about Kendig's supposed French passport and they'd be covering the intervals between Chartermain's suave troops and the Yard's stubborn flat-feet. No doubt the delegations of half a dozen smaller powers in London had got the word through one source or another and had alerted their personnel.

The longer he kept them at bay the more desperate they'd become. It wouldn't be long—if it hadn't happened already—before the orders would come down to take off the last of the kid gloves; probably the orders would be to make it look like an accident. They wouldn't shoot him in a public place.

They were governed by no code except expedience. There were no Commandments except Thou Shalt Succeed. Some of them had consciences of one kind or another but they all were caught in the gears of their great machinery. They believed in using any necessary means to preserve what they thought of as the greater good. It was a curious sinister idealism that motivated the best of them; the rest didn't count, they were merely Good Germans, they'd do as they were told—lost souls who'd settled years ago for the usual hypocrisies and specious rationalizations.

He'd always recognized the weakness in himself and that was why he saw it in the rest of them. In his own case it had never been put to the test. He had never been ordered to kill anyone. Lurid fictions to the contrary it was not part of the usual plays of espionage to commit murder; there had been assassinations, politically motivated, of which he had knowledge afterward and of which he had written with feelings of genuine outrage in his book. But he had never participated in any effort to take out a person, whether an ally or an enemy agent. It simply wasn't done. The objective nearly always was to obtain information or to plant false information. In either case it had to be done without the other side's realizing it had been done. Ideally the operative worked in such a way that nobody found out he'd been there at all. That sort of ideal couldn't be achieved if he left the landscape littered behind him with dead bodies.

Kendig was not certain what he might have done if Myerson had given him a kill order. He'd had training in the use of weapons and the tactics of unarmed combat but he'd never had to use them; last night's football yardage in the police station had been the most violent escape of his life except for the night he'd taken a bullet in the head on the Czech border wire; and he'd done no one any real injury. The game was one of wits, not of brute strength or ruthlessness.

But now they meant to kill him. This was something he'd known all along but the full realization had been creeping up on him for a while that there was a point at which they were bound to succeed if he kept playing the game with them: time, numbers and all the probabilities were in their favor. A matter of ten minutes one way or the other this morning might have delivered him onto Mikhail Yaskov's chopping block.

He visualized himself walking through a door and into the guns. It would happen sooner or later. And what then?

It distressed him in an almost comical way to realize how ordinary he was after all. Neither a pacifist nor a first-strike Neanderthal; merely a man who believed in self-defense. He knew, studying it as honestly as he was able, that if they tried to kill him he would try to kill them first.

A squall rattled the windows; it had become a cloudburst, the rain oiled across the panes and shattered in a haze on the surface of the street, cars spraying high turbulent wakes from the spitting puddles. A man sprinted out holding a tent of newspaper over his head; dodged a car and dashed across the street to catch the tall red double-decker that swayed around the corner.

He saw no point going out into that. He had no dry clothes to change into.

The place had a saloon bar and he was able to get a drink at his table; he ordered Dewar's straight up. He finished the meal, enjoying it, and when the whiskey came he sipped it and took pleasure in the flavor. His appetite had been ravenous for weeks— the voracity of a condemned man eating his last meal—but now he was luxuriating in the subtler tastes and textures of things.

The Dewar's was Carla Fleming's brand. He'd been flashing images of her. He'd no passion to rejoin her; she hadn't been or done anything extraordinary; it wasn't infatuation. But she was a vivid bookmark, marking the place where he'd turned a page. That night in Birmingham he'd begun to look at things beyond self-pity and the escape from boredom. That was when he'd discovered the moral outcry of the book he was writing.

The joy she took from flying had triggered something in him. It hadn't been superficial; it was the genuine joy with which she justified her existence and in some profound osmotic way it had communicated itself to him: the rediscovery of pleasure in the simple act of living.

The challenge of the game had begun as a desperate lunge against the blackness of his terrible ennui. He'd been greedy for the matching of wits. He might have gone on enjoying it indefinitely if he'd been able to sustain it as an open-ended excuse for staying alive.

But he wasn't sure he needed the excuse any more. Being alive had become its own justification. That was what he'd re-learned: that was what the Dewar's reminded him of.

He was thinking too clearly today, no longer overcharged by the surge of emotionalism that had carried him soaring through the heady weeks of writing and running. The ability to reason coldly was bringing him to a logical conclusion he'd been able to evade before. He'd not speculated on the finalities of the endgame; he'd shied away from it consistently but it had crept up on him anyhow.

Of course Chartermain or Yaskov might get to him first but most likely it would be Joe Cutter who'd end up facing Kendig over gunsights—literal or figurative; pull the trigger or order it pulled, it came down to the same thing. But Joe Cutter was no more a killer than Kendig was. What gnawed Kendig was that he'd put Cutter in an intolerable dilemma. He was making a murderer of Cutter.

The irony was inescapable. He'd set the avalanche in motion; it was too late to get out from under it; and Cutter would be buried with him through no fault of Cutter's own.

He ordered another Dewar's and thought the thing the whole way through. There was no calling it off, not in the usual sense; he couldn't simply phone them and tell them where to pick up the manuscript and say he was stopping the game. They'd come after him anyway—they could never trust him not to start it up again.

But there was a way it might be done. It depended on a number of things but most of all it depended on Joe Cutter's willingness to be fooled as a means of escaping from his dilemma.

He paid his bill and went out, carrying his umbrella and the empty school-book briefcase. The rain had moved on; the air was fresh and wet. He went up the street almost jauntily.

| 23 |

Cutter came into the storeroom, ducking his head to clear the doorway; Ross looked up from the scribbled note in his hand—*Better luck next time. M.K.*—and tossed it disgustedly back into the empty carton; and Myerson shot a bitter look at Cutter. "Have you ever considered shining shoes as a trade, Joe? Maybe you ought to keep it in mind—maybe you're equipped for it."

Cutter said, "I grant you in the long parade of stupid mistakes we've made this one deserves a special float all to itself."

Myerson pulled the cigarette from his mouth with a perceptible tremor of his plump fingers. "By God this is enough. I want the bastard dead, you hear me?" It was the first time he'd seen one of Kendig's pranks firsthand and he was distressed.

"All right," Cutter said. He was squinting as if the light was too strong. "It's got to be done but let's not rationalize it into one of God's Commandments."

Myerson stood unsteady, the muscles of his feet making constant corrections in his balance. Abruptly Cutter smiled at him. Ross thought it wasn't because there was anything worth smiling about; it was just that Myerson was already discomfited and Cutter's smile was designed to make him more so.

Kendig had pulled the storeroom apart with a vengeance—to make sure it didn't escape anyone's notice that he'd been there. The housekeeper had reported it to the desk at breakfast time and the manager had reported it to the Yard and Myerson had been in Merritt's office at the time; Myerson had collected Ross and they'd left a message for Cutter and now here they were looking at the strewn soap cartons and the amiable little note from Kendig in the box where the manuscript must have been.

"Under our noses," Myerson grouched. "Right here under our noses all the time."

He was talking to Cutter but Cutter was listening with a lack of interest that he didn't bother to conceal. He was pensive; Myerson walked around him in a circle, too agitated to stand still, but Cutter didn't turn to keep facing him and Myerson had to come around again to see Cutter's face. Myerson began to shout but Cutter cut across him: "Spare me the recriminations, all right?"

The skin on Myerson's ruddy face tightened. "I suppose you've got a rabbit to pull out of the hat now, have you? Because if you don't Joe, I have a very strong premonition that you're likely to spend the rest of your career decoding signals from the Russian scientific base in Antarctica." Myerson beamed wickedly but the quality of Cutter's answering glance smothered the smile quickly from his face.

"There aren't any rabbits," Cutter said quietly. "There's only a fabric of assumptions and suppositions and surmises. He left it here forty-eight hours and then he collected it. He could have left it here indefinitely but he collected it. That means something."

"Does it? I'll ask my Ouija board."

"It means one of two things," Cutter went on. "Either he wants to mail out another chapter or he's planning to leave the country."

"Give that man a cigar."

"Am I still running this show?"

Myerson dropped his cigarette and ground it out under the sole of his shoe. "Hell Joe, of course you are."

"Then I want more men. I want to double the cover on every airplane and boat that leaves this island. And I want to double up on Follett's idea, covering the post offices."

"Makes sense," Myerson conceded. He turned a final distasteful glance on the jumbled array of overturned cartons, fished Kendig's note out of the empty one and dropped it gingerly into an envelope, glanced bleakly at Ross, scowled again at Cutter and went.

Ross said, "I have a feeling it's the post office idea that's going to do the trick. I don't mean anything personal, Joe."

"I misjudged Follett. It was a brilliant idea. Don't apologize."

The Yard technicians arrived. Cutter and Ross relinquished the basement to them and went upstairs through the lobby to the car. Ross got behind the wheel. "Where to?"

"Chartermain's office."

Ross put it in gear and vectored into the traffic. The sun was a pale disk in the haze. Last night he'd dropped by Cutter's room to ask him something. Cutter had been reading the Bible. Ross had picked it up and glanced at the open pages. *Deuteronomy.* Something had leaped out at him. *I have set before thee life and death, blessing and curse. Therefore choose life.*

Suspicion wormed in him. "Sometimes I get the feeling Kendig thinks if he just charges head-on hard enough at death it'll get out of his way."

Cutter said, "There's a classic rat-psychology experiment where they send a hungry rat down a tunnel. There's food at the far end of the tunnel. But to get to the food the rat has to walk across an electric grid. The shock current is increased as he gets closer to the food. They keep testing the rat, increasing the current. The rat has to decide for himself how hungry he is—whether the reward's worth the pain."

Ross pulled up in the jammed lane of traffic. He looked straight at Cutter. "Who are you talking about, Joe—you or Kendig?"

"When I was a little kid there was a fight on my street. A couple of kids a little older than me—maybe they were eight or nine. I don't know what the fight was about. One of them hit the other one in the nose and the kid fell down flat on his back. He was a little dazed—I mean an eight-year-old can't hit very hard. But the kid died. They told us later if we'd turned him over on his side he'd have been fine. But the blood ran back in his throat, he drew it into his lungs and strangled on it."

"Christ."

"It wasn't anybody's fault. But sometimes you get the feeling it's all been written down in the book long before you were born," Cutter said. "I think I was talking about Kendig before. If there's food in sight you can't starve to death. He'll cross the grid sooner or later, even though he knows the shock current's too high to survive. But he's got no choice. It's an inevitable accident—like the kid dying because the rest of us were too ignorant to turn him over."

Ross said, "You could duck it. You could tell Myerson to pull you off the job."

"Wouldn't help. I'm still the most likely one to catch him. If it's not me it might be Yaskov and we don't want to think about what Yaskov's people would do to him before he died."

"I'm sorry, Joe. But he brought it on himself, didn't he?"

"Sure he did. Just like the rat in the tunnel."

| 2 4 |

He had pads in his cheeks again; he dyed his hair jet black, trimmed and blackened the eyebrows, made himself up swarthy with a pencil mustache and a dark mole on the left cheek.

It was October eighteenth, Friday evening; the West London Terminal was crowded with weekenders on their way to and from the airports. His cursory study fixed at least five stakeouts holding up walls, reading newspapers on benches and standing in queues at the airline counters. He passed a pair of them close enough to hear their Russian dialogue; they were deciding whether the bald man at BOAC check-in was their quarry in disguise. They stood face to face so that between them they had a 360-degree field of view. Their eyes slid across Kendig and moved right on as if he weren't there. Disguise was only minimally a matter of makeup; attitude was at least half of it and Kendig moved at a hunched shuffle like a mongrel dog who'd begun life by making friendly overtures and been kicked hard and spent the rest of his lifetime being reprimanded for violations he didn't comprehend. His expression in repose was a cowardly half-smile and he was ready at all times to burst into apologies. He stopped as if uncertain of his bearings and snatched off his hat and clutched it in both hands, looking around anxiously—a man who'd come here to meet his nephew and didn't see the lad anywhere.

Ready to cringe at the slightest hint of reproof he sized up the stakeouts. He wouldn't get a crack at anyone nearly as ideal as Dwight Liddell had been but whoever he picked had to be in the right physical ball park. They'd be checking the passport descriptions closely these days. He'd already drawn blanks at Waterloo and Euston Stations; both of them were crawling with hunters but none had been suitable. One trouble was that most of them were far too young.

Outside, night had come right down. He'd spent forty minutes in the reserved car park a block away until a stewardess had driven her own car into the lot, locked it up and walked to the terminal. He'd come in five minutes behind her. Now he saw her come out of the ladies' loo dropping a crumpled lipstick-smeared tissue into the open maw of her handbag. She carried a smart shoulder bag as well, not an airline job but a chic leather affair; but the handbag was not shoulder-strapped and that was why he'd picked her.

He had his awed attention on a big-breasted tourist in an outrageous skintight outfit; he wasn't looking where he was going and that was why he banged into the stewardess. Her open handbag fell tumbling, spewing its contents.

Kendig gushed profusely with Italian-accented apologies; he dropped in anguished sorrow to his knees to help her pick up wallet and hairpins and tissues and lipstick and a dozen other possessions. He flooded her with obsequious self-laceration and the girl impatiently checked to make sure he hadn't pilfered money out of her wallet; she stuffed everything irritably into the handbag, brushed off his anxious flow of apologies with a quick, "It's quite

all right, there's no harm done," and strode away clicking, hips un-
dulating because she knew people were watching.

Kendig shuffled away, dropping the car keys into his pocket.
She wouldn't miss them right away. If she did she wouldn't worry
about it until she returned to London.

He moved around the place like a park pigeon, still searching
for his nephew. One of the stakeouts was tipped on one shoulder
against the wall, bored, sipping a Coke out of a paper cup. Kendig
logged the man point by point: five-eleven, 170 pounds, dark hair,
rectangular face.

He wasn't going to do much better than this one.

The American gave him a brief uninterested glance. Kendig
spoke softly through an agonized smile.

"You'll save a lot of lives if you stand still and listen. I've put a
bomb in this building. Don't show your surprise. Take a sip of
your Coke."

The American's eyes went bright like an animal at night pinioned by headlight beams. "You're Kendig." He drank; and held
Kendig's stare over the rim of the cup.

"The bomb goes off if I don't disarm it. And I don't disarm it
unless you obey my instructions to the letter."

"You bloodless bastard."

Kendig shrugged nervously, sorry the man hadn't seen his
nephew. "The timer's set close. You could blow the whistle on me
but you'd never have time to screw the information out of me before it blows. You wouldn't even have time to evacuate the building. You understand me?"

"You're bluffing."

"No." Kendig dipped his head obeisantly but held his glance.
"I'm not bluffing, friend. I've got too much to lose—you know
that as well as I do."

The man deflated slowly. "What do you want?"

"What's your name?"

". . . Oakley."

"All right Oakley. I'm going to walk out to the street. I want you right behind me all the way. Don't flash any signals to anybody at all. Just stay with me. Have you got it?"

Reluctant and bleak: "I've got it."

"Come on then."

He went ahead of Oakley because he didn't want anybody to suspect he had a gun in his pocket covering Oakley. Oakley was just one of those friendly Americans and he'd agreed to help the Italian look for his nephew—that was the way it would look and Oakley's expression could be taken for the impatient disgust of a kindhearted fellow who'd let himself get roped into a boring act of mercy.

In plain sight of at least five men whose express purpose was to cut him down, Kendig shuffled across the terminal and went through the door, stopping politely to hold it open for Oakley. "Now we go this way."

"Where the hell are we going?"

"Just around the corner. Take it easy."

"Take it easy? Kendig I'd like you to know something. This isn't official, this is purely personal. In my book extortion by bomb threat is the lowest and vilest crime there is. Any man who uses innocent people for hostages is a filthy monster who deserves—"

"Shut up, Oakley."

The car park was deserted and there wasn't much light. Kendig took the crumpled coat hanger from his pocket and stretched the wire out; it was an implement he'd learned long ago was amazingly useful.

"What's this?"

"I'm going to tie your hands behind you. Don't make a fuss."

He saw it when Oakley thought about making a fight of it

but it was only a passing wistfulness; it had been decided back there in the terminal when Oakley hadn't raised the alarm. Kendig made the wire fast and unlocked the stewardess's Volkswagen. "Get in."

"What the hell is this? What about the bomb for God's sake?"

"There's plenty of time for everything, Oakley. Let me worry about it, all right? Try not to strain your mind, that's a good boy."

He slammed the door on Oakley and went around to the driver's seat; and reached across Oakley to push down the door-lock button. With his hands bound behind him Oakley wasn't going to be able to get the door open to jump out.

He switched on the sidelights and had a look at the gauge. There was half a tank; it was enough. He didn't turn the key yet. "You look like a man who's got kids in college."

"In the Air Force Academy. What's it to you?"

"Both of them dedicated to making a world where people like you and me won't be necessary."

"Yes, by God. For Christ's sake, Kendig, the bomb—"

"You raised your kids upright, I imagine. Men to whom truth and honor are important?"

"What the hell are you—"

"Some people think keeping your word depends on who you gave it to. Some others think your word of honor is your word of honor regardless. Which are you, Oakley?"

"You belong in a Goddamned rubber room, you know that?"

"I could put a gag in your mouth. But then I'd have to hide you down in the back seat so nobody'd see it. It wouldn't be comfortable for you. Or you could give me your word of honor not to yell to anybody."

"Where are you taking me, Kendig?"

"Do I have your oath?"

"All right. I won't try to attract anybody's attention. My word on it." Oakley said it reluctantly but without hesitation. Kendig decided to buy it.

He ran a piece of wire from Oakley's left ankle to the metal frame under the passenger seat. Then he started the car. "There isn't any bomb. It was a bluff."

Oakley stared at him momentarily and then nodded his head. "Okay. No, no indignation. I'd rather be fooled that way than go on worrying about innocent people getting blown sky-high. It was a neat trick—you handled it beautifully, I really believed it."

The engine kicked over with its characteristic washing-machine sound. He drove out of the lot and turned into the Cromwell Road.

"You're a ballsy bastard," Oakley said. "What happens now?"

"Settle back. It's a bit of a ride."

"You haven't got a chance you know. I suppose I'm obliged to say something like that."

"All right. You've said it."

"What did you steal that they're so anxious to get back?"

Kendig didn't answer. Oakley had decided to play it friendly; he was trying to make himself look like the truistic rape victim—if it's inevitable you may as well lie back and enjoy it—but in fact he was trying to draw Kendig out and Kendig didn't want to be drawn. He wanted to keep Oakley occupied, all the same; it would keep Oakley's mind off other things. "You're a little long in the tooth to be pulling routine stakeout shifts, aren't you?"

"Fortunes of war," Oakley said without rancor. "I stuck my neck out on a couple of predictions and the wind shifted on me. But it's not that much of a punishment right now—they've pulled a hell of a lot of stringers off good jobs to look for you. You're about the hottest item since the Lindbergh baby."

"You one of Follett's people?"

"No comment, I guess."

"Tell me about your family then."

Like many of them the color photo in Oakley's passport had been taken with flat lighting that washed out the planes of the features. The exposure had been a little too small and the result was a burned print with dazzling reflections off cheeks and forehead. Kendig laid out his makeup kit, stripped off the mustache and pulled out the cheek pads and went to work with theatrical putty on his jaw line and nose and the shape of his eyes. He took his time. When he compared himself with Oakley in the pocket mirror there wasn't much resemblance but he looked enough like the poor photograph to fool anybody who didn't know the real Oakley.

Oakley lay on the bed on his left side, hands wired behind him, ankles wired together, a length of wire fixed between wrists and ankles to prevent him from kicking; two more lengths of wire trussed him to the bed frame, passing around the edges of the mattress. He could bounce up and down a little but not enough to make much noise. Nobody would get those wires off him without a pair of pliers; Kendig had used one to twist the wire ends tight and he left the pliers on the writing desk across the room. He said, "I'm not hanging out the do-not-disturb sign. The chambermaid will be in sometime in the morning. I'm going to have to stuff a gag in your mouth. A word of advice—don't strain on the wire and don't panic for breath. You could choke to death on your own vomit, you could get a hell of a painful cramp in your legs and arms. Just lie easy and try to sleep—it'll be the best way to get through the night."

"Much obliged," Oakley said, very dry.

"Tell them they can save some money by taking surveillance off the post offices. I've mailed my packages from the hotel desk."

Oakley's face changed; in a different voice he said, "Thanks." It was genuine; Kendig had given him a piece of information his superiors would find useful and it meant they might not come down so hard on him for letting Kendig make a fool of him.

Kendig said, "You size up pretty well. I'm sorry I've made things hard for you. I'd like you to get a message to Joe Cutter for me. He probably won't believe a word of it but tell him anyway. Tell him he may as well call it off because I'm going to ground."

———

He reached Dover at five in the morning and racked the Volks into a curb space on a quiet street. He walked down to the waterfront and went into an all-night sailors' eatery where he had a cup of too-strong coffee and brought out the handcuffs. He'd bought them in a magic shop—they were trick manacles for escape acts. He didn't have any legerdermain in mind but it had been the handiest place to buy handcuffs that looked real. He locked one cuff to the handle of the heavy briefcase and chained it to his left wrist.

At six-forty he was in the dawn queue at the hovercraft landing. He bought his ticket and walked toward the customs-and-immigration door. It was close cover by three stakeouts he could discern; he picked the American one and walked right up to him and flashed Oakley's ID. It wasn't that much of a risk; the Agency had nearly 200,000 employees and the likelihood this man knew Oakley was remote.

The man was young, blond, brisk. Kendig said drily, "It's official business and I'd kind of like a countersign, fellow."

The youth flushed to his hairline and showed Kendig his card. Kendig said, "The Comrade over there giving you any hassle?"

"No sir."

"We're setting up a CP in Calais, we'll be posting men along the Channel ports. If you're at all uneasy about anybody you let pass through here, give us a ring across the Channel and we'll double-check them as they come off. Make a note of the number."

The youth got out a pocket note-pad and pulled the attached

pencil out of its tube in the pad's hinge. Kendig rattled off a number and glanced around. "It's a lousy patchwork arrangement but it's the best we can do for now. Pass that number on to your relief, all right?"

"Yes sir. But he won't get through here."

The fact that the Agency stringer accepted him meant that the Russian and Chartermain's man wouldn't detain him. He walked past both of them, cold-shouldering the Russian and nodding briefly to the Englishman; he cleared customs with his official-business passport and went on board ten minutes before departure time.

At the French end they were stuffy. He wasn't State; he didn't have diplomatic immunity; they insisted on opening the briefcase. He put the key in the flimsy lock and showed the manuscript. He'd spent an hour in the British Museum at the public typewriter yesterday, typing a phony cover-page and a few introductory pages. *Report on United States Immigration Policy Western Europe, Updated 7/17/74.* And a covering half-page: *Copy 14. To: United States Consulate, Paris, France. Not classified. Hand-deliver. Priority Five.*

There was no surveillance at the French end; they thought they had him bottled up in England. He discarded Oakley's face in the ferry pier's men's room and walked off the pier ready to begin the final phase of the game.

| 25 |

Ross could sense the tension in Glenn Follett, who crouched like a beast ready to spring. Myerson watched Cutter, his eyes distended with rage. Myerson lowered himself cautiously between the arms of the chair as though he feared there was a bomb under it—or inside himself.

Nerves near snapping point, Ross jumped when Cutter walked past the back of his chair and sat down in the next one. Cutter's suit looked slept in; his shoes were scuffed. He rotated the fingertips of both hands against his temples and dropped his hands onto the chair arms. His shoulders seemed to droop or perhaps it was only Ross's imagination; for the first time Cutter looked as if he could be beaten. He looked drab and uneasy, almost listless. To Ross it made him a little more real, more human.

The walls were thick but there was the thin stink of kerosene fuel pervasively in the room and dimly Ross could hear the jets whining outside. The chartered Lear was fueling up for them and there wasn't much time.

Ross had been talking; now he went on:

"According to the introductory material it's probably the chapter on how the Agency first installed Magsaysay as President of the Philippines and then decided he wasn't playing ball and had him assassinated. Incidentally is that true?"

"I wouldn't know," Myerson murmured. "It wouldn't have been our department."

Cutter said, "Everything else has been true so far. He'd have had no reason to make it up."

Ross said, "It was mailed two days ago in the post office two blocks from the hotel. One of the desk clerks did it. Kendig gave him a big tip. It'll probably start showing up in today's mail deliveries."

There was no damming the flood of Myerson's anger. "What the hell difference does it make what the chapter's about? The man walked out right under our noses. He's on the Continent right now and we're sitting here with hundreds of people holding empty bags." His face congested with blood. "He walks right into a public building and kidnaps one of our own agents in full view of fifty people. He uses our own man's identification to get himself out of the country. He's carrying the rest of the Goddamned manuscript around in a little brown case as if it was a bag of groceries. He's one stinking man, unarmed and fifty-three years old and none of you high-paid geniuses can lay a finger on the son of a bitch. It's *my* head that's going to roll but I'm going to make good and God-damn sure it's not the only one. You *comprenez* that, Joe?"

Cutter spoke; he sounded as hoarse as if he'd spent weeks in a cell without talking. "There's one thing I can still try."

"Then you'd by God better try it because it's your neck that needs saving right now. What is it?"

"We've played him by the book right along. We've used cold logic and detective work and saturation manpower. We've made all the right moves. But he's anticipated every one of them—precisely because they *were* the right moves. Like the FBI trap, the post offices."

Follett said, "Don't tell me, let me guess. You want to make a wrong move on purpose."

Cutter ignored it. "I want to forget forensics and go after him on sheer instinct."

Myerson snorted. "Toss a coin? Throw darts at a map? That's easy to say—what's it mean?"

"I'm not getting anywhere trying to manage this stinking huge field army. I want to dump the command structure and the impedimenta and get out there on the pavement. I think you ought to turn my job over to Glenn here—turn me loose on my own. I'll take Ross and we'll see what we can smell out."

"That's clutching at straws for God's sake."

"Can you think of anything better to clutch at right now?"

Glenn Follett said, "I can. I already have."

Myerson glared at him. "Well? Do you need to be prompted?"

"I called Laurier this morning, SDECE Paris. I've asked him to put a crowd into every bank in the city."

"Why?" Myerson snapped.

"Before he started this caper he withdrew a lot of money from his bank in Zurich. He was living in Paris at the time. He laid out his plans there. It's his most logical base of operations, and so far it's the only place he's returned to since he started playing hopscotch." Follett held out his hand and jiggled the fingers as if he were bouncing a ball on his palm. "He gave your man Liddell a lot of cash to pay him for taking that ocean voyage for him. There's a limit to how much cash a man can carry around. Stands to reason he must have been pretty broke by the time he went from Georgia to Spain. But someplace between Madrid and London he replenished his finances—remember the money belt? Well when he flew from Madrid to Copenhagen he picked a flight that gave him several hours' stopover in Paris. It's a pretty good bet he's got a bank in Paris—a cash account or a safe-deposit box. And right now he's flat broke except for whatever small change he's boosted to keep himself going. If he told Oakley the truth about going to ground then he'll want to clean out his stash—but even if he was lying he's still got to have money. I'm betting the money's in a bank in Paris. I've had SDECE saturation on every bank in town since they opened their doors this morning."

"That's shrewd enough," Cutter said, "but he'll walk right past them the same way he walked past our people last night."

Myerson slapped the arm of his chair. "Even if he does I agree we've got to assume he's in Paris. I think we've got to bottle up the damn city the way it's never been bottled before."

Follett waved his big arms wildly. "There's a thousand roads out of Paris. It can't be done."

Myerson glared at him and then shifted the glare to Cutter. "And you want to go out on your own and sniff like a bloodhound. That's your last and best shot, is it?"

"If I get close to him I'll feel it. I can't get more exact than that."

Ross said, "Is he really going under, do you think?"

"Maybe," Cutter said. "He's changed his tactics—it means he's changed his mind. He doesn't want to die any more, if he ever really did. What he's got left is knowing he won't give up and lie down and die. But he may have been telling the truth about going into hiding. I think he's tired of the hectoring game."

"That doesn't change anything for us," Myerson said.

"I realize that."

Myerson gave him a cold look and sank the knife, twisting it: "Give it your best, Joe. Because I'm going to phone Mikhail Yaskov and give him every scrap we've got."

Ross said, "What?"

"Yaskov was right all along," Myerson said, not without bitterness. "The important thing was to stop Kendig—not *who* stopped him. I'm going to bring Yaskov right up to date and wish him luck. And if he gets in there ahead of you, Joe, you can kiss everything good-bye."

———

They sent the overnight bags on with Follett and took a taxi in from Le Bourget; Cutter told the driver to let them off at the Place de l'Opéra and Ross followed him into the American Express and Cutter sat down on a bench on the mezzanine.

"Okay," Ross said, "what now?"

"Put yourself in his shoes. You're here in Paris and the whole world's gunning for you. You want to disappear. You pick up whatever money you've got left in your stash. Then what do you do?"

"I don't know. What do you do?"

"I don't know either," Cutter said. "Let's just think a while."

"Why'd you pick this place? Because he used to have a checking account here?"

"He still has it," Cutter said. "But there's only a few hundred francs in it. He won't come here."

"Then we shouldn't be here either."

"All right Ross, where should we be?"

"Put it this way. He knows we're looking for him. He'd go where he didn't expect us to go."

"Where's that?"

"The Folies? The bar at the Ritz?"

"Kendig? No."

"It won't be any kind of public transportation. He might steal a car—it wouldn't be the first time."

"I think he really wants to get away clean this time. He won't steal a car—it could be traced, somebody might remember he bought gas or stopped for lunch. He'd have to abandon the car somewhere and that would give us a place to start looking if we ever connected the car with him."

"Climb into the back of a truck full of lettuce."

"And go where?"

"Some country village where we'd never look for him in a hundred years."

Cutter said, "He's a chameleon but he's a deep-rooted American. He won't settle down in a place where English isn't the native tongue. It's not the language, it's the way the language makes you function. He speaks good Spanish but he's never had any empathy with the way the Latin mind works. It's the same with the others. If he's going to ground for the rest of his life it'll be in English-speaking surroundings. Australia, New Zealand, South Africa, the United States."

"He tried that before. . . ."

"We knew he was there. If we didn't think he was there would we have any chance of finding him there?"

"Is this getting us anywhere, Joe?"

"Maybe it is. I think we're psyching him about right. He'll want to get far away from this corner of the world without anyone ever knowing he's done it."

"I don't see how that tells us where to start looking for him."

Cutter didn't answer right away. Tourists and expatriates drifted through the building. Ross saw a lot of furs and long suede coats; it was a cold autumn. Downstairs there was a queue at the postal delivery window but it was nothing like as long as the one in the summer.

"Come on," Cutter said; he uncoiled as if he had hinges and walked away.

Ross caught up and followed him outside. Traffic clotted the square. He had to hurry to keep up. Cutter had his hands thrust deep in his pockets; he was walking with long strides—down the Madeleine and the rue Royale, around the corner of the Place de la Concorde, past the palace gardens and up the Champs-Elysées. He crossed over with the light and cut off the Champs and Ross said, "Where are we going?"

"Follett's office."

"What for?"

"I want to be there when Kendig says good-bye."

| 26 |

There was a malignant cloud cover and a raiding wind howled along the Seine, Kendig went up the moss-slick steps with his suitcase and across the quai into the rue Seguier.

Strauss seemed to have gained more weight; he led Kendig downstairs to the vault and Kendig took the black box into the private cubicle. Mainly what he needed was the Alexandre Vaneau passport. But he took all the money out of the box, put it in the suitcase and returned the black box empty to the vault. Strauss escorted him past the two armed guards up the stairs; Kendig went back along the quai to where he'd parked the 2CV van, tossed the suitcase inside and drove down through the sinuous boulevards of the left bank.

He had a room in a *pension* in the fifteenth arrondissement; he opened the suitcase and dumped the money out on the bed. He filled one of the two money belts he'd bought in the morning when he'd bought the comfortable pair of shoes and the overcoat with the velvet collar; he was still wearing Oakley's suit under it.

He transferred the remaining chapters of the manuscript from the school-book case into the suitcase and on top of the pages he put something over a hundred thousand dollars and all Oakley's papers. Then he went out again to finish his daylight errands.

He bought a *bâtard* loaf, a chunk of cheese, a bottle of Vittel water that had a screw-on cap, and a box of wooden matches. Then he walked on to a workman's clothiery where he outfitted himself with dungarees, flannel shirt, a beret, rubber-soled waterproof boots and a drab leather jacket with elastic waist and cuffs. He carried his parcels along the avenue Felix Faure until he found a florist's where houseplants were a specialty; he bought a tin of powdered fertilizer which had a high concentration of sulfuric acid.

He returned to the *pension*, left his purchases on the bed and had to go out once more; this time to the Caltex filling station near the quai. He told the attendant he'd run dry six blocks away. The attendant sold him a four-liter can at an exorbitant price and filled it from the pump. Kendig left it on the floor of his stolen 2CV van before he went upstairs.

He broke open the loaf and made a meal of that and the cheese, washing it down with the Vittel water. He poured the rest of the water into a tumbler and then carefully tipped a good share of the chemical fertilizer powder into the empty bottle. He filled it the rest of the way from the sink tap. Then he broke off a piece of his shoelace and dipped it in the solution. The acid was not too concentrated but it ate the leather away after a while; it would do. He capped the bottle carefully and placed it upright on the bureau.

He made a fuse from one of the wall candles, stripping the candle away until all that remained was the wick thinly coated with wax.

He stripped down to his underwear and changed into the workingman's outfit he'd just bought. After he'd laced up the boots he folded Oakley's suit carefully and laid it in the suitcase along with Oakley's topcoat. He tossed his toilet gear in and then gathered the remaining money on the bed; this went into the second money belt and he laid that on the topcoat and closed the suitcase over it.

There was nothing left to do but wait; he couldn't make the next move until after midnight. He pushed the suitcase aside to make room for himself and lay back with his hands laced behind his head. After a while he drowsed.

———

In the middle of each night the *gendarmerie*'s meat wagon made its rounds slowly, its crew stopping by the hunched *clochard* figures who sprawled in rags on the streets and gutters and doorways of Paris. If the *clochard* was drunk, asleep or merely deathly ill the *flic* passed him by because there wasn't manpower, facility, time or inclination to render assistance. But if the *clochard* happened to be dead the meat wagon would collect him and he would be taken to the morgue where medical students could learn something from his cadaver before his dissected remains were disposed of by the city. On a normal night there would be about twenty dead ones in the streets.

Tonight a high-pressure weather system had dropped down the globe from the northwest and the cold was more than autumnal; it was intense, several degrees below frost point, and it had caught the *clochards* of Paris unprepared. There would be an uncommon number of deaths.

Kendig had a general idea of the route the meat wagon took in the fifteenth arrondissement. He set out in the clanking little 2CV van a good two hours ahead of the meat wagon; it was just short of midnight. The frigid cold kept most pedestrians off the streets. The weather gave him a bit of an advantage but he'd have managed without it. He cruised the route slowly, making room courteously for impatient drivers who burst past him in a demented rush.

Here and there he double-parked the van and got out to have a close look at a prone figure or a shadow propped in a nook. Kendig's penance was the folded fifty-franc note he would slip into the hand or pocket of each drowsing *clochard*. He found a woman dead, all skin and bones and tattered rags; he went on. There was a man dead in the place de Lourmel but he was very small and skinny and Kendig passed him by; there was another in a passage off the rue Emeriau but that one was much too tall.

The fifty-franc note awakened a dozing fat woman and he hurried away from her profusions with his chin sunk in the heavy collar of his overcoat. He drove the van on, making a concentric circuit of the district, invading the *clochards'* privacy and apologizing for the intrusion with his money. There was a corpse on the curb of the rue Varet that met the requirements of size and build but the man was missing his left leg; there was another two blocks away but he was toothless and had a misshapen arm that was evidently the result of an old fracture that had healed unevenly. Kendig moved on. There was no urgent timetable. If he didn't find one tonight he'd go out again tomorrow night.

He found the right one less than half an hour later in a passage half a block from the *Convention métro* station. The man's dead face was ravaged with age but that was the accelerated deterioration of the life he'd led; the backs of the hands were not severely veined or mottled. The man was nearly bald but that wouldn't matter. Kendig went back to the van and moved it to a position where it masked him from the mouth of the passage when he picked up the odorous corpse. He placed the body gently in the back of the van and locked the rear doors. The smell filled the small Citroën immediately and he had to drive with the sliding window wide open in spite of the icy cold. He parked it behind his *pension* and went inside to get the suitcase and Oakley's topcoat; he brought them downstairs and checked out, paying the sleepy *concierge* in cash and leaving a tip for the char.

He carried his things out to the van and went around to the right-hand side to feed the case and coat into the passenger seat. He set the bottle of acid against the outside rim of the seat frame and closed the door gently against it to wedge it upright in place. Then he locked the door and stepped around the back of the van.

A car swung into the street from the intersection. Its beams arced along the row of parked cars and caught him in the face before he had time to turn. It came forward with a bit of a lurch and then the lights dipped when the car braked and he didn't need more than that to know the numerical odds had caught up with him. He was about-facing when the car stopped and he started to run when he heard the doors chunk shut.

They didn't bother to shout at him but when he threw a glance over his shoulder he saw the fragmentary ripple of reflected light along the pistol barrel. Two of them were out of the car but there was still a man inside it; it was moving again.

A weakening rush of panic; and he rushed across into the narrow foot passage beyond. He could hear their running footsteps; he pounded the length of the alley and the car had already gone around the end of the block; it was swinging around the corner too fast, leaning against the centripetal tug. Kendig ran right toward it; he dodged to one side as the car straightened in the street and then he was up on the curb diving down the steps into the *métro* subway station. It was shut down; no trains ran this late at night; he had to vault the chain at the foot of the stairs. A few work lights made faint illumination along the platform and several drunks slept on the benches. He dropped into the cut and danced across the tracks staying off the electrified rails and boosted himself up onto the opposite platform; he was at the foot of the exit stair when the two pursuers came in sight behind him but he was up into the shadows before they had time to take aim. He bolted up into the cold empty intersection. Their car was gone; odds were it had returned to keep watch on the street where they'd disclosed him: they might not know which car he'd been about to get into but they'd have seen the car keys in his hand. If there was a two-way radio in their car he didn't have much time.

On the northwest corner of the intersection stood a modern apartment building with a supermarket in its ground floor. Three steps led up to the lobby doors and you could see straight through to another set of doors that let out onto a passage behind the building where the parking lot was. He went right up the steps and across the lobby into the parking lot. The two pistols were coming up from the *métro* and he wasn't in time to get out of their sight; they came sprinting up the steps and Kendig ran down into the parking lot.

A high fence ran around it and the gates were locked up. The railing was topped with blunt metal spikes and he swarmed up it wildly. He heard gristle snap in his shoulder. He went over fast, ripping his coat on a spike; he dropped lightly on the asphalt and moved away swiftly, knees bent, pulse slamming.

The alley behind the lot twisted among low old buildings and he put a jutting corner between him and the guns; he went over a courtyard wall with the acrobatic strength of terror and batted his way through invisible clotheslines and found a gate that he scaled blindly; he dropped from his fingertips into a cobbled passage not more than four feet wide and ran on his toes to its mouth.

It was a narrow street with a *charcuterie* at the corner and he ran to it without sound and whipped around into the alley beside it where there had to be a crowd of garbage cans; he climbed into the midst of them and nested down surrounded by their stink and watched the street through the vertical slits between them.

The two of them came in sight; he saw them hesitate and then begin to spread out like hounds abruptly deprived of their scent. Kendig crouched bolt still, in total stasis; his scalp shrank and his forehead blistered with sweat.

They moved right and left. When the building corners hid them Kendig straightened up and climbed over the cans very carefully to avoid sound. He backed away close to the masonry wall, fingertips dragging it lightly, wrapped in darkness. Tenement flats back here. A door yielded to him with a dry groan; he slipped into a rancid hallway. Somewhere on the floor above an infant yowled. Kendig went through to the back and found a broken-out window; he picked shards of glass from the sill and set them down softly on the littered floor and climbed outside—another cobbled passageway crowded with a bumper-to-bumper line of small cars with their right wheels up on the curb and their doors close along the building walls. He went along the parked line trying doors and when a Renault admitted him he jammed his thumb on the plunger in the hinge wall to extinguish the interior dome light and held his thumb there while he crawled into the car and searched for the switch that would disengage the light permanently; he found it and then extricated his thumb and pulled the door shut silently. He locked both doors and climbed over the transmission hump into the backseat and settled his rump on the floor. His eyes were just above sill level and he watched the street filled with unease, willing his pulse to slow.

When the tall one came in sight at the end of the passage Kendig shrank down as flat as he could go. There was nothing to do but wait it out. After a while he heard the man's soles prowl toward him, crunching grit. Then the man's head and shoulders loomed beyond the rear side-window. He stopped and swiveled in a full circle, searching, bouncing the automatic in his fist. Kuyk-endall, Kendig recalled; one of Follett's junior agents—no wonder he'd been recognized so quickly. Hatless, puffing out steam clouds of breath, Kuykendall stood as if rooted, his head turning slowly and his scowl deepening. Kendig heard a door slam somewhere; it drew Kuykendall's immediate attention but still he didn't move off the spot and if the light had been just a little better he'd have known he was staring his quarry in the face over a distance of not more than eight feet; he might sense it anyway. Kendig lay still, hardly breathing, not even blinking.

Kuykendall's head veered around and his chin lifted question-ingly; then he shrugged and lifted both arms—a signal to his part-ner at the far end. Kuykendall made a sweeping motion with his left hand, ordering the partner around the block; then Kuykendall trotted away, forward along the line of cars to go around the op-posite end of the block.

Kendig watched until Kuykendall turned the corner. He looked back through the rear window but the partner was long gone. He climbed out of the Renault and went back in through the broken window, back along the stinking hallway and out the unlocked door; back past the garbage cans and then across the street swiftly, retracing his exact path because it was least likely they'd look for him where they knew he'd already been and gone.

In just a few more minutes they'd know for certain they'd lost him and they'd beat their way back to their car and stake out the street because they'd reason that he might have some-thing in one of the cars there that he'd have to come back for. In the meantime if there was a two-way they'd want to be there to brief the reinforcements the minute they arrived; after that the whole area would be suicidal for him because the SDECE and the *Sureté* and half the *flics* in Paris would comb it house to house.

He threw off the overcoat in the alley and hunched his back like an old man and moved purposefully afoot into the street where he'd left the van. There was no car double-parked and none of the parked cars had light on but spotting their car was ludicrously easy; the frigid cold gave it away. It was one among many parked vehicles but the driver had the engine running to warm himself and the windshield was clear from the defroster.

As if he had business there Kendig walked straight along the sidewalk with his old man's stoop. They were looking for an erect fugitive in an overcoat.

He had the door open before the driver could react to his turn; he hauled the man right out of the seat. In that brief broken instant under the streetlight Kendig saw the wild-eyed look: he'd seen it on a man's face once before but that had been on a thundering battleground below Cassino. Kendig's jaws flexed; he hauled the driver right out against his own upraised knee and when the man fell back against the car Kendig locked his left hand around his right fist and drove his right elbow into the driver's ribs. It collapsed the wind out of the man and when his head dipped in anguish Kendig pushed him right down onto the sidewalk and got a surgical grip around the base of the skull and pressed firmly with fingers and thumb. It closed off the flow of the carotid artery and starved the brain and after a moment the driver went limp. He wouldn't stay unconscious for more than two or three minutes but he'd be dazed for a while after that.

Kendig pulled the ignition key partway out and broke it off with the tip jammed in the lock. He plucked the microphone off the two-way and tore it out by the cord and dropped it on the seat. Then he pushed the door shut and walked swiftly the twenty paces to his 2CV van and drove away.

They might have a make on the van; he couldn't keep it. There were thousands of the cheap Citroëns in Paris but they'd be distraught enough to tear into every one of them at this point.

He drove as far as the tangle of streets behind the Invalides and parked the van in a dark side-passage. It took him fifteen minutes to walk to the Laennec Hospital. A handful of cars stood parked on the doctors' lot near the emergency entrance. A doctor in a hurry to reach a critical case didn't always lock his car or take his keys; Kendig was counting on that and he found a Peugeot still warm and ready to go and he drove it off the lot without looking back. The owner would find it missing pretty fast but what counted was that the theft wouldn't be connected with Kendig for a while.

He parked right behind the van and transferred everything into the Peugeot. He put the dead *clochard* in the trunk, slammed the lid and drove away into the boulevard Montparnasse, forcing himself to drive at moderate speed.

He left Paris by way of Charenton and the Bois de Vincennes; he ran along southeast with the map imprinted on his eyelids. It was somewhere past three in the morning; the well-tuned sedan ran eagerly and there was no traffic on the curving country road. Farmhouses rushed by vaguely, smeared by speed; heavy trees blurred and vanished into the onrushing darkness.

Around four o'clock he crossed the Yonne at Auxerre and took the road toward Chablis: The vineyards made an icy spindle tracery above the highway; occasionally a chateau loomed on the hill.

The gate was fastened with a padlocked chain—he was reminded of the bootleggers' road in Georgia. He drove right through it, splintering the gate and extinguishing one of the Peugeot's headlights. He switched them off. It didn't matter if he left evidence of destruction now; he expected them to trace him this far.

The Lafayette Escadrille had used it, and then the French training commands and then the *Luftwaffe* and the American Warhawks; after the war it had been judged too short for the jet generation and it had passed out of government hands into the private aviation sector. The wineries kept their executive planes here and there were planes of all sizes belonging to—and sometimes built by—Sunday fliers. The flying school had three single-engine trainers and a twin Apache.

The field had two runways laid out in an X; they were graded earth strips and there was no radar or strobe-light strip—it was strictly a daylight field for small craft. There were two maintenance hangars but if you wanted major work done you had to go to one of the bigger airstrips that had overhauling facilities. The planes were parked at hard-stands along the verges of the runways in high yellow grass. Some of them were tied down against the danger of high winds that might tip them over and snap a wing.

They'd never kept a night watchman and he assumed they'd had no reason to hire one since he'd taken his lessons here. He drove without lights right up to the dark hangars and switched off.

According to Oakley's watch it was four-twenty. This time of year nothing would begin stirring here until at least seven-thirty, more likely eight. There was plenty of time. He checked out the hangars cursorily and then went down the line of aircraft to pick out a plane. He knew what sort he wanted but he wasn't sure there'd be one. He'd settle for something else in that case.

But there was one. It was an old PBY Catalina amphibian—a small twin-engine flying boat on wheels. Some of the vintners liked to use amphibians because it made for handy access to quiet shores along the inlets of Lake Geneva on trips to Swiss banks they preferred not to advertise. It was a service Kendig had used a few times to get his money in and out of Zurich.

He took note of the civil air numbers painted on the plane and he went back to the hangar and broke into the office. He didn't want to turn on a light; there were two chateaus on heights within less than a mile. He lighted a wooden match and found the key on the pegboard by the number on its tag. Nobody stole airplanes; they were too traceable; so there was no security imposed.

He pocketed the PBY key and got back in the car and drove it out the runway, racked it alongside the Catalina and got to work. He checked the fuel gauges and found it full; that was standard procedure—you filled after you landed, not before you took off; that way you were ready to go on short notice. He took out the three logbooks—by regulation there was one for the airframe and a separate one for each engine—and left them askew on the floor by the right-seat rudder pedals. He didn't care what shape the plane was in but it had to look as if he did. Cutter wasn't going to give him any help if he left too many doors open.

He put the suitcase in the plane, belt-strapping it onto one of the pry-rigged passenger seats in the midships blister. The manuscript was in the suitcase. He had to give it up to them or they wouldn't buy any of it; and it had to be the real manuscript, not a fake and not a partial—no tricks, nothing withheld.

He took the *clochard* out of the trunk and laid him out on the grass under the high wing. He stripped the *clochard* to the skin. There were scars here and there—it hadn't been an easy life for the *clochard*—but none of that would matter. He brought the four-liter can of gasoline out of the Peugeot and bathed the corpse with the stuff to get rid of any telltales that might have adhered. The *clochard*'s filthy rags had to disappear; Kendig bundled them up and set the bundle aside.

He poured the acid solution out of the Vittel bottle onto the *clochard*'s face. He wasn't cold-blooded enough to do it without a cringing nausea. When the acid had done a fair job of eradicating features he washed it away with gasoline. Then he dressed the body in his own old underwear and socks and Oakley's suit and topcoat; he put Oakley's identification and wallet in the clothes along with the passport photo of himself that he'd rescued from the London police sergeant's desk. Then he added the Alexandre Vaneau passport—again with his own photo in it—to the contents of the dead man's pockets.

The *clochard* was stiffening with rigor by now and that was all to Kendig's advantage. He dragged the corpse forward, closing his mind to the ghoulishness of it and the reek of gasoline. He propped the body in the pilot's seat and belted it in.

Outside on the grass he opened the bundle of filthy clothes and spread the coat out flat. He piled into the center of it the rest of the clothes, the empty Vittel bottle and his own spare pair of shoes. He tied up the arms and skirt of the coat and carried the bundle into the plane together with the can of gasoline. Then he went back outside again and explored in the trunk of the Peugeot. It was slightly redolent of the dead but that would dissipate. He found a combination windshield-scraper and brush; it would do. He used it to rake the grass where he'd been working. He left no sign in the earth except a set of vague foot-impressions to show he'd walked from the car to the plane; he left the trunk lid ajar with the keys in it both to air it out and to indicate he'd been in a hurry.

When he climbed in the waist door he latched it shut behind him and went forward up the steeply tilted companionway into the cockpit. He tested the *clochard*'s limbs but they hadn't stiffened quite enough yet. He couldn't bear the thought of sitting beside the ghastly dead man for any length of time; he went back into the fuselage and sat under the blister watching the night. Along the edge of the field bare branches were silhouetted against the dark sky, as jagged as cracks in a porcelain surface. Scarves of cloud hung low in the southwest but the clear intense cold held.

He felt a vague urge: the impulse to communicate his grati-
tude to Carla Fleming. He remembered her soft self-assured voice,
her long-boned Modigliani features. He'd never get in touch with
her; he couldn't take the chance.

More than half his money was in the *clochard*'s money belt
and the suitcase but he had about forty thousand dollars in his own
belt and pockets and when it ran out he had the talent to make
more. He had no papers of any kind but that wasn't a problem either. This would be a poor time to try to make long-term plans.
He'd drift a while and think about what he wanted to do with the
rest of his years. There was plenty of time for it. He wouldn't get
bored; he'd got over that, he'd changed too much to fear it. He
was capable of life now; perhaps even capable of love—he'd find
out about that someday.

He stripped Oakley's watch off his wrist. After six now; he
couldn't wait longer. He moved at a crouch into the cockpit and
got the watch onto the dead wrist. The joints were so stiff he had a
lot of trouble moving them; that was how he wanted it.

It had to be done with great caution because if there was a
spark at the wrong moment it could incinerate him. He threw all
the windows wide open before he began to splash the gasoline
around. He poured it liberally around the cockpit, over the
corpse and the upholstery. Then he capped the gasoline can and
stuffed it into the bundle of things he couldn't leave behind. He
took the candlewick fuse from his shirt pocket and wedged it
into a metal seam by the edge of the soaked carpeting. Now he
had to wait again while the wind carried the fumes off and evap-
orated the surface petrol and the rest of it soaked deep into
things.

It was a risk but he had to take it and when he judged enough
time had passed he turned the ignition switch on and pressed the
Mesh button for the Number One engine. The flywheel spun with
a grinding effort but the engine didn't catch right away and he

pushed the mixture control to full rich. No sparks in the cockpit; this wouldn't have worked with a plane that had the engine in the nose of the fuselage. Both engines were in nacelles high on the wings and outboard of the cockpit.

The flywheel struggled and he heard the cylinders catch; he revved it a bit and then got the starboard engine running.

He unlocked the brake and ran the engines up and the PBY started to bounce, rolling slowly out of its parking space onto the strip. He kicked the pedal hard and she turned sedately to the right; he lined her up on the runway and taxied slowly to the far end and made the U-turn wide and slow. Now he had the length of the runway in front of him and a row of high trees at the far end. He remembered the strain with which the instructors regarded student takeoffs; if you didn't get the nose up fast enough you'd go right into those trees or the power lines beyond.

The emergency hatch was in the bow forward of the windshield; you had to crawl under the dash-board to get to it. That wouldn't be fast enough. He broke the half-window out of its frame on his right and judged he could work it from there. He set the bundle on his lap and ran up both engines against the brakes. When the plane began to shudder and lurch he released the brakes. It rolled forward and he throttled back; this had to be done precisely and he couldn't have a lot of speed at first. He bounced forward at twenty miles an hour or so, steering with his feet while he leaned across the aisle and fixed the *clochard*'s dead fingers to the crescent wheel. He locked both the fists onto the control yoke and jammed the *clochard*'s feet under the rudder pedals so that they couldn't kick back and send the plane into a ground loop.

Bumping along on the uneven ground he had a hard time climbing out the window but finally he was hanging there with both shoulders wedged into the opening so that he wouldn't fall out before he wanted to. The starboard propeller was frighteningly close behind him but he could avoid that easily enough; it was the wing strut and the landing gear he'd have to worry about when he made his drop.

He had two matches in his left hand, pressed together. With that hand he reached the throttles and thrust them all the way forward to emergency speed. There was about a quarter mile of runway left. He struck the two matches and touched the flame to the gasoline-soaked tip of the candlewick. The flame soared bright; he had only a glimpse of it and then he was hunching his shoulders, clutching the dead matchsticks in his left hand and the bundle of oddments in his right.

When he compressed his shoulders he slid down out of the jouncing window. He let go and dropped with his legs all gone to rubber; he felt his feet touch down and he willed himself to collapse and he was still dropping when he saw the strut coming at him but it only glanced off his upraised arm and then the starboard wheel was rutting past him and he was under it and free.

He rolled over and lay flat while the tail surface rumbled overhead, the tail wheel bouncing and veering a little from side to side. He didn't move after that: he lay prone on his belly and watched, uncaring of the blunt pain in his corded forearm; waiting with his eyes wide stark staring and the breath hung up in his throat.

Gathering speed the PBY began to yaw dangerously and he feared the ground loop but the *clochard*'s stiff joints held it on something like a course and it kept wobbling toward the end of the runway with a high angry whine of overaccelerated engines. He saw the flames burst alight in the cockpit, fueled by the gasoline-soaked carpeting and Oakley's saturated clothes. Perhaps it had been unnecessary but he had to make sure the plane caught fire to mask the work he'd done on the *clochard* with the acid. . . . It veered right and then left but it didn't flip over and it didn't loop around and it must have been doing at least seventy miles an hour when it smashed head-on into the trees. It was an earsplitting crash and there was afterecho and silence before the flames tongued into a ruptured tank and the whole thing went up with a spectacular thundering conflagration: even from where he lay he felt the heat of it on his cheeks.

He picked up the bundle and backed his way to the edge of the runway, dragging the bundle to erase his footprints; he faded into the brush, walking with care and rubbing it out when he left any signs.

At the vineyard fence he went through the staves carefully and then he turned and walked uphill, a bit jaunty and smiling without reservation, toward the violet smear along the east that predicted the dawn.

| 27 |

The afternoon sun broke through but it remained bitter cold and the wind went right through Ross's coat. He watched the technicians sift through the rubble. Wisps of smoke still curled from the charred surreal sculpture of the wreckage.

The body—the remains of it—lay on a litter near his feet. Follett spoke across it to Cutter; the wind almost carried his words away. "I don't like coincidences—I don't like handy accidents."

"He only had a few flying lessons," Cutter said. "He didn't know how to handle a plane that big. You couldn't call it an accident."

"I still don't believe he's dead just like that. It's too easy."

"Everybody dies. It was his turn."

"Overdue for that matter. But it's still hard to absorb. Son of a bitch made monkeys of us right up to the end."

Cutter laughed—a dryish cackle.

Follett made way for the SDECE medical examiner; he moved around the corpse and looked at his watch. "You said you'd follow through on the autopsy business, Joe?"

"Yes. It was my case—I might as well handle the rest of it."

"Then I'd better get back to the salt mines. I've got a lot of unfinished jobs to reheat." Follett turned away, picked up his driver and walked back toward the cars, out of step with his companion.

Cutter watched the medical examiner and Ross watched Cutter: his lean mentor looked stupefied. He looked away from the body, studied the backs of his hands and then turned them over and studied the palms.

Cutter turned to face the ruins of the plane. Ross turned with him. They watched the crew extracting the remains of the luggage; the fire hadn't done too much damage that far back in the fuselage. They walked forward and the technician set the suitcase down on the grass. The lid was buckled and scorched. Cutter tipped it up; a hinge corner snapped off and the lid fell askew onto the grass. There was a lot of ash inside; most of it was money. Ross had no trouble recognizing the manuscript for what it was; the edges were burned and curled up but it was still a manuscript. When sheets of paper were compacted together in thick stacks it was remarkable how fire-resistant they could be.

Cutter seemed restless. He walked back to the litter. The ambulance stood where it had been backed up with its doors open but the remains were fragile and the medical examiner wanted to make his preliminary investigation before it was moved. Cutter said, "What does it show, doctor?"

"It will tell us very little, *M'sieur*. The face is burned beyond recognition. If there were distinguishing marks on the body the fire has obliterated them. There was this."

It was a charred wallet with the black partial remains of two passports folded into it. Cutter said, "Oakley's wallet, I imagine. And we knew he had a French passport. Look at this."

The edges were gone and it had blistered but it was recognizably a photograph of Miles Kendig in the passport.

"First photograph I've ever seen of him," Cutter said. "Except for that basic-training group shot. And it looks like it'll be the last."

The medical examiner said, "As soon as possible we shall provide you with the fingerprints and the dental survey."

Ross thought, that meant nothing; they had no fingerprints to compare, no dental records on him.

The sunshine was brittle on the rolling vineyards. Cutter's flat stare drew Ross's eyes up from the ugly remains: Cutter was watching him with a curious fixed intensity. "Well, Ross—what do you think?"

He knew well enough what he thought. He'd traveled so closely with Cutter that he had the feeling he'd developed an ability to read Cutter's mind. Cutter had no more factual knowledge than Ross had but that didn't matter. Ross knew what Cutter believed instinctively: that it wasn't Kendig's body. He didn't see how the hell Kendig could have done it.

Abandoning the manuscript—that could be an olive branch: Kendig's farewell message, the assurance he was quitting the game. But if he was alive he still had it all in his head. He could start the whole business all over again any time he wanted to.

Cutter's eyes bored deep into him: a plea. Cutter was asking his complicity. It was no good asking himself why; if it had to be explained then probably it wasn't worth deciding.

A rage to survive was a natural thing, he thought; everybody had it. Everybody had a right to it.

He wondered if someday he'd earn a friend as good as Cutter was to Kendig.

He spoke: a strangled exclamation that escaped from him in a burst. "As far as I'm concerned that's Miles Kendig's corpse."

Cutter nodded slowly.

Ross threw his shoulders back and squinted into the sky, wondering.